Dead End

Dead End

By

Carol W. Hazelwood

Published by Aventine Press
55 East Emerson St.
Chula Vista CA, 91911
www.aventinepress.com

ISBN: 978-1-59330-872-8

Cover photograph by

Tracy Daniels Parker

Other books by Carol Hazelwood

Dark Legacy
Assume Nothing
The Beastly Island Murder
Twilight in the Garden
Web of Obsessions
View from the Jury Box
Coyoacan Hill

and co-author of
Tigers in a cage, the Memoir of Wu Tek Ying

Acknowledgements

Many thanks to Dorran Nadeau, Nancy Poss-Hatchl,
Adele Kopecky, Joan Blue, and Marcia Tungate.
A special thank you to Janice Clark,
who lost her fight against scleroderma,
for her diligent line by line editing and her friendship.
She will be greatly missed.
Thanks also to Tina Wilson,
who showed me how she lives a full life
with the aide of her guide dog.

Chapter 1

On this bleak Minnesota winter day, all Patty Harkin had left in the world was her father's new truck. As she walked into Maggie's Diner, the warmth, along with the heady aroma of fresh bread, engulfed her. Her senses reeled with anticipation of a hot meal, yet she knew the money in her pocket wouldn't go far.

"Man, it's cold out there," she mumbled, climbing onto one of the few empty stools at the counter. The old man next to her nodded, but kept spooning soup into his eager mouth. She took off her worn fleece-lined leather gloves, and when whipped off her wool cap, her wavy brunette hair tumbled onto her shoulders. Although the hour was early for dinner patrons, the place was humming. She checked the specials on the chalkboard next to the pass-through to the kitchen.

From the end of the long green Formica counter, Maggie called out, "Be with you in a sec. Want the usual?"

Patty fingered the five dollars and change in her parka pocket. No, she mouthed, shaking her head. The soup of the day, beef barley, wasn't her favorite, but she couldn't be choosey. It would keep her going until tomorrow. Then what?

Maggie moved down the inside of the counter, checking on each customer's needs. The woman was so short that her ample breasts brushed the counter top; her weathered, sixty-year-old face beamed with a merry glint. "Something different?" she asked Patty. "That's a first. I always set a bowl of stew aside just for you."

"Today, a bowl of soup'll do."

"You need more than soup to keep you going in this weather. You're as skinny as a pipe." She grinned, showing a neat set of dentures. "And as long to boot."

"Soup's fine." She took out a tissue and blew her nose. "I'll wash up. Keep my place, okay?"

"Will do." Maggie put a reserved cardboard sign on the counter, then called to the kitchen cook, "One soup special, extra beef and biscuits."

On the way to the restrooms, Patty passed the local team pictures with their sponsor's plaques on the beige wall and the bulletin board that was riddled with holes from tacked up business cards and postcards sent from visitors who thought Maggie Gordon and her diner were the best. In the ladies' room, Patty bathed her face in hot water, a treat after spending the day driving to surrounding towns and farms looking for work. She could barely feel her toes inside her heavy boots. The high price of gas had eaten most of her cash, and her credit cards had been discontinued. This morning Bromont's finest had bodily evicted her from the only home she'd known. Everything she owned was jammed into her truck. As she brushed her hair, the mirror reflected her pale complexion and brown eyes with their gold flecks. *God, what am I going to do? I'm twenty-six, no family, no home, no job, no money, and mechanic skills without credentials.*

She dried her hands and returned to her seat at the counter where Maggie placed a large bowl of soup and two oversized buttermilk biscuits, dripping with butter. "Maggie, I only ordered soup." Patty disliked taking charity from anyone, including Maggie.

"The biscuits are on the house." She winked at Patty and went off to serve other customers.

"Hey," the old man next to Patty called out to Maggie. "How come I didn't get extra biscuits?"

Over her shoulder, Maggie said, "That was the last of 'em, boyo."

Patty was glad she didn't catch what the old man muttered. She'd probably have clobbered him if he'd said something nasty about Maggie. After taking off her parka and putting it on the back of her stool, she ate and felt her insides warm. In between mouthfuls, she watched Maggie make her rounds, put orders in to the two cooks, and all the while keeping an eye on the only waitress. The girl was a new hire, a little slow and dimwitted, but Maggie's big heart wouldn't let her fire anyone unless they cheated her.

When there was a lull, Maggie came back to Patty. "The service for your dad was real nice. How are things with you?"

Patty stared into her empty bowl. "You don't want to know."

"I do too. Aren't I like an aunt to you?"

A man called out by the register. "Maggie, do I eat for free or are you going to take my money?"

"Okay, coming." She tapped Patty's hand. "Be right back."

The old man next to Patty grunted, grabbed his check, and after leaving a skimpy tip, headed toward the cash register.

She munched on the last biscuit, licked the butter off her fingers, then used a paper napkin. She couldn't ask Maggie for a job. Besides, she'd be a lousy waitress, and Maggie wasn't exactly rolling in dough.

Despite skills as a mechanic, there wasn't a job opening for her in the area. The last place she worked she'd given the boss's son a black eye when he tried to rape her in the office after hours. The guy claimed she'd asked for it. Police Chief Dankbar wasn't interested in her side of the story and arrested her for assault and battery, then relented and released her after a night in jail. Patti couldn't figure out why women didn't rally to her defense, but then she never had understood women. She'd been brought up by her father, and, except for Maggie, she'd been surrounded by men. Women were an enigma to her.

Maggie returned, swept the coins the old man had left into her pocket and began cleaning up the counter. "So tell me what's going on. You get a job yet?"

"No."

"The house?"

"Dankbar did the bank's bidding and kicked me out this morning."

"Dirty business. Got any money left?"

"Not much."

"You could sell your truck. The only bet your dad ever made that paid off. Glad he bought it and gave it to you. Finally something good came from his gambling." Maggie lowered her voice. "You could probably get a lot for that truck."

"Selling the truck is out of the question."

With arms akimbo, Maggie stared at Patty. "What're you going to do then?"

Patty leaned back and shrugged. "I might have to try another state."

"Honey, you gotta stop clonking every guy who makes a pass at you. You're a beauty. Face it. Guys will always go after you. You're just like your mother. She was a looker, too, but she handled men so smooth they never knew they'd been turned down flatter than an iron, and they never held it against her either."

"Well, since I never knew her, I never learned the art of evading rape through charm."

"Wish you'd known her." Maggie cocked her head. "Terrible her dying so young, and you only a toddler. Your dad did his level best to make a good life for you."

"He taught me all about engines."

"Yeah, but not much about social graces."

Patty sighed deep and long. "I miss him." She fiddled with the salt shaker.

"I do too." Maggie stroked the top of Patty's hand. "Now don't get down on yourself. You're a fine mechanic. You fixed my Oldsmobile's transmission, and I've never had a problem since."

A new customer slid onto the stool at the counter vacated by the old man. The fellow gave Patty a warm smile. "Hi. Cold day," he said in a rich baritone voice as he unfolded the local paper.

He removed the classified section and was about to shuffle them to the bottom of his stack of reading material, when Patty asked, "Mind if I look at the classifieds?"

"Help yourself." He handed her the section. "You live around here?"

She wondered if that was a pickup line. "Yes." She turned away and kept her eyes on the newspaper.

"Just trying to be friendly. My name's Camden McMillan."

"Nice to meet you." She didn't give her name. "Look, mister, if I don't seem real friendly, it's because I have a lot on my mind."

"Okay. You've eaten here before?"

She nodded.

"What do you recommend?"

"Meatloaf's always great." Her mouth watered just thinking about the dish.

Maggie came over to take his order. "Evening. What'll it be?"

"I hear the meatloaf's great."

Maggie grinned and nodded in Patty's direction. "Some of the locals say so. It comes with a side order of salad. How about homemade apple cobbler for dessert?"

"Sold."

"You're easy. Anything to drink?"

"You don't serve wine or beer, do you?"

"Nope."

"Okay. Hot tea."

Maggie left to put in the order, and he went back to flipping through the newspaper.

Patty scanned the help wanted section and had almost given up when her finger rested on a strange ad. *Driver with truck needed to tow trailer south. Salary negotiable.* She hoped the guy didn't live too far away.

She began to think how she should apply for the position. He'd expect a man. She had to get an interview. She'd stopped her cell phone service a month ago, and the only public phone was back by the restrooms. "Keep my seat for me, won't you mister? I'll be right back." She made her way to the pay phone, but before she pushed in the numbers, she sent up a little prayer. "Please, Lord, I need this one."

When the party on the other end answered, she used a deep voice. "I'm calling about your ad wanting a driver with a truck. My name's Pat Harkin. I have a truck with a tow hookup and I got the time to drive south."

"What kind of truck?" the male voice asked.

"Denali with a 5.3-liter V8 engine. Plenty of power for towing. How big is your trailer?"

"A travel trailer. About nine thousand pounds loaded. Sounds like your engine should handle it. I plan to leave before the next storm hits. Can you come out tonight to see if we can agree to terms?"

"Sure." Her heart beat faster. Here was a chance, a hope, an answer to a prayer.

He gave directions, and she said she'd be there within the hour. After hanging up, she rubbed her hands together, then realized she hadn't gotten the guy's name. No matter. Exiting this town would be a godsend. What could possibly be worse than freezing her buns off in a town that had given her nothing but grief the last few years?

Back at her seat at the counter, she found a slice of chocolate cake set out for her. Maggie would be hurt if she declined to eat it, so she dug in with relish.

The man next to her sipped his tea and studied the sports section. "Oh, my God." He banged his fist on the counter. "It can't be."

Startled, Patty asked, "What?"

"Mike Garrick died four days ago."

Patty frowned. The name seemed familiar, but she couldn't remember why. "Who's he?"

The man half-turned to her, as he folded the paper. "Sorry, I didn't mean to bother you."

"It's okay. I was a little abrupt earlier."

He nodded. His warm hazel eyes, behind black-rimmed glasses, held bewilderment. "I can't believe this. It's impossible. I'd hoped to get together with him on my way to Canada."

"That's tough," she said and added, "I know what it's like to lose someone."

His shoulders sagged. "Yeah. Sometimes life keeps tossing you rocks." The man was lean with a narrow scar tracing down his cheek from his right temple to the side of his mouth. It would have given him an ominous look, except that the rest of his features countered the effect. "Mike was the greatest left-handed quarterback Minnesota State College ever had. He could've gone pro." As he spoke, he took off his glasses and rubbed the bridge of his thin nose. "Died in a car accident." He tapped the newspaper. "His truck went over an embankment and caught fire."

Despite feeling that she should listen to the man's story, her thoughts were on her own troubles. "Sorry about your loss, mister, but I got an appointment. Take care."

"Of course, thanks for listening." He took a small address book out of his jacket pocket.

Patty gave Maggie a nod.

Maggie hurried over. "Why don't you stay? Take an empty booth and relax until closing time. You can spend the night at my place. You don't have to head out in this freezing weather."

"Thanks, but no. I have a job interview."

Maggie raised an eyebrow. "A job interview at this time of night? Seems kinda suspicious. You be careful."

"Gotta be first in line." After Patty paid Maggie, she slid off the stool and donned her parka. Tucking her hair under her wool hat, she said, "I just might be headed south."

"There's a big snowstorm headed our way," Maggie said. "I'd like to go with you, My bones are beginning to creak with the very idea."

Patty pulled on her gloves and waved as she went out the door. If her luck turned, she just might be headed for a warmer climate. Wherever she went it was bound to be better than Bromont.

Chapter 2

After the girl left, Camden continued to stare at the newspaper, unable to accept what he'd read. Before he'd driven up to Bromont, he'd tried Mike's cell number. Now he knew why he hadn't gotten a response. Flipping open his address book, he looked up Mike's address: a Post Office Box with a side annotation—Clive's RV Park.

Camden had written Mike that he'd be free during the Christmas holidays and suggested they go snowshoeing together. Mike's answer came in a postcard: *Great. I need to talk to you. Something important.*

While Camden waited for his meal, he reflected on his first meeting with Mike. It had been late spring four years ago when Camden had taken to running at dawn through the wooded grounds near the college. His thoughts had been deep in the shroud of his mind when he turned onto a side path and almost collided with another runner.

"Sorry," he'd said, moving aside, yet continuing to run.

The man had nodded and kept pace with him, an unusual occurrence since Camden ran fast.

"Nice day," the man said. "How far you going?"

"Up to Dover Hill." He'd thought that would put the man off.

"Great run, that last mile is steep," the man said without even a catch in his breath. "Mind if I tag along? Name's Mike. Yours?"

"Camden."

They ran on through the pines, across the bridge spanning the creek that fed the river running down to the town below. The buildings from the college and the Veterans' Hospital were towers of stone set amongst the surrounding forest. Wildflowers edged the gravel path, moss hugged the ground, and ferns softened the barks of trees. The men, well-matched, glided through the still morning as the sun rose. Neither gave ground to the other and neither pressed the other to compete.

At the top of the hill, they rested, their breath causing whispers of fog. "Not too many people run this far or this early." Camden stretched his hamstrings.

Mike glanced at him under his black eyebrows. "I jumped ship." He smiled. "Needed to get out of the VA loony bin they call the recovery ward." He laughed. "Don't worry, I'm about to be released." As if afraid he'd said too much, he added, "It's beautiful up here."

Camden laughed. "Fresh air is always helpful. I'm a history professor at the college." Although ostensibly with the university, his recent line of work made for a lonely life, but helped him deal with his grief. Some called it revenge, others patriotism. "You?" he asked the man.

Mike shrugged. "Vet in rehab."

"You seem very fit."

"Physically, I am. My buddy wasn't so lucky. Those of us who saw combat are given therapy for PSTD to get us back to normal, if there is such a thing." Mike jogged in place on the dew-laden grass.

Camden wiped the sweat from his forehead with the sleeve of his cotton shirt. "Sorry about your friend. Is he going to be all right?"

"He's blind, but he's getting a guide dog. Hope it helps."

"Damn, that's tough. Can't imagine what that would be like. I think I'd go berserk." He looked toward the rising sun and knew it was time to turn back. "I run everyday to drive out…memories. It helps a little." He couldn't speak of the accident that had killed his wife and daughter five years ago. The pain was too deep, too raw.

Mike stretched his calves. "Okay if I join your daily runs? I have my own devil."

Camden smiled and tilted his head, thinking how odd, but normal that sounded. "Look forward to a companion dealing with hell."

Every day as they ran, they exchanged ideas and beliefs, and the friendship that was born that early morning deepened, neither judging, both frank and easy with the other.

When Maggie placed his order in front of him, he looked up startled. Leaning back, he frowned, took off his glasses, and rubbed the scar on the side of his face.

"You okay?" she asked.

He sighed. "I was better before I read the paper. A friend of mine died recently in a car accident. Did you know Mike Garrick? He lived at Clive's trailer park with a buddy, Josh Peterson."

"Names don't sound familiar. You just get in town?"

"Yes." He picked up his fork. "Can you recommend a place to stay? I'm not sure how long I'll be here."

Maggie wiped the counter where Patty had been and picked up the classifieds. "You want these?"

He shook his head, so she gathered them up and put them under her arm. "There's Alice and Chuck's B&B if you like that kind of thing. Better than a motel and they're friendly without being nosey. That's hard to come by in a small town like Bromont." She left him as he began to eat.

The meatloaf was spicy and hot, not like the usual diner fare, and the food seemed to fill the void that the news about Mike had caused. Odd, how tragedy affected him.

He glanced at the article again and felt an odd sense of responsibility concerning Josh. How could the blind man get along without Mike? Camden wouldn't leave town without checking on Josh and finding answers about Mike's death.

Chapter 3

It was five above zero when Patty pulled into the trailer park next to number seventeen. She sized up the thirty foot long trailer sure her truck could tow it. The trailer looked new, so it might be ready to go, but her dad had talked about trailers needing an anti-sway stabilizer bar and brake control. If this guy didn't have one on his trailer, he'd have to get one. She bit her lower lip, thinking how long the delay might be if he needed to install one. She wasn't going to risk her truck without it, especially under stormy conditions.

The wind banged against her truck, and ice crusted the window edges. She cut the engine and rubbed her gloved hands together. When she stepped outside, cold knifed through her parka. Even before she knocked on the trailer door, a dog from inside emitted a growl. She hesitated. Ever since a dog had bitten her when she was a kid, she'd been apprehensive around them. She swallowed and rapped harder, hoping the owner would keep the hound under control.

"Come in," a deep voice said.

Slowly, she pulled the door open. The trailer was warm, but the dim light and the dog made her pause.

"Harkin?" She heard the man's voice, but could only make out his outline seated at the far end of the room.

"Yeah, I'm Harkin," she said, pitching her voice low.

"Well, come in and shut the door. You're letting in the cold."

A yellow dog with long fur came over to her, sniffing and wagging its fluffy tail. Patty remained standing half in and half out of the trailer. "What about your dog?"

"She's friendly. Close the damn door."

Patty obeyed. The dog sniffed her boots, her crotch, and then lifted its face to look Patty in the eye.

"Good dog, good dog," Patty muttered, steeling herself from backing out the door.

"She's a golden retriever and sweet," the man said. "If Kallie doesn't take to you, the deal's off."

"Oh." Patty's chin went up and her stubborn streak kicked in. "I'm not much of a dog person."

"Hold out your hand palm down and let Kallie sniff."

Patty did as she was told. Kallie seemed to like what she smelled, since she began to lick her hand. But after a few licks, Patty pulled her hand away and wiped it on her jeans.

"If you get the job, you'll know all about dogs by the time we get to Tucson."

"She seems to like my taste for all the licking she's done."

"Well, I guess Kallie thinks you're all right then."

As if on cue, the dog plopped down on a blanket under a Formica table opposite the kitchen sink. "Have a seat," the man said.

Patty edged past the dog, swiveled a chair around to face the couch, but remained standing. The man wore dark glasses. It didn't take long for her to put the dim lighting, the dog, and the glasses together. He was blind. Should she say something?

"Do you want a cup of coffee?" he asked. "There's a pot on the burner. Mugs are just above in the cupboard on your right."

"Thanks, I will." Patty rose, took a mug out and poured herself a cup. "You want some more?"

"Yeah. Thanks."

She took the five steps to where he sat. He pushed his mug forward, keeping his hand on it, and she filled it, returned the pot to the burner. "I never did get your name," she said and eased into the chair.

He smiled, showing beautiful white teeth. "Didn't give it. Name's Josh Peterson." He held out his hand and she leaned forward to shake it. Instead of letting go, he traced this thumb across the back of her hand. "You're a woman."

Patty pulled her hand away. "I didn't say I wasn't."

"Yeah, but on the phone you led me to believe you were a guy. You said your name was Pat."

"Right. Patty Harkin."

"What did you think you were doing answering my ad?"

Patty's temper kicked in. She took off her wool hat and dropped it on the table. Her hair tumbled down around her face. "I answered your ad because I got a truck—a damn fine truck, I might add." She leaned forward, her palms on the table. "It's got Quadrasteer with a trailer-tow package. That reduces curb turning if you don't know. I'm a mechanic. I know engines." She took a deep breath. "And I can tow your trailer south." She couldn't see his eyes, but his square jaw was set, and she felt his eyes bore in on her. But that was silly. After all, he was blind.

"There has to be enough room in the cab for me and my dog," he said.

"Why? You aren't going, are you?"

"Of course. You think I'd let some stranger tow my trailer without going along. Hell, I want to get me and my trailer out of this place." He leaned forward. "Now, what about the truck's cab?"

"Plenty of room. Got an extended cab and the rear seats fold down." She didn't mention that at the moment her stuff took up most of the space, but she could toss some and rearrange the rest.

"Sounds good."

"I keep it clean. Never had a dog inside." She glanced at Kallie, whose doleful eyes watched her.

"Not sure you will, yet. I wasn't expecting a woman. I'd planned to share my trailer with the driver. I can't have the added expense of a motel. You'd have to sleep in here or pay for your own digs every night."

Patty glanced around the trailer which was none too roomy. A doorway past the kitchen led through a narrow hall into a room with a queen-size bed. She walked over and glanced into the two side areas, noting a toilet, a shower and basin behind a door. She turned and asked, "Where did you plan on the driver sleeping?"

"This couch converts to a bed. You can keep some of your things in the space that used to house the TV." He motioned to his right.

"Okay."

"You still want the job?"

"So far so good. What about the pay?" She walked back to her chair. "Your ad said the salary was negotiable."

"All expenses paid plus twenty-five dollars a day."

"You gotta be kidding."

"Expenses include food and gas."

"Oil?"

"Yeah, whatever."

"All repairs to the truck, if it breaks down?"

"You said your truck was in mint condition."

"It is, but stuff happens on the road."

"Okay. Any breakdown up to a thousand. After that, you're on your own. You got insurance?"

Patty wiggled in her seat. She had insurance, but not for long. Still, it shouldn't take but two weeks max to get south. "Yes," she finally said.

"Sounds like you're lying."

"No. I got insurance. It doesn't come up for renewal for another two months."

He nodded and ran a hand through his dark curly hair. "I got a few rules. No smoking, no drugs, and no booze."

"No problem."

"Good. What about the law? You have a record? Don't lie. I might be blind, but I can tell a lie from the way people speak."

"I got picked up for shoplifting when I was fifteen."

"How old are you now?"

"Twenty-eight." Adding a year or two didn't hurt. She'd be there soon enough.

"Okay. So it's settled. Twenty-five dollars in salary."

"Twenty-five plus five dollars for incidentals."

"What incidentals?"

"Whatever comes up."

"Just like a woman to haggle over particulars." He leaned back and stretched out his legs, which Patty noticed were very long.

"When do I get paid?"

"I'll pay you at the end of the first week, the rest when we arrive at our destination."

"How about paying the five dollars for incidentals every two days?" Patty rubbed her hands along her jeans.

"You're hard up, aren't you?"

"I didn't say that."

"You didn't have to. It's obvious." He nodded. "Okay. It's a deal."

"Cash. No check."

"Suits me," he said.

Patty realized she'd been holding her breath and slowly exhaled.

"Storm's coming in," Josh said. "We'll head out tomorrow, first light. Is that a problem?"

She grinned. "Nope. What about provisions? Are the propane tanks filled?"

"Everything's ready to go."

"You got the anti-sway and brake control…"

"Yes." His brow furrowed. "I told you everything's ready."

"Guess you were sure you were going to get an answer to your ad. It wasn't in the paper yesterday. This must be the first day it ran. Any other takers?"

"None of your business. I like to be prepared. You want the job or not?"

"I'll take it, but it means I'll have to bunk here tonight."

"Right. Your pay period starts tomorrow."

"Got it. I'll need to get gas. Can you give me cash for that now?"

"No."

"No? How am I going to drive us out of here in the morning without gas?"

"I'll give you my credit card."

"Really? You'd trust me with that?"

"Trust is something I have to do. I figure I can have the police after you in a jiffy if you take the card and run."

"Well, I wouldn't do that." She held out her hand, then realized he couldn't see what she was doing. She tapped the table. "You'll have to give it to me."

He reached into his back pocket, pulled out a wallet and extracted a credit card.

She got up and took it. "What's your zip code? I'll need to know it."

He sighed and told her. "You sure you can hitch up the trailer by yourself?"

"I'll need someone to guide me into the hook up; otherwise it might take a long time. How will we manage that?"

"I'll get the manager's son to help. He can crank in the trailer's stabilizers, too." He rubbed his clean-shaven jaw as if he were trying to decide something. "If at any time you can't hack the job, you forfeit the remainder of your salary."

"Like hell."

"I gotta have some assurance you won't cut and run on me."

"We'll shake on the deal or isn't my handshake good enough?"

He didn't answer. He held his coffee mug in his left hand and stood. His head was only a few inches from the ceiling.

"Now there's another rule you gotta agree to. Nothing—and I mean nothing—gets moved from where I put it. Understand?"

"Yes." She could see her reflection in his dark glasses.

He held his head high, his shoulders back. A man, though blind, completely comfortable in his skin. "There might be times on the trip that it'll be awkward for you and me. Kallie is my eyes, but outside this trailer I need some info on directions. Like which door leads to the men's room, how many steps to some place. Can you do that?"

"I don't know why not. I had to show my dad the men's room many a time when he was drunk."

Josh smiled. "I think you'll do."

Chapter 4

After Patty filled up her truck with gas at a nearby station, she was tempted to drive to Maggie's to tell her about her new job, but decided against it. The guy had trusted her with his credit card, and she wasn't going to take advantage of him by driving extra miles. Instead, she'd send a postcard from a stop along the road south.

Her spirits were high as she drove back to the trailer park. When she pulled up next to number seventeen, she was surprised to see the trailer door wide open with the interior light flooding the frozen ground. Josh stood in the doorway with a blanket wrapped around his shoulders.

She grabbed a small gym bag with stuff she'd need for the night and got out of her truck. "What's going on?" Patty asked as she started up the steps into the trailer.

"Kallie decided to take an extra lap around the park and doesn't want to come back inside."

"She's nuts. It's freezing." Patty began to push past Josh, but he barred the door and held a leash out to her.

"Corral her for me, won't you?"

"Me?"

"Yeah, you."

"I'm not your servant."

"I hired you, didn't I?"

"To be a driver, not your dog handler."

"I was a bit abrupt. Please, go after Kallie, put on her leash and bring her inside."

"Better." She took the leash and shoved her bag into his hands. "Take my bag, and I'll go dog hunting." When she got near Kallie, the dog loped farther away. Patty called her name, but the dog continued to trot to another trailer with her nose to the ground. "You stupid mutt. You have a fur coat; I don't." There seemed no end to Kallie's desire to roam. Patty followed the dog, her patience growing thin, and her fingers, toes, and nose growing numb. "This is stupid. If you don't come back now, I'm leaving you out here," she yelled. As these words hit the air, Patty slipped on an icy spot and fell onto her back. She lay stunned, looking up at the inky night sky. Then she felt a hot wet tongue licking her cheek.

Before Kallie could bolt, Patty grabbed her collar and hooked on the leash. "Is that what it takes to make you come? I won't fall again just to catch you. This is the last time I go after you. From now on, you come or you get left behind or else your master will have to fetch you." Patty got to her feet and arched her back. Come morning, she'd be sore. Kallie, now totally compliant, trotted alongside Patty back to the trailer. Once inside with the door closed, Patty removed the leash.

Patty began to have doubts about the arrangement she'd agreed to. "Wait a sec. What's the deal?" She asked, dropping the leash on the table. "I thought Kallie was a guide dog. Aren't they supposed to do their master's bidding?"

"She's like any other dog, when she's not in harness," Josh said, while he sat in a chair at the dinette table.

"So how come you let her out on her own?" Patty blew on her hands to warm them.

"Too cold for me and she had to go. She knows something's up and has been a little odd ever since my friend left."

Patty arched her brow. God, he's blind and gay to boot, she thought. "Your friend?"

He laughed. "I can hear it in your voice. He was a friend, not a lover. Why is it people always think that if two people of the same sex share space, they must be gay?"

"Cuz that's usually the case nowadays." She picked up her bag from the chair and put it on the floor.

His chin came up. "You moved your bag. Where did you put it?"

"On the floor."

"Don't. I might trip over it."

"Oh, sorry." She carried her bag to the couch and dropped it. "Small quarters. Any room in the bathroom for stuff?"

"There's some space in a cabinet next to the sink. It's all yours."

Patty rose and went to peek inside the cabinet. "Gee, thanks. I might be able to put my toothbrush in there."

"Are you always so sarcastic?"

"Hell, no. But I've never lived in a tiny trailer with a dog either."

"Well, get used to it. That is, if you still want the job."

"I said I'd take it."

"You must be even harder up than I thought."

Patty looked around inspecting her surroundings. "Your offer came at a fortuitous time."

"Fortuitous? My, that's a big word."

Patty jammed her fists on her waist. "Just because I needed a job doesn't mean I'm uneducated, you oaf. I got my A.A. and would've gotten my Bachelor's degree, except my dad needed me and times got tough." She caught her breath, then added, "And another thing. I'll help you out when you need it, but don't expect me to be your girl Friday."

"Okay. Okay. I'm upset and Kallie's acting weird. Maybe it's all about leaving here." He held out his hand. "Peace?"

She moved forward and took his hand. "Peace," she agreed, feeling the strength of his grip.

"Put Kallie's leash on the peg by the door." He pointed toward the entry door. "Please."

She walked over and did as he'd asked, then joined him at the table. "How did you and your friend manage to live in such close quarters? I mean, there's only one bedroom and I think it would've gotten claustrophobic."

"He was gone a lot. Worked nights and at times slept there during the day. Otherwise he'd bunk exactly where you're going to."

She wanted to know what his friend did, and what happened to him, but knew he'd think she was nosey. Of course, she was, but this wasn't the time to be pushy. She took note of the maps and papers strewn on the table. She fingered one. "What's all this?"

"I thought we'd go over our itinerary before morning."

She leaned forward. The map was marked and there was a printed page with directions and facilities at each stop. "How'd you do this?"

"My friend did it before he left."

"He was thorough." Her finger traced the roads they'd travel, and she checked the mileage. "The first day is a long haul. If the storm comes in, we might not get that far."

"We'll see."

"How about a backup plan?" Looking into his dark glasses made her feel peculiar. "I mean just in case. Seven hours of driving time is a lot with a tow. If it snows, there's no way we can make that first stop."

He frowned and ran a hand through his hair that curled down onto the nape of his neck. "Where do you see us stopping instead?"

"How about here?" She put a finger on a city with a small trailer park.

"Where's that?"

"Oh, sorry. Let's see. It's two hundred and fifty miles south of here." She squinted to read the fine print. "Glory Hole Trailer Park."

"Sounds awful." He grimaced.

She laughed. "It does, doesn't it? Let's hope we get past Glory Hole." She continued to study the route. "There's a place called Oldorf's farther south. That might be possible." She ran the mileage miles through her mind. "Looks like we can get to Tucson in about a week and a half."

"That's what I figure."

"Where do you plan to park the trailer in Tucson?"

"I'll let you know when we get there." He put out his hand palm up. "You never returned my credit card."

"Oh. I forgot." She reached into her jeans' back pocket and pulled out his card and the receipts. "I had to use two different pumps with the limit set at the station for the card."

"You must have been near empty. At the cost of gas we'd better get south fast before I go broke." He took out his wallet and inserted the card without fumbling for the slot.

"It's a thirty gallon tank."

"What kind of mileage do you expect to get?"

"Depends on the road and the tow. We'll have to see; maybe twelve to fifteen miles per gallon if we're lucky."

"Yeah. If we're lucky. Haven't had much of that lately."

"Me neither."

"Want some dinner? Stew's on the burner."

She glanced at the stove. "That's sounds wonderful." Although she'd eaten at Maggie's earlier, turning down a free meal wasn't in her DNA, especially when she never knew when the next one might come.

"Mind dishing it up?" He began folding the maps.

"Heck, no." She rose, went to the burners and took off the lid. "Boy, it smells great and looks good." She noticed plastic bumps glued on each burner knob at the off point. "Hey, these markings are clever." She took down two plates from a cabinet, dished up the stew, and set them on the table with utensils and paper napkins she found in a drawer.

He held the plate with his right hand and he ate with his left.

"Have you always been a lefty?" she asked before taking a mouthful of stew.

"You're observant."

She shrugged. "My dad was left-handed. He said lefties were more gifted than right-handed people. Course I don't know where that put me. In the ungifted area I guess. He never thought about people's feelings." She took another bite, swallowed, and said, "This is good, sharp, and tasty. How do you manage to cook?"

He set down his fork. "Always put the spices back in the same place. If you check closely, you'll notice that each has a different raised mark. I've memorized them. I make things up as I go. Before I lost my sight, I was a good cook."

"You still are." She took another mouthful. "How'd you go blind?"

He picked up his fork and started eating again. She waited, but apparently he wasn't going to answer her question. They finished the meal in silence. Afterward, she offered to wash the dishes while he remained seated.

Her back was to him when she heard him say, "I was in Iraq. Flash shrapnel to the face." His voice was clipped with a hint of despair—or was it bitterness?

She turned around. "I'm sorry. That had to be tough."

He didn't add anything, but stood and headed to his bedroom in the front of the trailer. "Let's get up at six and try to start by seven. The manager's son knows the routine and can help. Might have to rouse him from bed though." He hesitated. "Do you need anything?"

"No." She glanced at Kallie. "Where does the dog sleep?"

"Anywhere she wants." He chuckled. "Her mat's under the table. She seems to like it there. If you have to use the john during the night, don't worry about waking me, I'll slide the pocket door shut. We'll have to make some timeline arrangement for the use of the shower. Goodnight."

After placing her things in the cupboard that used to hold the TV, she pulled open the sofa bed. Sheets were clean, and she found a pillow behind one of the cushions and a down quilt in another cupboard. Pleased her life had taken a positive turn, she crawled into bed and fell into a deep sleep. Sometime during the night, she awoke to find Kallie snuggled up against her and a light coming from under Josh's door. Odd. Why would he need a light? She pushed Kallie off the bed, got up, walked part way to Josh's room and called out softly. "You up?"

"What?" Josh asked.

"Your light's on. I figured you didn't know it."

"Of course, I don't know. The lights are on timers, so it always looks like someone's in the trailer. If it bothers you, you can change the settings in the morning."

"It doesn't bother me. I just thought it strange."

"You think too much."

Patty went back to bed, feeling foolish. There was a lot she had to learn about living with a blind person. She couldn't imagine what it must be like to lose your sight. Kallie put her muzzle on the side of the bed. "Aren't you supposed to be more concerned with your master than with me?" Patty shook her head, stroked the dog's soft coat, and fell back asleep.

She awoke to nudges of Kallie's cold nose. With bleary eyes, Patty stared at her watch. Six o'clock. "You must have a clock in your head." Stretching her sore back muscles from the previous night's fall, she lay in bed for a few minutes and heard Josh in the shower. She washed up at the kitchen sink.

While she was brushing her teeth, Josh came out. "You about through? It's snowing, and Kallie needs to go out."

"So?" came her garbled reply. After rinsing her mouth, she asked, "Don't you usually take her out yourself?"

"I thought you could take her and let the manager's son know we need him ASAP."

Patty dried her face and peered through the window and saw big flakes falling. "How did you know it was snowing?"

"Radio. We gotta move fast if we want to get out of here today." He was at the kitchen counter, starting to make coffee.

The idea of coffee gave her pause to stay and have a cup, but Kallie had her nose against the door and whined. "Okay, okay." Patty bundled up and grabbed Kallie's leash from the hook.

As she went out, Josh said, "I'll have breakfast for you when you get back."

It was a tad warmer out than last night and heavy wet snowflakes coated the ground. She rang the bell at the manager's office, stamped her boots on the bottom step and waited. Finally a freckled-faced young man came to the door.

"I'm Patty Harkin, Josh's driver. We need your help to hook up my truck."

The fellow rubbed a sleeve across his face and said, "God, it's early. Come in for a sec."

She didn't need prompting to get out of the cold, and Kallie joined her inside the small office that had probably been a sitting room at one time.

"I'm Howard," the young man said. "My dad runs the place, but he's on vacation. You from around here?"

"Yeah, but I no longer have ties here, unless you can call Maggie a tie."

"Maggie?"

"Yeah. You know Maggie's Diner?"

"Doesn't everyone?" He rubbed his pale cheeks with both hands. "You sure you want to take off today? It's going to be a heck of a storm—blizzard strength they say."

"Josh wants to leave by seven."

He pulled back a heavy red drape and glanced out the window. "I'll come over in about twenty minutes."

She started to leave, when he said, "I told my dad about what happened to Mike. He sure was surprised. He always thought Josh would die before Mike."

Her hand was on the doorknob. "Mike was his friend?"

"Yeah."

"He died?"

"Yeah. I never met the guys, but I took care of everything just like my dad told me to. He'll be real sorry to see Josh leave. He doesn't think Josh can make it on his own. It's good he has you."

"Well, he's got Kallie, too." Patty left and headed back to the trailer. No wonder Josh and Kallie are in turmoil. She knew what the death of someone close did to your mental state. After her dad died, at times she didn't know what she was doing or if she should be doing whatever it was she did. Boy, even her thinking and words got mixed up.

Back in the trailer, the aroma of fresh coffee greeted her. She took off her parka and settled in to eat a hot, flavorful seven grain hot cereal, toast, coffee, and juice. The pay might not be great on this job but the food was good. In between bites, she told Josh that Howard would be over soon.

Josh poured kibbles into a bowl for Kallie. "While you two hook up the trailer, and retract the stabilizer pads, I'll make sandwiches and a thermos of coffee. The stabilizer crank's in the storage unit on the left side of the door. Howard should know that. I'll hit the button to retract the slide outs when I leave the trailer."

"It's going to be rough driving today," she said, relaxing in her chair after finishing her coffee. "Might not get as far as you figured."

He shrugged his broad shoulders. "It doesn't matter as long as we get a ways down the road ahead of the storm."

"Even if it means staying at Glory Hole?" She laughed.

"Yeah. Even Glory Hole is better than here."

She felt the same way, but knew Maggie would scold her and say you can't run away from your troubles. Her thoughts were interrupted by Howard's banging on the door. She jumped to her feet, realizing she still had to make room in the truck's cab for Josh and Kallie.

Chapter 5

It took longer to clear space in her truck's cab, make the trailer hookup and retract the stabilizers than Patty had figured. By the time everything was set, it was after eight o'clock. The howling wind had blown snow over the entrance to the trailer park, making their exit tricky. With the storm coming in, the snowplows were already out trying to keep the main streets drivable, but their effort had built up berms on side streets. Unless Howard started shoveling, the park entrance would soon be impassable. Although Patty was glad to be heading south, she wished the driving conditions were better. It was her first time towing anything as long as thirty feet, but she wasn't about to tell Josh that.

Kallie sat behind Josh and Patty in the extended cab with her head between them. The dog's breath warmed the back of her neck. She pushed the dog's head away, but her concentration on driving precluded fussing too much about Kallie.

Josh remained quiet, facing forward, his dark glasses in place. Patty wondered what he looked like without them. She couldn't resist asking, "Why do you wear dark glasses? I don't mean to be rude. I was just wondering."

He didn't answer for a long time, but finally said, "You don't need to know what I look like."

Rebuffed, she shut up, but remained curious about his shrapnel burns. She drove onto the main highway leading out of town. The wind shook the truck and pushed the tow sideways. "That was a big gust."

Josh seemed oblivious. Of course, he couldn't see the almost whiteout conditions, but he must hear and feel the wind blasting against the truck.

"This storm's a ripper." Patty gripped the steering wheel tighter. "Not sure we can even make Glory Hole."

"We can't go back. So keep going as long as you can."

She glanced down at the radio and pushed a button for the news station. The weather was the main topic.

"The first blizzard of winter is giving the area a jolt. It will continue snowing through the night and into the morning. Snow accumulation eight to ten inches, wind gusts up to forty miles an hour."

"Jesus," Patty said.

"You called?"

"Ha. Ha." She clicked off the radio. "You can't see the conditions outside, but this is not a day to be traveling on the highway with a trailer."

"Sometimes it's best not to ponder what could happen. Keep driving." His voice held anger—or was it tension. Kallie whined, and he reached up to scratch her behind the ears. "It's okay, girl. We got an A-number-one chauffeur."

Patty smiled. "Thanks for the title, but eventually, I think the road will be shut down."

"How far have we gone?"

"Thirty miles."

"We're crawling. Can't you go faster?"

"Not if you want to remain upright." As she said this a wind gust hit them, sending the vehicle skidding sideways. She worked the steering wheel, turning into the skid. The road's shoulder dropped off sharply. Patty's heart pounded as she bit her lower lip. With only inches to spare, she got the rig under control. Slowly, they moved back into the center of their lane. Patty exhaled. "That was close."

"Yeah, I felt it. You did a good job."

He clung to the handhold above the door and leaned back into his seat. Kallie hunkered down with her muzzle resting on his shoulder. Time passed. The flakes flying against the windshield blinded Patty, and she had to blink often to keep her focus on the road ahead. The windshield wipers became sluggish against the accumulated snow on the front windows. Few cars or trucks were out. "If there's a whiteout, I'm stopping. We can only hope no one's stupid enough to keep going." She glanced at him, but he didn't respond. "Are you asleep?"

"No."

"Okay. I couldn't tell. You're so quiet."

He shrugged, and she continued to fight the swirling wind and snow. When the wind abated a bit, she asked, "Did you know your friend Mike a long time?" He didn't answer, so she continued, "How did he die?"

"Are you just making conversation or do you really want to know?"

She thought about this for a second, then said, "We're going to be together for over a week, so I'd like to get a handle on you."

He turned away to face the side window. His words came out slow and exact. "We knew each other from high school. We both got scholarships to state college, football for him, academic for me. After college, I persuaded him to sign up. I was full of patriotic energy. We joined the Marines." He leaned his head back. "Stupid waste."

He stopped speaking and she waited. Finally, she couldn't stand it anymore. "Okay and then what?"

"We got sent to southern Iraq. We thought we were invincible till we ran into a firefight–snipers, shelling. I got hit. Mike pulled me into a building. A grenade went off. I got sent back to the states for rehab, and he finished his tour. It was Mike's idea to set up house together, so we bought the trailer and moved around the country. Got to Bromont for the fishing. Mike got a night job and we stayed longer than we should have. He'd been a football player, but he started drinking. The car accident might have been his fault. I'm not sure. Truck caught fire. Kallie and I got out, he didn't."

"A fellow said a football player named Mike Garrick had died. Was that him?"

"Yeah. I guess it must have been in the papers. Mike had athletic potential, but he got screwed up in Iraq. It happens."

"The guy who told me about Mike said he was a friend of his."

"Oh?"

"Camden something. I don't remember his last name." She laughed. "The only reason I remember his first name was because it's different. He had a scar on the side of his face."

Josh's body sagged as if he'd expelled all his air.

"You know him?"

"No." His voice was curt.

"So why the heavy gasp?"

"I'm tired."

"I don't buy that." She kept glancing over at him from time to time. Oh, he knew the guy all right. He just didn't want to say so. Why?

"Stop being such a yenta. Just drive, damn it."

"I might be a nag, but you're a liar and a clam."

"I can't be both at the same time."

"Oh, shut up."

"Glad to."

Silence filled the cab. The defroster kept the window from fogging, but the snowfall thickened, and the wipers labored. She spotted flashing red lights ahead. "Looks like the police have closed the road and are diverting traffic to an off ramp."

"How far have we gone?"

She checked the mileage gauge. "A little over a hundred miles. Guess we can't even make it to Glory Hole." She tapped the brakes as she neared the flashing lights and slowed the truck to a crawl behind a large semi, then followed it down the off ramp to a large truck stop across the road. After finding a somewhat sheltered spot between two large trucks, she shut down the engine. Leaning back, she breathed a heavy sigh. "Looks like this is home for the night."

She described the area to him. "A diner and gas station combo about fifty feet ahead of us. Trucks parked all over and a few cars too." She peered out one window and then the other. "There's a big red rig hauling some kind of machinery on our left and a moving van on our right."

"Good. The trucks should shield us from the wind." He unbuckled his seat belt, zipped up his jacket, and snapped on Kallie's leash, not her harness. "Will you take Kallie? She probably needs to go. I need to set the stabilizer pads. I can feel my way." Before she could answer, he went outside, letting the wind whistle into the cab.

Patty glared after him, then turned to Kallie. "I guess I'm driver and dog walker." She zipped up her parka, pulled the wool hat over her thick hair and entered the world of swirling snow. Kallie was ecstatic and pulled on the leash, but Patty had no intention of straying far from the truck. She could barely make out the diner or the gas pumps. After walking Kallie around the nearby trucks, she made her way to the trailer door and swung it open. Josh had already opened the slide outs and turned on the heat.

She unhooked Kallie, hung the leash on the hook, and hung her parka on the peg next to it. Only when she worked on cars was she so precise and neat whereas her habits away from a job tended to be helter-skelter.

Josh sat at the table unpacking the lunch he'd made earlier. "Grab some cups, will you?" he said, fumbling with the thermos.

Patty grabbed the tilting thermos and set it upright, then retrieved cups from the cabinet. It was past noon and she was hungry. "Tell me," she said, sitting opposite him and unwrapping a sandwich. "Why don't you take Kallie for walks? Ever since I've been around, I'm walking her."

"I told you. When she's not in harness, she's like any other dog and wants to run, sniff, and play. With what's happened to Mike, I think she needs more of that sort of thing. You can handle that better than I can." He unscrewed the thermos and pushed it in her direction.

She poured the steaming coffee into two cups. "You seem to handle the crank and other mechanical stuff easily."

"You can do that by feel. Finding a dog that wants to run and play is a different matter."

"So did Mike usually take Kallie for romps?"

"All the time. He spoiled her. I think that's why she's acting strange. He's gone, and she's confused or else she's in mourning." He hesitated. "Dogs do mourn, you know."

Patty focused on Kallie who was sprawled on her belly, her eyes glued to the food on the table. "She's looking mighty hungry. How often do you feed her?"

"Morning and around dinner time. Don't go for that sad-eyed look." He took a bite of his ham and cheese sandwich. "Mike said that's how she always looked at him whenever he ate."

They continued eating in companionable silence. When they'd finished, Josh said, "Let's find out about the road closures. They ought to know something at the diner or the gas station."

"I thought of that, but I'm not taking Kallie with me."

"I don't expect you to."

Patty rose and put on her parka. "Anything you want me to get while I'm there?"

"Nothing, thanks. We've got plenty of provisions."

With the warmth of the trailer behind her, she struggled against the whipping wind. Burrowing her neck deeper into her parka, she jammed her gloved hands into her pockets. Despite the wind and freezing temperature, she was glad to be outside. Living in the trailer seemed like a sentence to boredom. She wondered how Mike could have lived in it, even if he'd been away a lot.

She walked to the diner, keeping near the semis for protection from the wind. At the diner's door, she bumped into a man coming out. They grunted, danced around one another, and went their separate ways. Inside she unzipped her parka, removed her gloves and hat. The smell of fried foods, grilled meat, sweat, and wet clothing accosted her senses. People milled around a small grocery store and a café across from it. High on one wall, a TV blared out a soap opera. Nobody was watching except the obese middle-aged cashier.

"Any news about the roads?" she asked the gray-haired woman.

Keeping her eyes glued to the TV, the woman said, "Maybe they'll open tomorrow. Storm ain't lettin' up. With my luck, the electricity'll go out before I get to see all my shows."

Patty turned away and wandered around trying to find someone who might have a better handle on the situation. She saw a couple of truckers talking and went over to them. "Any info on the road heading south?"

"You stuck in your car, little lady?" a large-bellied man asked as he leered at her.

"No. I just landed my UFO and trying to figure when I can take off again for Mars."

A younger man with a crew cut grinned. "Don't take offense. He's just surprised to see an attractive woman in this hole." He toyed with the zipper of his expensive parka.

Patty nodded, refusing to react to his comment. No need to rile the guys. "No one seems to know much about the conditions. Any ideas when the roads will open up?"

"Not yet," a man with a thick full beard said. "Police shut down all roads in the area. Weatherman claims the storm's stalled and will dump over a foot and a half of snow before it moves off to the east."

"Nothin's moving," the potbellied man said. "This place might run out of food before we get out."

The bearded fellow laughed. "Hey, you can afford to lighten up on the groceries." He glanced at Patty. "Not sure this gal can handle not eating for long though."

She smiled. "Not to worry fellas. I'm in a trailer with plenty to eat." She backed away. "See ya." She noted that the crew cut young fellow raised his head and stared after her. Maybe she shouldn't have said anything about having food in a trailer. If food ran short, tempers could too, and you never knew what people might do.

She took her time, looking at the different items still left in the grocery aisles. The potbellied guy was right. There wasn't much left on the shelves now, and several dishes on the diner's blackboard menu were crossed out. She wondered how much food the diner had on hand. All the booths were full as well as the stools at the counter. She knew from Maggie that most diners didn't keep a large food inventory, since keeping deliveries small meant longer time frames to pay bills. No deliveries meant a low food stock. Not good under these conditions.

Near the exit, the crew cut fellow came up to her. "If you need help while you're here, come on over. I'm in the yellow truck towing a reefer, a refrigerator trailer to you. Third row back." He put his hand on her arm. His clean-shaven face came close to her, his eyes seemed cloudy as if he might be on something.

She ignored his hand, pulled on her hat, and zipped up her parka. "Thanks, but I've got everything under control."

He grinned. "Well, honey, you never know. Trailers are known to have all kinds of trouble in the snow and cold."

"Really?"

"Yeah. The transmissions freeze up. You might need a tow."

"It's a travel trailer and doesn't have a transmission."

He wasn't to be put off. "But your truck does and it can jam on you. I can fix it if it does."

"You're a mechanic?"

"Hey, I'm a truck driver and know everything there is to know about engines."

"You're a real winner." She turned and went out the door. What a jerk, she thought. I wonder how many women he's pulled that one on. She didn't look back, but had the uncomfortable feeling that he was watching her.

Back in the trailer, she found Josh sitting on the couch. "Not much to tell. Nobody knows anything. All the roads are shut down. I guess we just sit tight until tomorrow." She took off her boots and left them by the door, hung up her parka and stuffed her gloves, hat, and scarf in its pockets. "What do you do to occupy yourself?"

He tapped the audio cassette on his lap. "I used to read a lot, but now I resort to books on tape. It's not the same, but that's the way it is."

"What about Braille? Did they teach you that in rehab?"

He laughed. "That's not easy to learn. Not patient enough. The whole experience drove me nuts. I know I should, but..."

Kallie growled, the door banged open, and the crew cut fellow barged inside.

Snow blasted into the trailer. Kallie barked with raised hackles. The intruder stood transfixed in the doorway, staring at Kallie. Patty backed up against the far wall.

Josh's voice roared above the noise. "Shut the god damn door! What's with Kallie?"

"She's barking at a man who just busted in," Patty yelled back.

"What do you want?" Josh's body stiffened.

The man stared at Josh.

"Well?" Josh insisted. "Shut the door. Kallie hush up."

Kallie stopped barking, but her growl rumbled low as she faced the man. Patty was pleased the dog was willing to launch herself at the man.

"Look, I meant no harm," the stranger mumbled as he struggled to close the door against the blasts of wind. When he finally succeeded, he turned toward Josh, ignoring Patty and Kallie. "Sorry about the sudden entrance. I followed the little lady and saw the door wasn't properly latched. When I turned the handle, it flew open. Really didn't mean to barge in, mister."

Patty opened her mouth to tell him he was a damn liar, but Josh interjected. "You can see all is well."

The man glanced furtively around. "If you need any help, you can count on me."

"I can't imagine why we'd need your help, but thank you," Josh said in a monotone voice that held an edge.

"Which way you heading?" the man asked.

"What's your name?" Josh countered.

"Floyd Rickter. I got a reefer, running empty to Kansas."

"A reefer?" Josh asked.

"Sorry for the shorthand. A refrigerated trailer."

"Interesting," Josh said. "Thanks for stopping by, Floyd."

"Things might get tense around here if the snow doesn't let up," Floyd said. "How long can you last on your propane and batteries?"

"Long enough," Josh said.

The three stood in an uncomfortable silence with Kallie growling and the wind shaking the trailer.

Floyd finally said, "Coffee sure smells good."

"I'm sorry there isn't any more," Patty said, taking Josh's low-key approach to the stranger.

"Oh, well, sure. The diner's out of things, too."

"I noticed." Patty continued to stand next to Kallie.

Floyd turned again toward Josh. "You remind me of someone, especially your voice."

Josh's chin came up. "Really? You know many blind men?"

"Ah, no, that's not it. Sorry. I guess I'll be going then." Floyd stared at Patty.

Neither Patty nor Josh said anything, giving Floyd no choice but to leave. He turned the doorknob. "Take care." The wind whistled into the trailer as he went back into the cold.

After he left, Patty made sure the door was locked, put the chain on as well, then faced Josh. "He's a liar."

"I know, but getting angry wouldn't help, would it?"

She shook her head. "I wanted to slap him silly then shove him out."

"What would that have accomplished? He'd just want to get back at us."

"It would have made me feel better."

He sat with his hands clasped under his chin. "Perhaps you made him think you wanted him to follow you."

"Bull." She walked over and stood in front of him with her hands on her hips. "He started flirting the minute he met me, and I did nothing, I repeat, nothing to egg him on."

"Okay, but there's something about you that catches a man's interest."

"How the heck would you know? You don't even know what I look like. I could be a gross looking hag."

He smiled. "But you're not. I can tell. I'd say you were rough around the edges, but ugly, no."

"You don't know that."

He didn't respond.

Kallie came over and nudged Patty's knee. Without thinking, she stroked the dog's head. "I think Kallie would have torn Floyd apart if he'd made a move on you, Josh."

"Maybe she was defending you."

"She's not my dog."

"No. But dogs have good instincts about people. I think dogs have better sense than humans. Kallie is my leader-eye dog, but she liked Mike more."

"How can you be sure? You could have been wrong."

He shrugged, stood, and walked back to his room, leaving the pocket door open. Patty mulled over the situation. Finally, she walked back toward his room and leaned against the hallway's fake wood paneling. "That guy brought up a good point. How long will the batteries and propane last?"

"Not sure. I already cut the thermostat back. Haven't you noticed it's colder in here? Use the lights only when you have to. We don't want to have to move into the diner along with everyone else. Drawing attention to ourselves is not a good idea."

"Why? Is there something you haven't told me?"

As he sprawled on his bed, he said, "I have to trust people, but that doesn't mean I'm naive. Floyd now knows I'm blind, with a dog and a woman. You said there might be a shortage of food. I think we are in some danger. Not a lot, mind you, but some."

"I can take care of myself."

"To some extent so can Kallie, but you must admit there's some truth in what I'm saying."

She nodded. "You're right, but not sure what we can do about it. No one is going anywhere for a while."

"I'm not saying we should do anything but be wary. If anyone gets rough, we'll handle it."

"Well, you were a Marine."

"Yes, and I have a gun."

That gave Patty pause. Here she was stuck in a snowstorm with a blind man who had a gun. She almost laughed at the situation. Maggie would love to hear this story. Returning to the table, she took out a stamped postcard from her old collection and began to write. *I'm on my way to Tucson with a blind man....*

Chapter 6

A day after the storm blew through Bromont, Camden drove his silver-gray SUV through plowed streets to Clive's RV Park. He'd never met Josh, but he'd heard about him. How could Josh get along without Mike's help? Had Mike felt guilty about Josh's blindness? Why else had he stuck with him the past two years? Camden knew how guilt ate into the soul.

The road into the trailer park was blocked by a snowdrift, although a vehicle had already barged through the drift, leaving a hint of a path. His four-wheel-drive might get through, but he didn't want to chance it. He pulled to the side of the road and surveyed his options. Zipping his parka up to his chin and jamming on his plaid wool tam, he waded through the calf-high snow, thankful he'd had the foresight to wear heavy boots.

The three rows of various sized RVs and travel trailers were covered in a mantel of white and for the most part seemed unoccupied. It was hard for him to imagine Mike living in such a place with his blind friend. After making his way through the snow to the office, he knocked on the door. When a young man opened it, he said, "I'm Camden McMillan...."

"What can I do for you?" the fellow asked, not giving ground.

"I'm trying to get in touch with Josh Peterson. I understand he lives here."

"Used to. He left yesterday morning."

"In the middle of the snowstorm?"

"It's cold with the door open. You better come in. I'm Howard." He turned and retreated into the room.

Camden stepped into the warm room, closed the door and removed his hat.

"I'm sitting in for my dad." Howard moved behind the desk. "Josh left before the storm got bad."

"I was led to believe he's blind."

"He is. He got himself a driver, a gal with a big truck. Sweetest piece of machinery I ever saw." He blushed. "I mean the truck. Course she was good-looking, too. Some guys have all the luck."

"Ah, yes." Camden smiled. "Did he leave a forwarding address?"

"No. Said he was heading south and would be in touch." Howard shifted from one foot to the other. "My dad would have wanted an address, but the guy was paid up, so..." He raised his arms in a futile gesture.

"Your dad's the owner?" Camden took off his lined leather gloves as he spoke.

"Yeah. I'm managing the place while he's on vacation." Howard sat, raised his narrow chin and scratched his neck. "Dad knows he can count on me."

"I'm sure he appreciates the help." Camden hesitated. The story of Peterson's sudden departure right after Mike's death seemed strange. "Perhaps you can clear things up. When did Peterson decide to leave?"

"Not sure when he decided, but he left a message on the phone saying he'd be outta here as soon as he could. I was surprised when the gal came knocking and asked me to help hitch up her truck. I didn't know how he was going to manage, him being blind and all, but he got a driver and off he went."

"Do you know the driver's name?"

Howard brightened. "Patty Harkin. Lives locally, or did, anyway."

"Any other information about her you might have? Address, phone number." Camden took out a small notebook.

Howard's eyes narrowed. "You're the second guy that's come around asking about Mike and Josh. Why all the questions? Who are you?"

"I already told you, Camden McMillan. I'm trying to get in touch with Josh Peterson."

"Why? Is he in some kind of trouble? The last guy was real pushy, a jerk. Said Mike was in trouble at the Hitower Casino, but didn't say why. Mike did work there nights as a dealer and bouncer for Slocum."

"Slocum?"

"You're new around here or you wouldn't ask. Slocum owns the big gambling Hitower casino east of here on the Indian reservation. You don't fool with Slocum."

Camden shook his head. "I'm a friend of Mike Garrick's and hoped to visit him on my way north, but then I read about his death. I knew Mike was Josh's friend and helper." Camden paused. The other guy's connection to Slocum must have spooked the boy about giving out information.

Howard fiddled with the desk drawer. "Look, I'm just subbing for Dad. I never met Mike and only talked to Josh briefly, but Dad said they were good guys."

"I told Mike that if anything ever happened to him, I'd look after Josh," Camden lied.

"Well, Dad said he needed looking after. Said Mike was really good about taking care of him."

"You can understand why I feel I have an obligation." Camden paused. "Can you tell me anything about Patty Harkin?"

Howard shook his head. "I don't know much about the gal. I helped hook up her truck to the trailer. She mentioned knowing the owner of Maggie's Diner. Good food. Ever eat there?"

"Had dinner there last night. Friendly woman, Maggie. Did you get the girl's license number?"

"No." He frowned. "Didn't need to."

Camden looked around the bare-bones office and took note of the filing cabinet set in the corner. "You must have information on Peterson's trailer. Could you give me the make and its license number?"

Howard stuck his hands in his pocket. "How will that help you? You got connections with the cops?"

"Mike Garrick was a friend and I want to help Josh if I can. No hidden agenda."

Howard took a few steps to the gunmetal filing cabinet and opened it. "They were good guys. Always paid on time. No trouble. That's what Dad said, anyway." After rifling through manila folders, he pulled out a file and read off the information about the trailer. "The other guy who came in wanted the same stuff. I didn't give it to him even though he threatened me. I told him I'd call the cops, and he backed off."

"Good for you." Camden had written the particulars in his small spiral notebook and put it back in his pocket. "Were you here when Mike's accident happened?"

"Sure was. Cops brought Josh here afterward. The cops said they found Josh and his dog floundering in the snow. The truck had caught fire and Mike's body was badly burned. Gruesome, huh? I tried to look in on Josh from time to time, but he shut the door in my face." He shrugged. "I did what I could."

"It sounds like Josh was really upset."

"I guess. Anyway he's gone." Howard shifted papers around on the desk.

"You did what you could," Camden reassured him.

Howard gave a small smile. "Dad agrees. My dad thought Josh would die before Mike. Funny how life goes, isn't it?"

"Do you know anything more about the accident?"

"Mike must've swerved and went over the side of the road. They don't know why, but you gotta watch out for elk."

Camden asked, "Where did they take the body? There must be a morgue or coroner in town?"

"Dr. Whittier took over old Doc Clausman's practice. He acts as the coroner."

Camden rubbed the scar on the side of his face. Josh Peterson was headed south, but where exactly? Maybe Maggie would know where this Patty Harkin went. "You've been very helpful. If you hear from Peterson, would you please call me?" He handed Howard his card with his cell phone number and told him where he was staying.

As he turned to leave, Howard said, "Hey, you're an author! Wow." He glanced up from reading the card. "A professor, a PhD guy."

Camden smiled. "Don't let it make you star struck. I'm a history professor, and the book is on the Peloponnesian War."

"Yeah. Well, I've never met an author before."

After shaking hands, Camden asked, "By the way, who owned the RV?"

Howard flicked open the file. "It was registered to both Mike Garrick and Josh Peterson."

Camden pulled on his gloves. "What's this Slocum place like?"

"Rough and tumble, busy. My dad would kill me if I went near there," Howard said. "Especially with the latest stuff that's gone on there."

"What kind of stuff?"

"Big fight over some gal—Mike might have been involved. Two of the guys and the gal are missing."

As Camden walked out the door into the cold, he knew his next visit would be to Slocum's.

Chapter 7

The trailer grew colder and Patty settled onto the couch to read a book she'd found in the trailer. Kallie snuggled next to her. Dogs might not have been Patty's thing, but she welcomed Kallie's warmth. "If all dogs were like you, girl, I might have taken a shine to them." Kallie nuzzled her hand. "This book is about guide dogs, just like you." Patty noted the signature on an inside page. *Mike Garrick.* She studied the distinctive serifs on the M and G. Unusual, for a man. As Patty read, she became intrigued with the interaction of hand signals and voice commands between the blind and their dogs.

Josh came into the living area. "I'll take Kallie outside for her break." He hesitated. "Unless you want to do that while I make lunch."

"You're good at the food department. I'll take her." She drew on her parka, gloves, and hat. "Can you make something hot? In case you haven't noticed, it's getting chilly in here."

"Yeah and it might get colder. I'll heat some soup. Lentil, okay?"

"Great." She hooked on Kallie's leash and went outside. The wind had subsided and it had stopped snowing. Maybe they'd be out of here tomorrow. She glanced in the direction of the diner and was surprised to see no lights. No electricity was bad news.

A portly man in thick parka tromped through the snow and nodded to her as he reached the semi next to her truck and trailer. "How's it going?" he asked.

"Okay. How about you? Any news about the roads?"

"Nope. Electricity is out in the diner and people are getting riled up. Some young dude started a fight over a card game. Pulled a knife. I'm holing up in my cab till morning. I'll be running the engine most of the night to keep warm." He opened his cab door and climbed in.

Patty and Kallie circled the two semis, scuffing through the new fallen snow, and then went back inside the trailer. The aroma of toasting bread and garlic made her sigh with anticipation. After her short time outside, even the cool temperature inside seemed warm. No sooner had she hung up her parka and sat at the table than Josh placed a steaming bowl of soup on the table.

"The way you work in the kitchen is amazing."

He smiled and put the other bowl down. "As long as nothing is someplace that it shouldn't be, I'm fine." He set two plates on the table, laden with toast covered with melted brie and garlic.

Patty grinned. "I've died and gone to heaven." She needed no prodding to start eating.

Josh sat and lifted his spoon and held onto the edge of his bowl with the other hand. They ate in silence until Patty told him about the truck driver's comment about the incident in the diner. "Do you think it could have been Floyd?" she asked.

He shrugged. "It could be anyone."

"I'd like to find out."

"Why? You got a yen for him after all?"

"Oh, please, you can't be serious. Just curious." She took another bite, savoring the brie and garlic. "I guess I'm bored. We could take a walk up there and back. The wind isn't too bad. Stretch our legs, give Kallie a little more exercise, too." She could tell he was thinking about her proposal. He must be as antsy as she was.

"Okay, after we clean up the kitchen. But," he waved his spoon in the air, "we don't get involved with anyone and we don't go inside the diner."

"Right."

Kallie pranced about the trailer obviously aware something was up when Josh and Patty donned their outdoor clothing. Josh put Kallie's harness on and went out the door with his left hand holding the harness. When they were outside, Josh handed Patty the keys and told her to lock the door behind them. "Walk a pace ahead of me on my right side," he said. "That way I can put my hand on your arm. Kallie may be my eyes, but she doesn't know where we want to go."

They set out toward the darkened diner. Snowdrifts banked against the gas station pumps, forming human-like shapes. Across the open spaces beyond the parked vehicles, the pale afternoon light cast a gray sheen. Josh and Patty moved slowly through the snow as high as Kallie's shoulders. The dog lunged forward with Josh holding her harness.

"It wasn't such a workout the last time," Patty said between gasps.

"You wanted exercise." Josh wasn't even breathing hard.

"Maybe we should have left Kallie in the trailer," Patty said. "She's really struggling."

"It'll be easier on the way back. We'll have made a swath."

They continued until they were outside the diner's door. "I want to mail a postcard. I'll just be a second."

Josh's grip on her arm tightened. "You agreed we wouldn't go inside."

"Hey, that hurts."

His released her. "Sorry. Sometimes I forget I'm strong."

"Strong is an understatement." She rubbed her shoulder. "I'm just going to drop my postcard in the mail slot. I'll be right back." Once inside, the odor of urine overwhelmed her. The bathrooms must have overflowed. She made her way through the darkened interior to the post box, dropped her card to Maggie into it and turned to leave.

Floyd stood in her way. "I knew you'd come back to see me."

"Not hardly. We came out to get some exercise and post a card." She shoved past him, but he followed her out the door. He stopped when he saw Josh and Kallie. The dog's growl cracked the white silence.

Instead of backing off, Floyd moved forward and stood in front of Josh. "You ever been to Slocum's place in Bromont?" He studied Josh's face. "The guy I'm thinking of lived in a trailer," Floyd said.

"You've got me mixed up with someone else." Josh turned away.

Floyd grabbed Josh's arm, yanking him around.

Josh's dark glasses fell into the snow. In one swift move, Josh twisted Floyd's arm, spinning the man around so his back was to Josh.

"Kallie, sit!" Josh ordered with his head bent toward Floyd's immobile figure.

"He's got a knife in his free hand," Patty yelled.

Josh tightened his grip on Floyd's arm. "Drop the knife or I'll break your arm and then your neck."

"Christ, let go. I dropped it," Floyd said through clenched teeth.

"He did," Patty said.

"Patty, get my glasses and put them on for me, please." Josh's voice was so calm it was scary.

She found them, brushed off the snow, and placed them on Josh. In her hurry she hadn't even looked at his face. She stepped away from the two men. Josh thrust out one leg and shoved Floyd, sending him sprawling into the deep snow. Floyd lay stunned, staring up at Josh.

"Don't ever try that on me again." Josh's voice cut through the air like flint. "Next time I won't be so easy on you."

"Jeez, you broke my arm." Floyd whined, holding his arm close to his chest.

"I doubt it."

"I didn't mean anything. Just wanted to talk." Floyd floundered in the snow as he rose to his feet. "Learn more about you."

"Nothing about me is any of your damn business."

Floyd backed away nursing his arm. "Look, no harm done, okay? A little misunderstanding, that's all."

Josh's answer was interrupted as three men came out of the diner. One said, "Is this asshole bothering you, sir?"

"Not any more."

"He's caused enough trouble. Lousy gambler, a drinker and a sore loser. Threatened one of our friends with a knife." Patty recognized the speaker as one of the truckers she'd spoken to earlier.

The men glared at Floyd and he backed away. He turned, threw a last hateful glance over his shoulder, and slunk off toward his truck.

"Wish there was a cop around to take him in," one of the men said. "But they're busy with accidents and stuff."

"Is your friend hurt?" Patty asked.

"He's okay," another man said. "But that jackass shouldn't be loose."

"Not much we can do for now," the third man said.

"If I see that bum's truck," the man said, pointing at Floyd's retreating figure, "I just might run him off the road. He's probably a gear jammer."

The other two men put their hands on the brawny man's shoulder. "Come on, Brutus, no sense in making things worse. Let's forget it."

"No way." Brutus turned toward Josh. "I watched through the window on how fast you reacted to that s.o.b. For a blind guy, you're a hell of a fighter. Army?"

"Marines," Josh said.

"Figured something like that." Brutus fingered his gray beard that touched the top of his large chest. "You in the trailer over by the moving van?"

"Yes," Josh said, his voice flat, giving nothing away.

"You're lucky. It's getting bad inside." Brutus motioned with his head toward the café. "You take care. See ya around." The men turned and went back inside.

Patty heaved a sigh. "Sorry about wanting to go for a walk."

"Why you'd want to post a letter when the mail won't be picked up for days is beyond me." He shrugged. "Let's go back." He gripped Kallie's harness, faced the direction of the trailer, and said, "Kallie, forward."

As they walked, he asked, "I thought I knew slang, but what's a gear jammer?"

Patty laughed. "A reckless truck driver."

"You've been around truckers?"

She shrugged. "When you work around engines, you pick up the lingo."

When she unlocked the trailer's door, Josh said, "We'll have to shovel to get the snow out from around the tires, won't we?"

Patty looked and her heart sank. "Yeah. Especially around my truck's front wheels and…" She glanced at the trailer. "Probably the trailer's, too."

"I'll do it," Josh said.

"How?"

"With a snow shovel." As if reading her thoughts, he continued, "I can feel along the bumpers and the edge of the trailer. Get the shovel, please. You'll find it in the rear storage area."

As she left to get the shovel, she thought about Floyd and how he might know Josh through a connection to Slocum. There was a lot she didn't know about Josh, but one thing she'd learned was that despite being blind, he wasn't helpless.

Chapter 8

During the night the trailer swayed with the wind gusts, making a whooshing noise against the duel-paned windows. Josh had told her the trailer had an arctic package that improved the insulation. She put her head on the pillow and stared into the dark. Kallie had made herself comfortable on Patty's bed, but she didn't mind since the dog kept her feet warm. Odd how she'd been so afraid of dogs for so long and in just a short time she was becoming enamored of this golden retriever.

Kallie raised her head, a low growl vibrated in her throat. "Darn it, Kallie. Just when I get comfortable, you scare me." There was pounding on the door. Oh God, it's that stupid guy Floyd again, she thought. She threw back the covers, jammed her feet into her wooly slippers, grabbed the sweater she'd dropped on top of her blanket, and pulled on her jeans. The pounding continued and a muffled voice could be heard on the other side. She switched on the light by the table.

Josh, dressed in sweats, stood in the entrance to his room, his dark glasses in place, and a gun in his hand. What the hell was he going to do with the gun when he couldn't see his target?

"What should we do?" Patty asked, swallowing her fear. Kallie stood in front of the door, her growl deep and loud.

"Try opening the door a fraction. Only way we'll find out what's going on." His voice came hard, terse, yet calm, as if he was telling her what they'd eat for dinner.

"Put the gun away," Patty said.

"Don't worry. Its for scare tactics only, unless...."

Kallie barked as the pounding continued. "Just don't shoot willy-nilly." She unlocked the door and cracked it open an inch.

"Jesus, I thought you'd never open up. It's me, Brutus. We got a problem at the café. I think you can help."

"Let him in," Josh said.

When she opened the door wider, the wind tore it from her grasp and swung wide. Brutus exploded into the room carrying snow and cold with him.

"Down, Kallie," Josh ordered. The dog sat, but kept an eye on the uninvited guest.

Brutus shoved the door shut. "Sorry if I scared you, but I had no other way to get hold of you." The big man brushed snow off his beard with his gloved hand.

"You said there's a problem at the café. Not sure how we can help." Josh stepped forward, hiding the gun behind his back.

"I'll get right to the point. You know the electricity's been off for some time and food's almost gone. Most of the truckers have holed up in their semis with their motors running. But we got a young woman there with a two-month-old baby. She shouldn't be left in that freezing place. One of us could take her in, but we talked it over and thought it would be better if she bunked in here tonight."

"Who's we?" Josh asked.

Brutus shrugged. "A few truckers."

"This trailer is small, not set up for a baby." Josh said.

"Hell, it's paradise in comparison to what she's putting up with."

Patty wondered what Josh's response would be. She was about to speak up in defense of the woman when he said, "Okay, we'll help."

"Great." Brutus took a few steps forward and clapped a large hand on Josh's shoulder. "I knew an ex-Marine wouldn't turn down doing a good deed. Thanks. I'll bring her over."

Brutus was out the door, shutting it firmly behind him before Josh or Patty could react. It was as if a hurricane had entered and left behind an uneasy quiet.

"We haven't much time to reconfigure the sleeping arrangements," Josh said. "She'll have to take your bed."

"What?" Patty hadn't considered that.

"You can bunk in with me," Josh said.

"Now wait a minute." She put her hands on her hips.

"Look," he said. "I'm not sleeping on the floor. You want her to sleep on the floor or do you want to sleep on the floor?"

"No, but…."

"Okay then. Don't worry. I won't come on to you. We'll make a barrier in the bed between us. Get your stuff together and haul it into my room. When she comes, it'll be up to you to explain about not leaving things out of place or on the floor."

"And where will you be, oh big boss?"

"In my room out of the way. I'll talk to her in the morning. By then hopefully the storm will be over, and she can move out." He turned, leaving her slack-jawed. What could she say? Even if he was logical, he didn't have to be so dictatorial.

When she moved her things into Josh's room, she found him on the far side of the bed, his face to the wall, and a long bolster set at his back. She smiled at his idea of a barrier. Okay. She'd sleep on top of the sheet and under the blankets.

Before she had a chance to square away her gear, the trailer door opened and in walked Brutus, nudging a small frail figure in front of him. He closed the door and ushered his charge to a chair where she sagged into it with her arms cuddling her baby to her chest. Brutus set a small canvas bag on the floor next to her as Kallie sniffed its contents.

Her parka hood fell back revealing a wan-faced young girl. Her lips were thin and blue, her gray eyes round and dilated with what appeared to be fright or exhaustion.

"You look frozen through," Patty said, moving next to her. "Would you like some hot tea?"

"Thanks, yes," came the thready reply. Then she cringed as Kallie pushed her nose onto the girl's lap.

"Don't worry about Kallie, she's friendly. She's Josh's guide dog. He's the owner of the trailer. She just wants to get to know you and your baby." Patty wondered at her ability to talk about the dog as if she were her owner.

"I like dogs." The girl put her thin hand on Kallie's head and left it there for a moment.

"Looks like I'm leaving you in good hands," Brutus said. "You take care of yourself, young lady." He patted the girl's shoulder.

"I can't thank you enough, mister." The girl's words were swallowed by the storm as Brutus left. She sniffed and wiped her runny nose with the back of her hand.

Patty gave her a tissue and then started to boil the water. She placed a tea bag in a mug and reached for the cookie canister, thinking the girl looked as if she might keel over. When she turned back to the girl, she saw the baby had been placed on her back on the bed, its tiny face angelic in sleep. Kallie's chin rested on the mattress next to the baby, her brows quizzically furrowed, her nostrils twitching.

The girl stretched her arms wide then unzipped her parka. "Thanks for letting me stay here."

"The least we could do. I'm Patty. Josh is asleep in the back."

"Linda," the girl said, and nodded to the baby. "Arlet's two months old."

Patty peered at the small face. "Kinda young to be taking a car trip in the snow, isn't she?"

Linda shrugged. "I didn't know the storm would be this bad." She looked at the baby and added, "I'm going to meet my husband in Bromont."

"We just came from there." The kettle whistled and Patty poured the water into the mug.

"It's a small town, right? Do you know my husband, Peter Darby?"

"No, sorry." When Patty put the mug and cookies next to Linda, the young girl was weeping. "Hey, now," Patty said, taken aback. "Everything will be okay. The snow can't keep coming down forever, and you'll be on your way soon enough."

"Hope so." Linda took a sip of tea and nibbled on a cookie. "I'm breast feeding so I don't need formula or anything, but diapers are running low. Arlet's so little and a little sickly. Really glad you put us up."

"Glad to help. Things will look better when you're with your husband."

Linda nodded and continued to sip her tea, but her eyes maintained a sad, faraway look. Something was definitely not right with this girl. "How long have you been married?"

"I haven't seen him since he left to get a job."

The girl's answer was evasive, so Patty asked, "How long ago was that?" As usual her curiosity spun its own web.

"Five months. He said he'd send for me when he was settled, but I haven't heard anything since Arlet was born. I decided to come anyway. I have his address. Beaver Street."

"That's on the north side of town." Patty didn't add that it was the worst part of town. Perhaps it was her skewed view of men, but she doubted that Linda would find her husband. And if she did, she didn't think he'd be employed. The reunion might not go as Linda dreamed. "Tonight try to forget about everything and get a good night's sleep." Lord, I sound like Maggie, she thought. "The toilet's through that door on the left," she pointed. "Use the basin here in the kitchen, cuz you have to go through the hall that leads to the bedroom to get to the shower and washbasin. Please don't leave anything out of place or on the floor. Since Josh is blind, he needs to have everything out of the way."

After seeing Linda and her baby settled, Patty locked the trailer's door and went back to the bedroom where the small light on her side of the bed was lit. She started to slide the pocket door to the bedroom shut, but Kallie pushed her way in first. "Thought you might stay in the other room tonight," Patty said softly as the dog sprawled on the floor at the end of the bed. Patty took off her slippers, but kept her jeans on. Josh's even breathing was the last thing she heard as she burrowed under the blankets.

It wasn't Kallie who woke her in the early hours of the morning, but the loud wail of the baby. It was dark in the bedroom and the sun hadn't come up yet. She peered at the glowing dial of her watch: 5:40. The crying stopped abruptly.

"About time," Josh said, groaning.

"The baby's been good most of the night," Patty said.

"Yeah. Most."

"Her name's Linda. I mean the girl is Linda. The baby's Arlet."

"I don't need introductions at this hour."

"Sorry." Patty shut up, but lay on her back unable to go back to sleep. The bolster remained between them as if neither had moved an inch during the night. Kallie jumped up on the bed, nudged the bolster off the bed and plopped down between them. "Ugh. What do you think you're doing?" Patty pushed the dog's head off her thigh, but Kallie refused to be thwarted. Her chin rested on Patty's leg.

"Kallie's smitten with you," Josh said.

"She likes everyone, including the baby." She petted Kallie's soft fur until she felt Josh's hand on the dog as well. She withdrew hers.

"Didn't mean to scare you," he said. Silence hung between them. The wind moaned and snow pelted the windows. "Now that I'm awake, you want to tell me about our guests? Knowing you, you found out her entire history."

"Humph. You think I'm nosey, don't you?"

"A common trait of women."

"Lordy, but you're biased against us."

"And you? I seem to hear a few negative feelings about males."

"Yeah, well, experience is a heck of a teacher."

"Agreed."

She felt him roll over to face her. Although tempted to turn on the light to see his face without his dark glasses, she hesitated. "Why do you always wear dark glasses?"

"Are you trying to prove my point?"

"Okay. It's a fact. I'm nosey. So answer my question."

He sighed. "People have a difficult time looking into the face of the blind. Eyes are the portal to our souls. When you can't read the other through their eyes, you feel awkward. I want people to feel comfortable when they're around me."

That sounded so philosophical that she didn't have a retort. She wanted to say, it wouldn't bother her, but she wasn't sure. When had she been close to a blind person? Never.

"So tell me about our guests." In the dark his deep voice was soft and comforting.

"The girl's in trouble, and I don't mean from the storm. Before she had the baby, her so-called husband left to get a job. Claimed he'd send for her. He never did and never contacted her after the baby was born. She plans to meet him in Bromont. I don't think she's married. No ring. It sounds to me like the guy left her in the lurch."

"Not good." He rolled off the bed on his side. "From the sound of the wind, I think we'll be here at least another day. I'll shower now and get out of everyone's way." He moved about the room, gathering up his clothes and glided out of the room like a cat.

She pulled the blankets up around her shoulders and snuggled, enjoying the extra time alone. But even as she tried to go back to sleep, her thoughts turned to Linda's situation. The town of Bromont and the surrounding area had lost jobs, and more people were unemployed than ever. She planned to ask Linda a few hard questions. Maybe the girl could head back to where she'd come from. Being on your own was not an enviable position, especially with a new baby and no contacts. She punched the pillow, and tossed about, tangling the covers. Now wide awake, she switched on the bedside light, rummaged through her belongings and found her brush. Kallie stretched out on her back apparently delighted to have the queen-sized bed all to herself.

After using the toilet, Patty eased open the pocket door and saw Linda bathing her daughter in the kitchen sink. She moved next to the girl and viewed the squirming tiny body glistening with soap and water. As Linda cooed to her baby, her long red hair fell forward.

"You handle her with such sureness," Patty said.

Linda smiled. "I took care of my younger brothers and sisters."

"Sounds like heavy duty. I'm an only child and don't know the first thing about babies." Seeing only a blanket had been spread out on the couch to dry Arlet, Patty took a towel from a cupboard and laid it out. Linda lifted Arlet out of the basin onto the towel and swaddled her in it.

"She'll be clean and warm now." Linda dried her squirming infant. "I was getting worried, but she's fine," she said, diapering the baby.

Patty cleaned the basin and the kitchen area, knowing Josh would soon be out and might be upset with the mess. She checked the floor, pleased that Linda had kept her things out of the way and on the bed. While Linda cuddled Arlet to her breast, Patty made coffee and set the table for three.

Josh appeared and moved to the kitchen. "Linda," he said. "I'm Josh. Welcome to our humble abode. Hope it's not too cold in here for you, but we've kept the heat down so the butane will last through our stay."

"You're kind to have me." Linda gazed at Josh. "I'll try to stay out of your way."

"I'll fix breakfast, Patty, if you want to take a shower. Kallie can wait to go outside, but she'll probably just go out and come back in under the conditions."

When Patty came out from her shower, she found Kallie eating her kibbles, the bed remade into a couch with the baby asleep in a corner of it, and Linda and Josh sitting at the table enjoying oatmeal. "Well, I guess everything's under control." She dished out cereal for herself.

"Yes," Josh said. "Kallie stuck her nose out the door, jumped into a snow drift, yelped, and came back inside. We won't be going anywhere today."

"The radio said the storm's supposed to end tonight," Linda said.

"Good." Patty sat at the table and looked from Josh to Linda and thought they both seemed rather smug.

Josh held his coffee cup to his mouth, then put it down. "Linda and I have had a good talk."

"Have you thought about going back home, Linda?" Patty asked. "Under the circumstances, maybe…"

"It wouldn't be a good idea," Linda said, shaking her head. "Josh agrees. I'm headed to Bromont. I'll find Peter." She took a deep breath. "But it would be easier, if I knew someone there."

"Go to Maggie's Diner. Maggie Gordon's a good friend of mine." Patty knew how miserable it was to have no home and no one to turn to. "Tell her Patty Harkin sent you, and she'll help you out as best she can."

The room quieted with Josh sipping his coffee, Patty eating her cereal and making toast. When Arlet awoke, Linda rocked her, lulling her back into slumber. The silence inside the trailer was only disturbed by the howl of the wind.

"Could I use the shower?" Linda asked.

"Sure," Josh said, "Make it quick and remember it's gray water and shouldn't be ingested. Although we keep the water heater going to prevent freezing, we use antifreeze. There's drinking water in the kitchen. We have to conserve all our resources, since we don't know how long we'll be stuck here."

"I'll be quick." Linda rose and put Arlet on the sofa, then glanced at Patty. "Do you have an extra towel? All my things are in the trunk of my car."

"You'll find one in the cabinet next to the shower," Josh said.

Linda hurried off and Patty waited a short interval, before she said, "Seems you and Linda got acquainted real quick."

Josh nodded. "She's had it tough."

"I didn't realize you were such a softy." Patty rose and put on her parka. "Think I'll take a gander at how things are outside. Kallie might want to stick her nose out to get some air again too."

"Good idea," he stood to pour himself another cup of coffee.

After bundling up, Patty and Kallie ventured outside. The steps were covered with fluffy snow. Kallie dove into the powder and almost disappeared. She came up shaking and barking in what Patty deemed to be pure joy. Grabbing the snow shovel left upright by the door, Patty started to make a path to her truck. The wind came in soft gusts as if it had spent its energy and was pretending to still have power. The semi's engine next to them roared, a sound echoed by other trucks. Kallie frolicked while she shoveled. After she'd dug out the truck's back wheels, she took stock of the entire area. In some places vehicles were mere mounds of white. She shoveled for a few more minutes, then whistled for Kallie and the two of them went inside.

When she shook out her parka, snow scattered about the room. Kallie let loose a shake of her own, sending snowflakes and water droplets throughout the room.

"How deep is it?" Josh asked, turning down the radio next to him.

"Above my knees, the drifts are huge and some cars are totally buried. Most of the truckers are running their engines and the diner is still dark."

Before he could react to her news, the baby started to fuss, then let out a howl. Kallie looked at Josh, then Patty as if to say, "Do something."

Linda was still in the shower and would be no help. "What do we do?" Patty asked Josh.

"You're a woman. You ought to know."

"Well, I don't." She gazed at Arlet thrashing about, her round face bright red, screwed up in anger, or was it pain?

"Pick her up," Josh said. "That'll probably quiet her."

Patty leaned over Arlet and put one hand under her head and the other under the wiggling body and lifted. She was used to handling camshafts, not screaming babies. "Okay." She moved toward Josh and deposited the bawling infant onto his lap. "You do the fatherly thing and make her stop crying."

"What the heck do I know?" He slowly lifted Arlet to his chest and then to his shoulder. Arlet let out a huge burp and stopped crying. "She's not very ladylike, is she?" He had a wide grin on his face.

"I guess you have the daddy knack." Patty chuckled. "You're one surprise after another."

Josh let out a growl that sounded more like Kallie, than Kallie.

By the time Linda came back out, face scrubbed, and eyes shining, Arlet was fast asleep; her face snuggled into Josh's neck. "Hey, that's a great picture," she said.

"She needed to burp," Josh said. "Maybe you'd take her now."

"Sure." Linda cradled Arlet in her arms and moved to the couch where she sat with a satisfied expression on her face. "I feel like a new person. Amazing what a hot shower will do, isn't it?"

"The weather should let up this afternoon, so perhaps we'll be on our way tomorrow," Josh said, stroking Kallie.

"Gosh, I hope so." Linda frowned and searched in her bag by her feet. "I'll need more diapers for Arlet. Could you take care of her while I get them from the trunk of my car?"

"That might be easier said than done." Patty unlaced her boots. "Where'd you park?"

"Golly, let me think. I'm between a rig hauling farm equipment and another big semi with a yellow cab towing a refrigerated trailer." Linda puckered her lips in thought. "I'm about four trucks to the right of you as you face the diner."

Josh frowned and Patty wondered if he was thinking what she was. A yellow refrigerated rig could belong to asshole Floyd. "If you go, I think I ought to go along," she said.

"Patty said the snow's above knee level," Josh said.

"The gas pumps are obliterated," Patty added. "The cars are totally buried."

Linda's face fell. "I'll need diapers before morning and I'd love to change my clothes."

"Let's wait a couple hours and then give it a try," Patty said. "Maybe the wind will die down some."

"But if you go with me, what about Arlet?"

"Josh has proven to be a better baby sitter than yours truly."

"You're volunteering my services for a job I'm not suited for." He folded his arms across his chest, his jaw tight. "I'd be of better use shoveling the way to her car."

Patty didn't think it smart for her to tell him that was ridiculous. How could Josh find his way to a car that was completely buried? She'd tramped on his ego too often so she tried to be diplomatic. "What color is your car Linda?"

"Maroon. A Toyota Corolla."

"That'll help. Maybe if we walk straight toward the rig with the farm equipment, we'll spot it." Patty glanced at Josh. "It's going to be hard to see with all the snow that's fallen."

Josh hunched his shoulders and sank deeper into his chair. "I get your point. Kallie and I will stay here while you go car searching." He pulled Patty aside. "If you meet up with Floyd, don't get chummy, okay?"

Patty shook her head. "If I chat with the jerk, it's to get info, not for any other reason."

"Well, while you're chatting, don't give info to the enemy."

Enemy had an ominous sound.

Chapter 9

Later that afternoon Patty and Linda headed out to Linda's Corolla while Arlet napped on Josh's bed. Patty grabbed the snow shovel and began to wade through the knee-high snow with Linda behind her.

"Stay next to the front of the trucks," Josh yelled from the trailer's doorway.

Without turning around, Patty waved her hand above her head in acknowledgment, then realized Josh wouldn't notice. The semi's driver next to the trailer had killed his engine and was shoveling and checking his tires. She nodded to him and he gave her a halfhearted wave.

"Time to start digging out," he said. "Plows should be here first thing in the morning. They've already started to clear the main roads."

"Good news," Patty replied, poking her chin above the wool scarf wrapped round her neck.

After they passed two more trucks, Patty stopped. "How much farther do you think?"

Linda's smooth cheeks were rosy orbs. "Another three over, but I'm guessing."

Patty nodded and they continued tromping through the thick white fluff. When they stood in front of the third truck's grill, Patty saw a yellow Peterbilt cab with an attached reefer just beyond, but no visible signs of a car.

Linda patted her on the shoulder. "It's gotta be here."

"Maybe that's it under that mound," Patty pointed ten yards away.

"Oh no, it can't be. What'll I do?"

"Dig." Patty moved toward the mound, where she could just make out the car's maroon top. Linda wiped snow off the car's hood. After assessing the scene, Patty said, "We can dig out enough snow so you can get into the trunk, but you're going to need a tow to pull you out."

Linda waded around to Patty's side. "I can get into the car from here with a little digging. If I start the car, the snow will melt."

"Don't start the engine until we clear the area around the muffler. Otherwise, you'll asphyxiate yourself."

"I hadn't thought of that." With her hands Linda began to shove snow from around the passenger's door while Patty went to the back and shoveled. Her breath steamed into the cold air, and under her parka, sweat dampened her turtleneck shirt.

"Well, aren't you the industrious beavers." The voice came from a few yards away.

Patty knew from the unctuous tone that it was Floyd. She didn't answer or stop digging, but Linda had no such compunctions.

"Hi there," Linda said. "Care to give us a hand?"

"What's the return?"

"Excuse me?"

"What's in it for me?"

"You want money? I thought you might be kind enough to help."

Floyd move closer to Linda. Patty would have hit him with the snow shovel for what he'd implied, but she was too far away.

"I don't mean money, honey. I got a nice warm cab. Glad to have your company. There's plenty of time and I'll dig you out later."

Linda put her hands on her hips. "Thank you, but I want to get it done now."

Floyd shook his head. "I saw you with your baby in the diner, wanted everyone to help you. I see you got help."

Patty stopped shoveling. "Floyd, if you want to pitch in, okay, otherwise beat it."

His long thin face reddened. "Oh, it's you. You just can't stand to be away from me, can you?"

"Don't flatter yourself."

"Your blind boyfriend thought he was tough yesterday, but he's scared."

"Go play Eskimo in your truck and leave us alone. We've got better things to do than listen to you rant."

The heavy snow prevented him from moving toward her quickly, but she was ready to whack him with the shovel if he got physical. He strode through the snow and stopped a few feet away. Even from that distance the reek of alcohol was overwhelming.

"I'm trying to be friendly and you slam me. You're with a loser." He wiped the back of his hand across this mouth. "Maybe I should tell Slocum about your guy."

My guy? What's he thinking? Her temper kicked in. "Shove off. We're busy." She didn't add epithets lurking in her mind. For once she held back.

His eyes narrowed. "I could show you what happens to a gal who gets on the wrong side of Slocum." He waved his hand at his truck.

"What the hell does that mean?"

"Forget it," his voice slurred.

Patty rolled her eyes, picked up the shovel, and tossed a load of snow at his feet. "You're in my way."

He turned and moved toward Linda who stood with her mouth agape. "You want to stick with this stupid broad or come with me?" he asked, putting his hand on her arm.

Linda shoved his arm away. "I'm trying to get my car out of the snow. You want to help, help. If not, move on."

"You don't know what you're missing, babe." He shrugged, made his way back to his truck and stumbled into his cab. When he started his engine, the roar split the air as he intermittently gunned it.

Patty continued to shovel, ignoring the blasts of noise and fumes from Floyd's rig. With any luck he'd flood the engine. After a few minutes she walked through the trodden snow toward Linda, put her mouth close to the girl's ear, and said, "The muffler's clear. Give the engine a try, but don't floor it."

Linda unlocked the door and pushed it open wide enough to angle inside. Once in the passenger seat, she gazed up at Patty. "I can't believe he'd expect me to do what he suggested just to help me get my car out."

Patty leaned inside the car. "Don't spend a second thinking about him. Not worth it."

"You were really nasty to him."

"Sorry if I offended you, but creeps like that deserve to be on an island alone. A good man is hard to find and if you find one, don't let him get away."

Linda smiled weakly then started the car.

"How much gas do you have?" Patty asked.

"Half a tank."

"Good. That should get you to Bromont. I'm going to shovel out around the front wheels. Let the car idle while you get what you need from the trunk, then we'll shut her down, lock up, and go back to the trailer." Patty put her back into shoveling and hoped that Floyd wouldn't get any nasty ideas about damaging Linda's car. He'd have to know they'd report him, but his type was beyond figuring. No matter how much snow she shoveled, Linda would still need a tow. Brutus might help, but she had no idea which truck was his. Deep in thought, she hadn't heard Linda slam the trunk closed, but when the throb of the car's engine stopped, she looked up.

Linda locked the car and stood with a suitcase in one hand and a large plastic bag in the other. "I'm ready," she said.

Patty nodded, shouldered the shovel and started back through the path they'd made earlier. The sun dipped below a gray haze and the snow lost its glitter. By the time they got to the trailer their feet, hands, and faces were blue and icy.

Kallie greeted them with licks as they shed their coats. The warmth spread over them like a blanket and they both sighed.

"Have hot chocolate for both of you," Josh said as he stood in the kitchen. "Arlet's been an angel, fast asleep the entire time, but her breathing seems raspy."

"It's always been that way," Linda said.

Josh nodded. "I figured Arlet would be okay for that short a time. Kallie and I got a chance to chip ice from around the tires."

"How did you manage that?" Patty said with her hands hugging her hot mug of cocoa.

"Feel."

"I realize that, but what did you use? I had the shovel."

"The trucker next to us lent me his. We should be able to haul out of here after the road and ramp are plowed."

Patty hadn't noticed her truck's situation when she'd returned and was glad to hear Josh's assessment he'd gotten from the trucker. "Even though we shoveled out a lot, Linda will need a tow."

"We won't be able to tow her." Josh took a seat across from the women.

Patty turned to Linda. "What about Brutus? Do you know which truck is his?"

Linda shook her head. "No idea. What about the guy who lent you the shovel, Josh?"

"His truck's too big. He'd smash your little Corolla."

"I said, tow, not push," Patty said.

"I heard."

Linda seemed to ignore their spat; her shoulders slumped. "What'll I do?"

"If my truck weren't hooked up to the trailer, I could probably manage." Patty noted the downturn on Josh's mouth. "Course I'd need help getting it hitched back up to the trailer."

"Out of the question," Josh said. "We'll find someone in the morning. The police will be around and they might help."

For a time the three sat in silence, till Linda said, "We had a run-in with a nasty guy."

"Oh?" Josh's chin came up. "Anyone I know?"

"Yeah, Floyd," Patty said. "He made a crude pass at Linda."

"He said things about you, Josh," Linda said before taking a sip of cocoa.

"Like?"

Linda looked meaningfully at Patty, who only shook her head. "You brought up the subject, Linda, you tell him."

"I don't want to be rude."

"You'll be rude if you don't tell him."

"Cat got your tongue, Patty?" Josh asked.

"Never." She moved to the couch.

Arlet started crying from the bedroom and Linda, looking sheepish, rose. "She's probably hungry." She picked up the plastic bag she'd brought and disappeared into the bedroom.

"She got off easy." Josh's hand rested on Kallie's head while the dog had her muzzle resting on his knees. "So what was the slur?"

Patty straightened and leaned forward, her elbows on her thighs, her hands cupped around the hot mug. "You know he's a blowhard."

"I hope that's all he is," Josh said. "Give."

Patty sighed. "He claimed he was going to tell Slocum about you. Then he got way off base with Linda. So I let him have it, verbally that is."

Josh continued stroking Kallie. "I wonder if Floyd would really talk to Slocum. Bet it was a bluff."

"Maybe." Patty took a sip. "Floyd made a threat, but it was strange. Of course, he was stewed, so maybe that's why it didn't make much sense. He gives me the creeps."

"Can you remember his exact words?"

"Something like, let me show you what happens to a gal who tangles with Slocum. What do you think he meant?"

Josh sat back, his mouth drawn into a thin line.

Patty didn't know what to make of his reaction. He seemed to be holding himself together while rage swept over him. Thinking she could get him to open up, she said, "Slocum is not a guy I hold fondly."

"Oh? You know him?"

"My dad went to his casino all too often, especially after he got laid off. Gambling's a disease. Thanks to Slocum's place, we were broke and lost the house. The bank did what banks do best—foreclose."

"Times are tough." He stood and stretched. "Floyd's a windbag. We'll be on our way soon and Floyd will be a bad memory. He can't hurt us."

"Hope so," she muttered.

Chapter 10

Camden timed his visit to the diner after the surge of the afternoon crowd when Maggie might not be too busy. He scanned the postcards and advertisements on the bulletin board where Maggie posted friends' notes as well as community events. Would she tack up a card if she got one from Patty Harkin? Feeling the heat of the steamy interior, he removed his parka and ran his finger under the collar of his blue turtleneck. After sitting at the counter. he picked up a menu from the rack in front of him.

When Maggie came by, she offered him coffee. "Did you find the B&B?"

"Yes. You were right about the place. I appreciate the referral."

She held an order pad in her hand. "If you want something substantial for lunch, the lamb stew's on special. Normally it's expensive, but a driver dumped his entire inventory of frozen food and left before I noticed. The supplier's going to be mighty angry when he learns I'm not paying for the extra items."

"In that case, I'll have the lamb stew." He replaced the menu in the rack and waited for an opportune moment to broach the subject of Patty Harkin. He sipped his coffee, watching the waitress scrub down the tables under Maggie's supervision. The first time he'd come into Maggie's he'd noticed that the interior glistened and the aroma of fresh-baked bread masked the smell of fried food. He almost wished he'd relaxed in a booth, but decided it would be easier to talk with Maggie at the counter.

Maggie returned with a large plate of stew and a biscuit. "Homemade."

"Thought so. You seem to have many loyal customers."

She nodded. "A lot of new faces lately. Odd for this time of year."

"Patty Harkin one of your regulars?"

Maggie's wrinkled face suggested interest. "You know Patty?" She paused. "Of course you do. You sat next to her when you first came here."

"I did?"

"You were chatting with her."

"The slim, good-looking brunette. That was Patty? I didn't get her name."

Maggie grinned. "Is that right? Thought a handsome guy like you would have gotten her name and phone number."

Camden fingered his facial scar and wondered at Maggie's idea of handsome. "She's towing a truck south for a Josh Peterson. Do you know him?"

She frowned. "She went for a job interview, and I haven't seen or heard from her since." A customer waited at the register to pay his bill. "I'll be back in a sec." She hurried off, then took another order and walked back to the kitchen.

In the meantime he ate his stew, relishing its spicy curry flavor. It was several minutes before she returned and stood in front of him. "Lordy, I wish I had more help."

"Seems to me there are a lot of people who could use the job," he said.

"True, but my profit margin is low as it is." She folded her arms. "Now explain about this man, Josh Peterson, and why you want to know about Patty."

"As I said, she's towing a trailer for Josh. I need to talk to him. The kid at the RV Park said Patty came here often, so I thought you might know her plans."

"Wish I did. I've looked after her since she was a tiny tot." Her short frame straightened. "What about this guy Josh? Is he in trouble with the law?"

"Not to my knowledge. Mike Garrick shared the trailer with Josh. Garrick died recently in a car accident, and I want to learn how Josh is doing without him."

She tossed a towel over her shoulder. "I'd like to help you, but I really don't know much about your friends. Were they ex-military?"

He sat up straighter. "Yes, Marines."

Maggie leaned her arms on the counter. "The paper said that a bouncer at Slocum's was a soldier, and that he got in a ruckus with some guys about a woman. She and one of the fellows are missing. The bouncer died in a car accident."

"Did the paper give any names?"

Yes, but I don't remember them, sorry."

"Mike died in an accident and had a night job, but I don't know where." He bunched up his paper napkin. "What about this Slocum place?"

"Slocum owns the Hitower Casino on the Indian reservation." She chuckled. "Not that he's Indian, mind you. Why would this guy Josh need Patty to haul his trailer?"

"He's blind and needed someone with a truck. She must have answered his ad."

"Good for her. She needed a job and wanted out of this town."

"If you hear from Patty, would you let me know? I assure you I don't mean any harm to her or Josh. I need to know how Josh is."

"Depends," Maggie said. "I'd like to know more about you."

He took out his wallet and removed his business card. "Going to check me out?"

"You betcha."

"Here's my card. Call the college and talk to the dean."

She read his card, then studied him. "I'd never have taken you for a history professor."

"I hope that's a compliment. My cell number's on the card."

She smiled. "I'll let you know after I talk to the dean." She put his card in her pocket. "Want any dessert?"

He shook his head. "Just the check, please." He paid her and left a generous tip.

Heavy clouds hung over Bromont as Camden drove through icy streets to Dr. Whittier's office in an old brick building. He parked in the rear, made his way to the entry and opened the heavy wooden door. The lobby had a modern decor with hardwood floors; a bamboo waterfall and leafy potted plants in a corner, not what he'd expected to find in this northern Minnesota town.

Patients glanced up at him as he walked to the young red-haired woman receptionist and handed her his card. "My name's Camden McMillan. I'm inquiring about Mike Garrick's death. If the doctor's too busy, perhaps you could let me see the death certificate."

"Are you a relative?"

"A friend, but it's my understanding that death certificates are public information."

"Please wait. I'll check," the woman said and walked into the back. She returned in a few minutes. "Dr. Whittier will see you. Wait for the nurse to call you."

Camden was about to sit when the door opened and a nurse called his name. He followed her down the hall and into a cluttered office. "He'll be right with you, Mr. McMillan."

While he waited, Camden studied the diplomas and several pictures of children on the wall. No pictures of a woman so he assumed the doctor wasn't married.

"My young patients," the freckled-faced doctor said as he entered his office and closed the door. "Please sit down, Mr. McMillan. I'm glad someone has taken an interest in Mike Garrick's death. You were a close friend?"

He thought about that question and realized that although he and Mike had started out as running partners, their friendship had grown. "We were running partners," he said without going into further details.

"Oh?" He frowned, then pulled out a file from a cabinet and sat at his desk. "I keep the coroner files in here and the patient's records up front. That way they don't get cross-filed."

"Do doctors usually double as the coroner?"

"Part of the reason I opened a practice here was the extra duty and pay of coroner." After opening the file, Dr. Whittier said, "You were running partners? Odd." He tapped the top of the yellow folder.

The doctor's phone rang and he picked it up. "I'll be right there." He hung up. "Excuse me a minute, Mr. McMillan. I have a patient who is impatient." He chuckled at his joke and left the room.

Opportunities for snooping are rare. Camden rose, turned the file around and flipped through it: *Cirrhosis of the liver, emphysema, PTS.* Jesus, no way. This wasn't Mike. He heard footsteps, closed the file, turned it back around and returned to his seat.

Dr. Whittier opened the door. "Sorry for the interruption." He took his seat behind the desk and flipped open the folder again. "You understand I can't give you medical information about the deceased."

"Doesn't the death certificate state the cause of death?" Camden asked.

"Of course. He died of a broken neck, probably from hitting the windshield and then was burned. I did only a preliminary review. Since it was an auto accident, Police Chief Dankbar asked that I not do an autopsy. I saw no reason to counter that request."

"You must be able to tell me more."

"Josh Peterson, his blind roommate, gave the police Garrick's medical records and they gave it to me. He didn't have long to live. The auto accident might have been a blessing—a quick death versus a slow one." He leaned back and studied Camden. "War affects men in horrible ways." He rubbed his chin with his thin, pale hand. "I wished you'd come in earlier. Josh Peterson told the police Mike drank a lot."

Camden leaned forward in his chair. "That's news to me. Drinking was not one of his vices."When did you see him last?"

"About a year ago," Camden said. "But we kept in touch. I'd hoped to do some snow-shoeing with him during my visit."

The doctor frowned. "He was far too sick to have run, much less walk a quarter of a mile or snowshoe." He folded his hands in front of him on the desk. "Are you sure we are talking about the same man?"

"I'm beginning to wonder." Camden stood and moved behind his chair, his hands on its back. "Who identified the body as Mike Garrick?"

"Josh Peterson's statement about the accident. He was lucky to survive. The fire department found Josh and his guide dog floundering next to the burning truck. Mike's body was still in the truck."

"Did you compare Mike Garrick's face to his ID picture?"

"Not enough to ID from the burned remains. The police brought in his effects that included his wallet unscathed. It was in the glove compartment. The police told me the body was that of Mike Garrick." The doctor leaned back and studied Camden. "I had no reason to doubt them. Perhaps this is wishful thinking on your part. It's hard when someone you care about dies."

Camden shook his head. "I'm saddened, not grieving, at least not yet."

"The young man who manages the RV Park identified Mike Garrick as the man who drove the truck."

"A boy named Howard?"

He glanced through the file. "Yes."

"I talked with him. He claimed he never met Josh Peterson or Mike Garrick."

Dr. Whittier frowned. "Perhaps the police should have questioned him more closely, but under the circumstances they probably didn't think there was a need to do so. Are you trying to tell me that you don't think the man who died was Mike Garrick?"

"Not sure. Things just don't add up, that's all."

The doctor rubbed his forehead. "I had the dead man's medical records and there was no reason to conduct an autopsy under the circumstances. No sign of liquor or drugs according to the police." The doctor fiddled with the papers in front of him. "Look, I'm new in town. I took the word of the police. I saw no need to stir up trouble over a tragic auto death."

A rising anger built in Camden's chest. "Mike had been a college football star, a runner, kept in shape, didn't drink much, was a former Marine. I can't understand your findings."

"Your description doesn't match the man's medical records. I'm repeating myself, but war does terrible things to people, and perhaps you didn't know him as well as you thought."

"I think there's been a mix up. As a Marine he would have been given a free burial with honor."

"Everything was paid for."

"By who?"

"Josh Peterson."

"Could we exhume the body?"

The doctor sighed. "I'm afraid not. He was cremated."

Chapter 11

The rumble of trucks nudged Patty's sleep, but it was the high-pitched scraping noise that caused her to sit up. She rubbed the condensation off the window. Snowplows. She reached for her watch: seven-fifteen and the sun hadn't yet made its full appearance. She tossed back the covers and sprang to her feet as the trailer shook from a passing plow. Josh was in the bathroom. Kallie jumped off Josh's side of the bed and whined.

"Oh great. You gotta go. Me too. Under the circumstances, I'll have to wait." Patty struggled into her rumpled clothes, jammed her feet into her boots, and grabbed her parka. She stopped momentarily looking at the empty couch. Where was Linda? Arlet was asleep, cuddled into a corner, her shallow breathing raspy. The baby looked flushed, but then what did she know about babies.

After hooking Kallie to a leash, Patty went out into the biting cold. It had stopped snowing, but sullen clouds hung low. The sun would not win the battle today. The plows had cleared the gas pumps and a major part of the lot was scraped, leaving a sheen of ice on the pavement. Many trucks had already left and two were filling their tanks, which meant the electricity was back on.

She checked her truck's tires and marveled that they were clear of snow and ice. It surprised her that a blind person could be so capable and in such good physical condition. She remembered his grip on her shoulder and how he'd handled Floyd.

Once inside the trailer, she unhooked Kallie's leash and dashed to the bathroom. She came out to find Josh in the kitchen and the baby still asleep on the couch. "Where's Linda?"

"She went to find Brutus."

"I didn't see her. Guess I was too busy inspecting your great shoveling job. How will she find Brutus?"

"Relax. You aren't her mother. She needs to fend for herself. Let's wait and see who she drums up to help her."

"It's freezing out there. Maybe I should go look for her?"

"Listen up," Josh said. "Don't coddle her."

"You aren't being very helpful." She gazed out a window. The trucks on either side of them had moved out, leaving long patches of dirty snow. She spotted a lone figure dressed in a green parka next to a police car—Linda. Maybe she had more gumption than she'd shown earlier.

Patty turned her attention to Josh. "You need a haircut."

"I don't notice."

"Course you don't." Patty went over and pulled at long strands at the nape of his neck. "See, it's way long in the back. I could cut it for you."

"Can I trust you with scissors?"

"Well, you've trusted me with your trailer and your dog."

"Maybe tomorrow. We should get ready to leave."

"Sure." She went into the bathroom to brush her hair. "Linda's been gone a long time, don't you think?" she said over her shoulder.

"Stop worrying." He doled out kibbles for Kallie and set the dish down in the corner.

"I'll give Linda another fifteen minutes, then I'll go after her." She put her brush in her bag. "She can't have gone far."

Josh slapped the spoon down on the counter. "Don't keep looking for trouble where there isn't any."

"I'm not looking for trouble. I just want her to be safe."

"You stick your nose into everything and bring the world in here. I don't like that. You've got to look out for yourself, not mewl about others." The cooking timer buzzed and he removed a pan from the burners.

Something was wrong with Josh's approach to the world, but now was not the time to nag him about it. "What's for breakfast?"

"Cheese omelet and toast. Hope that will suffice. Pour our juice and coffee, will you? Linda already ate. She said she left the butter and jam on the table."

Patty poured two glasses of orange juice and two cups of coffee and placed them on the table. "Best food I've had on a job," she said, sitting down.

He put a plate topped with a fluffy omelet and rye toast in front of her, then turned back to the burners to pick up the other plate. He sat across from her. "Where are the drinks?" he asked with his hands resting on either side of his plate.

"On your right. Here." She moved the juice into his right hand and the mug into his left. "Okay?"

"Thanks." He drank his juice and set the glass down. "So what other jobs have you had? You know, the ones where the food wasn't so great."

She laughed. "Mostly I brought my lunch, but I'm not much of a cook."

"Didn't your mother teach you?"

Patty rested her forearms on the table and stared at her plate. "Mom died when I was five. Dad raised me." She shrugged. "That's why I know how to cut a man's hair and fix a car. I'm not much good at the lady-like stuff."

His fingers traced the sides of his coffee mug. "Maybe your life will improve."

She buttered her toast and noticed that Josh hadn't buttered his. "Want butter and jam on your toast? I can do it for you."

"Thanks. That would be easier."

While Patty spread jam on his toast, she said, "I'm not running away, you know. I hope to be running toward something. Like a good job. Then I can go to college and get a degree in mechanical engineering."

He nodded. "It's good to have goals."

"So what about you? Why'd you want to leave in such a hurry?"

"The storm was coming in."

"Bull. You could have waited it out and then left."

He swallowed his mouthful of toast, then took a gulp of coffee. His silence spoke more to Patty than if he'd answered her.

She shrugged. "You scared of what Slocum's thugs might do?" He ignored her, and they continued to eat in silence.

After he finished, he stood. "Are you through?" His voice was rough, demanding. "Time to get organized. The next place is still another 180 miles down the road. We'll need to get propane, fresh water, and flush the tanks before dark."

"What about Linda?"

"She's doing what she has to do. She'll be back."

"Well sure, her baby's here." She nodded at the sleeping infant. She gathered up the dishes and put them in the sink. "You cooked. I'll wash up." She stood at the sink and turned toward him. "We've got a long trip in front of us, Josh, and don't think for one minute I'm going to let you stay mum all the way to Arizona. Eventually you'll tell me about yourself."

He walked to where his parka hung by the door. "Don't push, Patty. You might not like what you learn."

"I have no preconceived ideas about you."

"Sure you do, if you're like most women."

"I already told you, I'm not like most women."

"Wanna bet? You think I'm a poor blind war vet, looking for a life, but I'm older than you and I've seen too much: blood, slaughtered civilians, you name it. I've killed men in battle. And I've done things I shouldn't have, things I'm not proud of. I haven't got a life and probably never will. Cuz let me tell you, when you do something wrong, there's no forgiving yourself. Just so you understand, you drive me to Arizona, then we part ways." He pulled on his parka and hat and went out the door.

Kallie stood by the closed door and whined.

"It's okay, girl. We'll find out what's bugging him." The trailer shuddered, and she realized Josh was cranking in the stabilizers. She hurried to wash the dishes and straighten out the inside of the trailer, so they could pull in the slide-outs. She wished Linda would hurry back. They couldn't leave until she did.

She heard voices outside and opened the door. Two lanky state troopers were talking to Josh while Linda stood next to them. "What's going on?" Patty asked.

Linda waved to her. "They pulled my car out. Someone broke in and stole my CD player."

"We know who probably stole it, right?" Patty motioned to the officers to come into the trailer.

With everyone huddled in the small living area, Patty told them a short version of the run-in she and Linda had with Floyd Rickter.

"Understand you and Mr. Peterson here," the trooper pointed at Josh, "also had trouble with this man."

"Right." Patty glanced at Josh who remained standing apart. She wondered how much he'd told them about his confrontation with Floyd. "Some truckers said Floyd pulled a knife and stabbed a guy."

"We have that report," the other officer said. "We'll be on the lookout for him, but we have our hands full with the remnants of this storm." He turned to Linda. "I doubt if you'll get your stereo and CDs back, Ms. Terrell, but we'll try."

Linda nodded. "I understand. At least my car runs."

The troopers left and Linda hurried to Arlet, changed her diaper, and dressed her in a wool sweater and leggings for the car trip.

Linda's last name had caught Patty's attention. So much for the girl being married to Peter Darby. The name Terrell struck a familiar note. She'd read a news story about a stepfather named Terrell who'd abused his wife's children. Had Josh known? Was that the reason he insisted Linda not return home as Patty had suggested? Why hadn't he told her?

After Linda gathered her things, Patty helped her stow them in her car, now parked next to the truck. They returned to the trailer to find Kallie resting her head near the baby, while Arlet grabbed a wad of fur. Without missing a beat, Linda disengaged the baby's hold and swaddled her in a blanket. Before picking up her daughter, she turned and hugged Josh. "You've been wonderful. I wish you were my brother."

A smile touched his lips. "Glad you said brother not father." He took a step back. "You'll do all right."

Linda nodded, leaned down, and stroked Kallie's head. "Maybe someday I'll find a dog as sweet as you."

"I think Kallie is in a league of her own," Patty said.

Linda came over to Patty and hugged her, too. "You're so gutsy," Linda said. "I hope I can be as brave."

Patty smiled. "You've already shown a lot of grit, Ms. Terrell."

Linda's mouth gaped, but Patty continued, pretending that she'd said nothing out of the ordinary. "Do look up Maggie at her diner. She's a treasure worth knowing."

"I will." Linda turned to Josh. "I'll give your friend your message, if I see him." She picked up Arlet and walked to her car. After settling Arlet in her car seat, Linda got in, waved, and drove slowly across the nearly deserted lot.

Josh and Patty finished rigging the trailer for the road and joined the caravan of trucks heading south. Patty shifted to a lower gear and glanced at Josh who had his arm draped around Kallie's shoulder as the dog stuck her head over the seat.

Patty shook her head in disbelief. "Why didn't you tell me about Linda's home situation? Did she tell you?"

He removed his arm from Kallie and put his hands in the pockets of his parka. "You're a nosey pest, you know that."

"My father used to say that." She shifted from low to second as the speed of the truck in front picked up. "You didn't answer my question."

"Have you ever thought that you don't need to know everything?"

"No." She grinned. "I learned early that if I didn't ask I'd never find out anything. People can be very tightlipped for no reason or the wrong reason."

"Patty Harkin's philosophy."

"Yep. And it's true."

He sighed and shook his head. "I can't believe I hired you for this long trip."

"You had no choice and neither did I. We were tossed together by fate."

"I don't believe in fate."

"What do you believe in?"

"I believe in getting to Tucson."

"Why Tucson and not, say, Phoenix?"

He shook his head. "Save me from prying women."

Patty refused to be put off. "So Tucson is more important than any other town in Arizona?"

"Yeah."

"What about this friend Linda talked about? You know the one who she was supposed to give a message to."

"I do have friends. As I said, you don't need to know everything. Now get off my back."

She shrugged and drove on in uncomfortable silence. They must have covered eighty miles when the trucks in front of them came to a halt.

"What's up?" Josh asked.

"I don't know." She leaned out the window. "Looks like a traffic jam."

The truck in front of her let out a hiss from its compressed air system. Patty turned off her motor. "I'll hop out and see what I can learn. The truckers will be chattering on their CBs." She got out and slammed the door shut. Slush slopped over her boots as she made her way forward and rapped on the other truck's door. When the trucker opened his window, she yelled to him, "What's going on?"

The driver leaned out. "Truck jackknifed. They're taking the injured driver out in a helicopter."

"How long do you think we'll be stuck?"

"They gotta bring in a wrecker, but they're shoving the rig off to the side, so not too long. If it ain't one thing it's another."

Patty looked down the line of traffic. "It sure messes up deliveries, doesn't it?"

"In spades. Time is money. It's a damn shame. Brutus was a good guy. Not like some of the young punks driving today."

"Damn! I know him. He was real helpful to a friend." Patty wished it had been Floyd instead. "How bad is he hurt?"

"Not sure. But his semi's mangled."

She turned away and went back to her truck. Once inside, she told him about Brutus.

"Brutus? Shit, that stinks. Is he badly hurt?"

"Not sure. A chopper's coming to take him out. Brutus had a kind heart."

Josh rested his head against Kallie and muttered, "So this is how it was for him."

"Excuse me." She settled herself in her seat. "What are you talking about?"

"Have you ever read or seen *Waiting for Godot?*" he asked.

Patty frowned. "I've heard of it."

He smiled. "A play by Beckett. Two characters wait for Godot, who never comes. The play reminds me of life as it is now: boring, repetitive, sad, aimless."

"But the play's characters were waiting. We're heading someplace. We have a goal."

"Can we meet our goal, and if we do, is it meaningless? Of late, I have no more illusions."

"God, you are depressed." She unzipped her parka. "Put your window down and get some air."

He laughed and sat up straighter. "Don't you ever get depressed?"

"Everyone does. Dad would whack me and tell me to get moving, cuz life wasn't something to dawdle over."

"You had a good dad."

"Yeah. He was great when he wasn't drunk or gambling. Maybe that's why he never got depressed, he was too stewed to know what that was like."

"Did he always drink heavily?"

"No. It wasn't until after he was let go five years ago. He couldn't find work, and we lived on what I made. Then he got sick. When he won at the tables last year he had the good sense to put his winnings into this truck. Only smart thing he ever did. Maybe it's just as well he died quick, but it sure was shit for me."

"My friend used to drink a lot. For a while he snapped out of it, but he was in bad shape at the end. I didn't understand why he didn't give a damn about living. I do now."

"Why now?"

Instead of answering, Josh felt for Kallie's leash. "Let's get out and give Kallie a pee break."

"It's icy, so watch out, and let me wipe off her paws before she gets back inside."

"My, my, little Miss Neatness."

"You're the same way about your trailer, everything tucked away in its place."

"That's a necessity." He put his hand on the door lever. "Come on." His feet hit the pavement and Kallie jumped out next to him.

The three of them walked off the road toward a pasture fence. In the distance the fields spread out flat and white like starched sheets. Josh stretched and did knee bends. Patty chatted. "Do you think Floyd could have forced Brutus off the road?"

"That's a big leap just because neither of us likes the guy," Josh said between knee bends.

"I was wondering about what Floyd said."

"You're like a dog with a bone—drop it."

"You are such a clam." The sound of engines revving up stopped her. "At last. Let's go." She grabbed Josh's hand and they hurried back to her truck.

Chapter 12

The sun hovered low in the west when Patty pulled off the main highway into Oldorf's Trailer Park and stopped at a hookup clear of snow. After cutting the engine, she emitted a long sigh, rubbed the nape of her neck, arched her back, and stretched her arms behind her head.

"Tough drive," Josh said. "You did a good job."

She nodded dumbly. "Even though we didn't put in many miles, I'm glad it's over." The drive had been a nightmare of icy patches, then slushy areas. "The place looks deserted, only a large RV and one beat-up trailer about two hundred yards to our right," she said, peering through the windshield. "I don't see anyone around. Wonder if they're open for business. The gas pumps haven't been cleared of snow."

"Any signs on the office door?"

"Can't tell. No lights. I'll check."

She was about to get out of the truck when Josh said, "Hold it a sec." He handed her his credit card. "Use this."

"Right." She slid to the ground and trudged through snow to the office. Wind whistled through the pines overhead. Pulling her parka tighter around her neck, she read the sign: *Ring bell in back*. Around the corner of the A-frame building, a snowbank blocked her way. Turning back, she tromped to the lee side of the building where a corrugated fence halted her progress. Under other circumstances, she might have been amused at the non sequitur between the sign and reality. Now she gritted her teeth, shook her head, walked back and rapped on the flimsy door. Impatiently, she pounded harder and yelled, "Anyone there?" No response. Looking back toward her truck, she saw Josh had gotten out with Kallie in harness by his side.

Shrugging, she rejoined him. "Nobody answers." She studied the other two vehicles and pondered the eerie quiet. "Shall I knock on the trailer doors?"

"Let's hook up to the electrical outlet," he said. "Somebody's bound to come and want his fee. In the meantime, we can get settled." He urged Kallie forward to the end of the trailer where he began feeling for the crank to lower the stabilizers.

"Want help?" she called out "No. Find where we can hook our hose to flush our sewage system."

Patty found the outlet on the trailer, connected the RV's hose and turned on the valve. The trailer shook as the stabilizers went into place. Josh went inside and extended the pop-outs. He leaned out the door. "Can you see where he keeps his propane tank refills?"

"Not a sign. Maybe it's behind the office, but a snowdrift is up against the house and a high fence is on the other side, so I can't get at it."

"We'll find out when the guy comes to collect his money. For now let's fill the water holding tanks. I'll add the antifreeze." With Kallie at his side, he stepped outside and began feeling his way along the trailer, his bare hands red and chaffed from the cold.

Patty went to the water dispenser and was thankful that the park owner had the heat on to allow the flow of water. As they finished their chores, the sun sagged to the edge of the gray horizon. A few flakes fell like wayward children without family. She gazed at the pale forbidding scene. Ice clung to the RV's entry steps and strange mounds of snow stood like sentinels in front of the old trailer beyond it.

"There's a cleared road parallel to the parking area. Do you want me to take Kallie for a quick walk?" she asked.

"Great. I'll take off her harness. Would you get the leash?" Before Patty handed the leash to him, Kallie wiggled out from under his hands. "Hey, hey. What's got into you, girl?"

Kallie moved a few feet away, her nose in the air, and ran down the icy road that curved behind the large RV. "Kallie, come," he ordered, but the dog ignored him and bounded through the white drifts surrounding the old trailer. She stopped, sniffed the air, then lunged forward, spraying snow in all directions.

Patty grabbed the leash from Josh and set out after the dog, taking the same route along the road. Josh continued calling Kallie's name, frustration riding his voice.

Kallie trotted down a beaten path through the snow to two mounds a few feet from one another jutting out from a drift. With a pounce, she landed at the base of one of them, sending snow flying.

By the time Patty stood next to her, the dog had excavated a large hole around the mound. "What are you up to?" Patty reached out and attached the leash to Kallie's collar. Curious to see what the dog had dug up, she peered closer and noted green fabric under a sheen of ice. Snow from on top of the sculpture fell off, exposing a red mop or wig, encrusted in ice. It looked like a Halloween snowman. Whatever it was, she had no interest in the grotesque object. "Come on, Kallie, it's getting dark. Your freedom has been terminated." Patty backed up through the snow, tugging on the leash. Kallie twirled, growled, and lunged toward the mound she'd dug up. The object toppled over.

Patty took a step back, but couldn't avert her eyes. She tried to swallow, breathe, but could only gasp. The face that stared back at her was human. She stifled a scream with her gloved hand. "Oh my God!" The words tore from her. A woman was frozen in a kneeling position. Patty gagged. Kallie's hackles rose. Patty held on tight to the leash and backed away. Despite the terror seizing her, she hesitated. Should she knock on the trailer's door? In the fading daylight, her nerve failed her. Her boots crunched on the ice as she tugged Kallie along. After they barged into the trailer, she slammed the door shut behind them.

When Josh turned to face them, Patty rushed forward and hugged him.

"Hey there," he said, his arms encircling her in a hesitant manner. "What brought this on? I mean, I like the attention, but—"

"Oh, shut up." Patty pushed away from him. "There's a dead woman by the trailer, kneeling, frozen, buried in the snow. Nobody dies like that." Her words tumbled out pushed by fear. "There's another snow-covered mound. It may be another body. What'll we do?"

"Is this a joke?"

"Hell, no. Why do you think Kallie tore off like she did?" Patty bent over, undid the leash and hugged Kallie, relishing the comfort of her soft fur. "She knew something wasn't right. Ran right to those hideous domes and started digging. When I tried to get her to come with me, she lunged at one of them and it fell over. Jesus, it was horrible."

"Anybody in the trailer or the RV?"

"Not that I could tell. The RV's steps are icy, like no one's used them. I couldn't bring myself to bang on the trailer door. I mean what would I say, for crying out loud? Did you misplace a body?" Patty started to hyperventilate. She could handle live rough guys, but dead bodies were out of her league. "Nobody's around this graveyard but us."

"Sit down," Josh said. "You're breathing like an express train."

Patty sagged into a chair at the table, and Josh put a cup of coffee in front of her. She watched the steam rise from the cup. "I can't believe what I saw."

"Give me details." He sat across from her, his thick dark glasses reflecting her worried frown.

"A woman, red hair, wearing a green coat or parka or some such." She hiccuped. "God, what a ghoulish scene."

"Red hair? No. Damn it!" Josh put his hands to his head.

"Where were her hands?"

"What do you mean?" She stared at him. "How the hell should I know."

"Were her arms by her side, in front, in back?"

"What kind of question is that?" She shook her head and rubbed her temples. "Jesus, I don't know. Let me think. Okay, okay, they were behind her."

"Tied?"

"I don't know," she screamed at him.

"Worse than I thought."

"What?" Patty asked.

"Nothing." He shook his head as if despondent. "We've got to leave. Now."

"Leave? How can we leave with frozen bodies cluttering the landscape?"

"You're exaggerating. Nothing we can do for them, and you said the place is deserted."

"Yeah, well, we ought to call the police."

"How? I haven't charged my cell phone, and you don't have one."

Her shoulders drooped. "We're probably the only two people in the world who aren't connected by cell phones." She tapped her fingers nervously on the table. "I can get into the office and phone from there." She started to rise, but Josh grabbed her arm with a firm grip.

"No way. You said the place was locked. You break and enter and there's no phone or it's disconnected, then you become a suspect. You might even mess up a crime scene."

"Well, what bright idea do you have?"

"I told you. We get the hell out of here and call the police from a gas station down the road."

"Ever since we drove up I've had this eerie feeling." She took a sip of hot coffee before asking, "How about you?"

"Let's just say the back of my neck prickles."

"Okay. We'll clear out, except…I could try the trailer and the RV doors to see if they're unlocked." She gulped back her fear even as she offered her idea.

"The same argument for the office applies to the trailers. What if you did find someone in one of them? He could be a killer."

Patty swallowed. "Yeah, that makes sense. That wouldn't be so good."

"To say the least. I know you're tired from driving that treacherous road all afternoon, but we can stop and stay overnight at a truck stop. We're okay except the propane tanks are low. How much gas does the truck have?"

"Enough for another hundred miles." Patty finished her coffee. "Okay, the sooner we leave, the happier I'll be."

Josh rose and got his parka. "I'll crank up the stabilizers. You unplug the electrical line and hoses after you pull in the pop-outs. Put Kallie in the truck. We don't want her running back to that graveyard."

Patty yanked on her gloves and followed him out the door with a leashed Kallie. The limbs of pine trees swayed like giant windmills. Bits of a frayed moon peeked from behind skittering clouds. It should've been a peaceful scene, but instead it felt spooky.

The light from their trailer shone like a beacon through the oncoming blackness. After putting Kallie in the truck, she arranged the trailer's furnishings and pushed the button to close the pop-outs. Outside, she unplugged the electrical hookup, plunging the trailer and surrounding area into darkness. She hurried into the cab and waited for Josh. She heard his jacket brushing against the side of the truck. When he opened the door, the cab light went on. After easing into the passenger seat, he slammed the door shut.

"You're a miracle worker the way you start the stabilizers." Patty's headlights traced a beam through the lot as she slowly maneuvered toward the entrance. She stopped, downshifted, and swung the truck around so her headlights shone on the vacant trailers.

While the truck idled, Josh asked, "What are you doing?"

"I want a last look at the scene."

"What do you see?"

"A tall snow dome and a dark clump that must be the body Kallie knocked over. It's damn scary." As she began to turn out of the lot, the headlights cut through the night spotlighting a man walking down the entrance road, his head covered in a battered hat and a long muffler covering his face and neck. "There's a guy walking toward the trailers. He looks kinda old and tired or maybe drunk. Shall we stop?"

"Leave. Now."

She accelerated slowly up the hill, and drove down the partially plowed side road. "He might have seen our plates."

"Doubtful," Josh muttered. "It's not as if we aren't going to notify the authorities."

"He'll have seen the kind of truck and trailer we drive."

"Stop worrying and drive."

"I don't know why I'm so scared." She shook her head trying to rid her mind of what she'd seen. "It was so creepy." Patty gripped the steering wheel with her gloved hands, turned onto the main highway, and settled in behind a large moving van. She chewed her lip, her thoughts on the macabre scene she'd witnessed. "I've been thinking about where we parked. It was the only cleared parking area, which means—"

"A truck had parked there recently," he finished her sentence. "Did you notice how large a spot it was?"

She thought a minute. "Our rig fit inside the outline of the other tire marks."

"Okay. The more details we give the police the better. Did the domes seem old or new?"

"Like had they been there long?" She thought a few moments. "Now that you ask, they couldn't have been there long. The path to them from the road wasn't covered with snow and the domes themselves looked like snow had been packed on, not fallen on top of them. That's why I thought they were snowmen." She shivered.

They drove in silence until Patty noticed a billboard. "Looks like we'll be able to make that phone call soon. Twenty miles farther there's a gas station and restaurant. I don't know about you, but I'm starved. Do you want to cook or eat out?"

"Out sounds good, and we can save the propane."

The miles passed quickly and soon she pulled off the highway and parked next to a large semi hauling a flatbed. "It's a trucker's spot," Patty told Josh.

"Great," he said sarcastically. "All we need is to run into Floyd hauling that reefer."

"Wonder what his cargo is?" She palmed the truck's key. "Beef a la mode?"

"Did you just make a half-assed joke?" He smiled. "Good for you. Thought I might have lost you to the demons of darkness."

"Momentarily, you did." She shuddered. "It'll be hard to keep that scene out of my dreams."

Before they got out, Josh put Kallie in her harness. The chill of the night air closed about them as they headed toward the restaurant seeking a pay phone and a meal.

The smell of greasy food assaulted them as they entered. Patty pulled Josh's sleeve. "Phone's in the back. Maybe I'd better lead. The aisles are a maze."

"Right." With Kallie guiding him on his left and his hand holding Patty's elbow, they moved forward through the aisles and stopped by the phone located between the restrooms.

Patty reached for the phone. "Okay. I'll dial 911."

"They'll be able to trace this number, so lets make it short without giving our names."

Patty dug coins from her pocket, punched in the number, and lifted the receiver.

"Let me talk to them." He pushed her aside, took her place, and grabbed the receiver from her.

She glared at him, then shrugged off his taking charge. This was no time to see who could be boss.

When Josh was connected, he said, "There's a serious problem, maybe a crime scene, at Oldorf's Trailer Park off Highway 59. Only person on-scene is an old bowlegged man dressed in jeans, tan oversized coat and a muffler," he said, repeating Patty's description she'd given him earlier. He hung up abruptly.

She grabbed for the receiver too late. "What are you doing? You didn't tell him about the bodies, who you were or where we are."

"If we mention the bodies and the police stop us, we'll have to confess we saw them. That will lead to further questions. The important thing is that they go out there and investigate. We can't tell them anything more, can we?"

"Why not?"

"Think about it. If we get involved, we could be stuck here answering questions for hours, maybe days. And I, for one, am not going to stay around waiting for the police to interrogate and investigate me." He stood facing her, his dark glasses gleaming in the light, his left hand holding onto the handle of Kallie's harness.

"And what if I don't drive?" She folded her arms across her chest.

"You will." He squared his shoulders.

"Damn it, Josh. We can't go on our merry way as if we, I mean I, didn't see anything." Patty turned away, yet part of her agreed with him. Cops were not her favorite people. They'd always been in her face in Bromont, blaming her whenever she'd had a run-in with some jerk. And her dad hadn't exactly been an upstanding citizen either, so they'd treated him like dirt.

She guided Josh to a booth where Kallie sprawled under his feet. Except for Patty reading the menu to Josh, they didn't speak until after the waitress came and took their order.

"There's enough propane to heat the trailer tonight, and we can pull out first thing in the morning." Josh kept his head bowed as if in prayer.

"I don't like leaving. What if that old guy tells them about us?" Patty fingered the ends of her paper napkin, curling its edges. "It doesn't feel right."

As if he hadn't heard her, Josh said, "Let's head over to Highway 29 through the Dakotas instead of going through Minneapolis."

"How do you know that route?"

"Mike and I talked about this trip. I have a good memory."

Drained of emotions, Patty leaned back and closed her eyes, her thoughts on the body at Oldorf's Trailer Park. She had no desire to be questioned by the police or delayed, but it bothered her to walk away from what in all likelihood was a murder. She opened her eyes and looked at Josh. "Aren't you even curious about what went down back there?"

"Sure, but not enough to stick my neck out."

The waitress brought their order, and Josh fingered the silverware. "Hand me the ketchup."

Patty placed it in his left hand. "What if they trace our call?"

"You've seen far too many crime movies." He splattered ketchup across the meat patty and put down the bottle. "We can't do anything for them, but knowing how curious you are, you'll probably ferret out news in the morning." His hand fumbled toward his bowl of soup.

She moved it into his outstretched palm.

"Eat your dinner." He picked up his spoon. "Let's see what the morning brings."

Patty tried the hot vegetable soup. It wasn't as good as Maggie's, but it warmed her. She was homesick for Bromont, an unbelievable idea, but it brought forth the image of Linda. "I hope Linda finds her man," she mused.

"From what Linda said, he's a cheat. She'll be better off without him."

"Yeah, but she had such hopes. I like to think things can work out between people. You know, the fairy tale image."

"Didn't realize you were such a romantic dreamer. Hope will take you just so far, then you need guts and luck. Of late her luck hasn't been so hot."

"What about you?" Patty poked at the opening into his life. "Maybe I'm wrong, but your luck seems kinda thin."

"I'm riding low, but not totally down. You?"

"I thought we were talking about you," she parried.

"You were. I wasn't." He took a bite of his hamburger as if to punctuate the finality of his words.

Chapter 13

During the night Patty had visions of corpses walking on top of snow banks. When dawn's weak light filtered through the trailer's windows, she got up, trying not to disturb Josh. Kallie greeted her with a wagging tail.

"Yes, I know you want out," Patty whispered. "Gotta get dressed." She reached down and rubbed the dog's shoulders. "Unlike you, I don't have a fur coat to keep me warm." Kallie sat by the door. It was almost eight by the time Patty went out the door with Kallie prancing next to her. On the way to the restaurant, they walked through lines of parked trucks, with their reassuring smells of oil and diesel. The throb of engines were her comfort zone, grounding her in her past.

She tied Kallie to a post, ordered her to stay, and entered the restaurant to see if she could pick up any scuttlebutt on Oldorf's Trailer Park. On the far side of the restaurant, the talking heads were relating the morning news on the TV. As she stood in front of the magazine rack, she overheard three men sitting in a nearby booth bantering with the skinny brown-haired waitress.

"Can you believe we got our own local murder," the waitress said. "I'm carrying my mace when I leave today."

"Hey, guys, have you heard the news? Those bodies had been frozen for a long time," a trucker with a Minnesota Twins cap said. "You got nothing to fear. The perp's probably long gone."

"Easy for you to say. You don't live here year round." The waitress looked over at Patty. "Take a seat anywhere, honey, I'll be with you in a sec." She finished pouring coffee for the men and went to the kitchen.

Patty went to the counter, keeping her ears tuned to the conversation in the booth.

"Poor old Jan," the trucker said, shoving back his cap. "Gets stuck in the snow, walks to his place, settles in, and wham, a bunch of cops descend on him."

"I bet they scared the crap out of the guy," a heavy set man, wearing a blue denim shirt, said.

"Well, if he wasn't scared then," said an older man with a red bandana around his neck, "he sure was after he was told he had frozen bodies in his lot. A woman and a man. Damnedest thing I ever heard. Who would do something like that?"

"If a body's frozen it could keep for years just like the deer in your freezer," the Twins fan added. "The only clue the police have is tire marks."

The heavy man chortled. "You mean that's the only clue they're giving out to the press. I bet the cops know a heck of a lot more."

"Yeah," the older man said. "Tread marks can give 'em the make of the tire. That's what they do on CSI."

The Twins fan said, "I'm deadheading to Chicago. No stopping for me this time."

The other men laughed. "You gotta do a flip-flop and that'll put you right back here."

The guy grimaced, then smiled. "They'll have the perp behind bars by that time."

Patty slid off her stool and went outside where Kallie waited impatiently. Trying not to run to the trailer with the news, she strode over the icy cement. She approached the trailer and smelled the heady aroma of brewing coffee.

"Thank God you're up, Josh," she said, after entering with Kallie at her heels. "We gotta get out of here quick."

He stood by the stove, unshaven, dressed in jeans and a navy blue sweatshirt with his ever-present dark glasses in place. "Did you get yourself into trouble again?"

"No. But I overheard the latest gossip about what went down at Oldorf's Trailer Park." Between sips of coffee from a mug Josh had put on the table for her, she reported what the truckers had said. "It's on TV. Maybe even the radio." Patty expected Josh to say something, but instead he went about putting kibbles in Kallie's bowl. Exasperated she said, "We have to leave now."

"Don't panic. Eat some breakfast and then we'll go."

"We need gas for the truck." Patty hurried to put two pieces of wheat bread in the toaster. "We should have filled up last night."

"Should have, but you were beat. We'll fill up this morning. Act normal." He sat and buttered his toast. "Would you pour the juice?"

She got the orange juice from the fridge. "We should get our story straight in case we're stopped. Shall we tell them the truth or what?"

"In this case, I think the whole truth isn't a good idea. Half truths might work better." He took a bite and munched for a time before continuing, "We did pull into the park, but we thought it was closed and drove on. Did we see anyone? No. Did anything look unusual? No. Did we fill our water tanks? Yes. Did our dog run around loose? Yes."

Patty nodded. It sounded normal and that was what they'd done except for her discovery of the body. She took out her toast, sat, and enjoyed her breakfast. He always seemed to make everything seem logical. How did he do it? Her world was frenetic, a constant fight. Josh had problems, but he glided through them, whereas she confronted issues as if she were at war. Figuring him out was becoming an obsession.

After they washed their dishes and readied the trailer for travel, they drove over to the gas pumps where Patty used Josh's credit card. She had to drive to a second pump and finish topping off because of the gasoline spending limit on each pump for his card. Afterward when she was back behind the wheel, she let out a sigh. Only then did she realize she'd been afraid of being approached by a state trooper.

"Okay," she announced. "We're off to North Dakota to pick up 75 south. I looked at the map earlier, and you're right. It's a highway they'll keep clear of snow." And we'll be out of Minnesota, she thought. Did Josh have the same idea?

They cruised along at the speed limit in light traffic. She turned on the radio and pushed a button to listen to western music.

"You like that stuff?" Josh asked.

"Stuff? I gather you don't."

"It's better than rap music or elevator music, but I'm a jazz fan and I don't mean Mick Jagger junk."

"You sound like my dad."

He gave a short hollow laugh. "Maybe I'm more his vintage than yours."

"Not quite." She dialed the music lower. "So how old are you?"

"Thirty-two, going on fifty." He turned to face the window as if he could watch the passing white pastures. "War and death turns your world upside down."

"Not every person comes back from war miserable and depressed," she said.

"True. A lot hide their feelings. My friend did and look what happened to him. I should've known. I should've intervened earlier." He banged his hand against the dashboard.

Patty jerked with surprise. It was the first time he'd shown emotion, and here she'd thought he was all Zen-like and able to deal with his blindness. "Could you have done something for him?"

"I can always depend on you to be blunt, can't I?"

"Sorry." She turned her concentrating back to driving but wondered what had happened to soft-spoken, even-tempered Josh Peterson.

"Don't try to analyze me, Patty. You won't know what to believe about me, and that's the way I like it."

She didn't know how to respond and instead burrowed into her thoughts, thinking of her future in Arizona. She'd decided it just might be the place to start over even if Josh didn't want anything to do with her. She was about to say she hadn't seen a trooper for a long time, when the traffic slowed to a crawl. Cars going in the opposite direction whizzed by. As she inched forward, she saw the lights and barricades. She sat up straighter. "It's a roadblock. Damn! We're going to be pulled over."

"Relax and tell the truth." He took out a baseball cap from his parka and put it on. Afterward, he fastened Kallie into her harness.

Patty clung to the steering wheel like it was a lifebuoy. A trooper waved them off to a side road where a wood barricade forced Patty to halt. When the trooper walked up, she powered down the window.

"Good morning, miss," he said. "May I see your license please?"

"Sure. What's going on?" She pulled her purse out from the seat behind her, rummaged through it, and found her wallet.

"A routine inspection," he said.

Routine, my foot, she thought. While she gave him her license, another trooper came up to Josh's window and motioned for him to put it down. "Josh, there's a trooper on your side who wants your window down," she said. "Can you find the switch?"

"Yes." He powered down the window.

The trooper, who had taken her license looked over, frowned, then looked at Kallie in her harness.

"Do you have a license, sir?" the trooper on Josh's side asked.

"I have an expired license that I use for identification," Josh said, facing straight ahead. "I also have my navy discharge paper if you want that?"

"The license will do. Thanks."

Josh pulled his wallet out of his back pocket and passed it to Patty. "Take out the license, will you?"

Her fingers felt numb as she extracted it and handed it to Josh who in turn handed it to the trooper. Both troopers left and got inside their patrol car.

"They're checking us out," Patty said.

"That's normal. Take a few deep breaths and pretend you're interviewing for a job."

She had to laugh. "That's a good one. A job being a prisoner." Kallie whined. "Oh great, she wants out."

"Might be a good diversion," Josh said.

She rubbed her cold hands together. "Do we tell them we made the call?"

"Stick to as much of the truth as you can. If they ask, we admit to it."

"Here they come," she muttered.

"You're now beginning your acting career," Josh said.

"We'd like you to get out of your vehicle, Miss Harkin. Mr. Peterson, you can stay in the truck," the trooper said.

"My dog needs to get out if that's all right," Josh said.

The troopers glanced at one another. "All right, Charlie, I'll stay with Mr. Peterson while you talk to Miss Harkin." He then waved to another trooper who came over to inspect the truck and trailer's tires.

"What's the matter?" Patty asked as she followed Trooper Charlie back to his patrol car.

He didn't answer until they were inside the backseat of the patrol car. "We need to ask you a few questions." He took out a notepad.

"Shoot. Oops. I didn't mean that literally." Her coyness had no affect on him.

"Where were you last night?"

"In the trailer."

"I mean, where did you park the trailer?"

"We stayed at a truck stop called Golden Wayside."

"Did you stop any place else?"

She frowned. "Yeah. We pulled into a trailer park up the road a piece, but it was closed, so we drove on."

"Do you remember the name of the trailer park?"

"Odendorf's or something like that."

"Could it have been Oldorf's?"

"Probably. Why?"

"What did you do there?"

"I told you it was closed so we drove on." She groaned. "Golly, is this about us dumping off our waste at that place? We'll pay. There wasn't anyone around so we hooked up the electricity, filled our water tanks, and dumped our waste. We would have paid the fee."

"Why didn't you just stay there instead of driving off?"

"No propane. We were running low and we needed gas. The place had a gas pump, but it was locked. We had dinner at the Golden Wayside restaurant."

"Your friend is blind."

"So?"

"Did he take his dog for a walk?"

"You gotta be kidding, right? I mean, how would the dog know where to guide him? He let Kallie run free for a while and then we took off. She minds real well, if you haven't noticed."

"Did you see anything odd at Oldorf's?"

"Odd? Only an RV and a rundown trailer."

"Anything else?"

She shook her head. "There was only one parking spot that was clear of snow and we took it. Another rig must have been there earlier." Patty worried that she was giving him too much information, but at least the patrol car was warm. She peeked out the window and saw Josh standing by her truck with one hand gripping the trooper's elbow and the other holding onto Kallie's harness.

Finally, Trooper Charlie had no more questions and she went back to her truck. When she got in next to Josh, she asked, "How you doing?"

"Not so good. Did you tell them we called them?"

"No. You?"

"No. It doesn't matter though. They're going to escort us back to Oldorf's Trailer Park."

"And you rolled over for that?" Patty said.

"Under the circumstances, I thought it best to give in."

"No way." Her ire climbed to another level. She turned on the ignition, started the engine, and then began to climb out. "You stay here and get warm, I'm going to get to the bottom of this."

"No. You'll make it worse," but his words were lost on Patty. She stepped to the frozen ground and slammed the truck door. She headed toward the four troopers huddled near one of their cars. "Who's in charge?"

"I am, Miss," the shortest of the state troopers stepped forward. "What can I do for you?"

"You can tell me why in blazes you want us to go back to the trailer park with you? I told you," she pointed to Charlie, "we'd pay what's his name for dumping our waste. That's got to be only a misdemeanor. Are we under arrest for that?"

"No ma'am."

"Then why should we go back with you?" She was cold and mad and not about to make it easy for the troopers.

"You're a witness," the trooper said.

"To what?" She wanted him to spell it out.

"There were two bodies back at the trailer park."

"Bodies? You mean dead people were at that trailer park?"

"Yes." The troopers' interest in her reaction would have been comical if she hadn't been so mad.

"Jeez, that's scary. Glad I didn't see 'em, and of course Josh couldn't have. Your man here," she pointed a finger at Charlie, "didn't say diddly about any bodies. Where were they?"

"In the snow near one of the trailers. A dog, we think your dog, dug up one of them."

"We let Kallie run while we were working on the trailer. When Josh whistled, she came back." Patty looked from one trooper to the next. "Obviously, she can't help you."

"We are treating the scene as a homicide. We need your cooperation." He moved toward her, but Patty stood her ground.

"You think we killed those people?" Patty didn't let him answer. "We were there for a half hour at most. And for the two nights before that we were snowed in at a truck stop about a hundred miles out of Bromont. In fact, if you check you'll know we were there because we had to report a theft. The troopers were even in our trailer. Now do you think we had bodies stored in our trailer? It's not that big and we took in a woman and her baby, cuz they needed a safe place." She continued her stream of info, figuring she had nothing to lose.

"We didn't say you killed them," the trooper began.

"Damn right we didn't. I'm freezing out here talking to you guys. I'm going back to my truck and wait for you to talk to the troopers up at that truck stop. If you want to arrest us, do it, but otherwise I'm not driving back up to that trailer park."

"Why the rush to get out of here?" the trooper asked.

She put her hands on her hips. "To keep ahead of the next storm, and Josh has a job waiting for him in Tucson. How easy do you think it is for a blind man to get a job these days?" She turned on her heels and left them to ponder their next move.

Back at the truck, she climbed in, and leaned back, soaking up the warmth and tried to stop trembling. "We'll see what they decide to do." She blew into her cupped hands.

"Okay, Annie Oakley. What happened?" Josh asked. "Are we going to jail?"

"Doubt it. They're trying to figure out what to do." She rubbed the top of Kallie's head.

"I told them we were on our way to Arizona," he said.

"Good. I told them you had a job offer there."

"You what?"

"It sounded like a good reason for us to be in a hurry."

"Did you tell them anything else?"

"They didn't ask. I spoke the truth with slight omissions."

"Did they buy your story?"

"I think so. I asked if we were under arrest for not paying to dump our waste. That's when they told me about the bodies."

"I wondered when they'd let that information out." His voice was more confident now. "Since neither of us mentioned that we called to alert them about Oldorf's, then we better not admit to it now. He put his hand on her arm. "You're gutsy, Patty. I made a good choice in hiring you."

"Choice? You had no choice. It was me or you'd still be in Bromont. Of course, the way things are going, maybe you wish you'd stayed put."

Before he could answer, the trooper in charge tapped on Patty's window, and she powered it down. "Your story's confirmed. You can continue on your way. But if you remember any details about the trailer park, call this number." He handed her a card. "Do either of you have a cell phone?"

"I do," Josh said.

"Give me the number."

Josh rattled off a phone number. Patty wondered if it was fake as she smiled sweetly.

"And what company will you be working for in Arizona, sir?"

Josh's chin rose. "Company? I don't have the job yet. It was an offer of one."

"I understand, but we'd like to have it for our records." The trooper kept his pencil hovering over the clipboard.

Pahchuco Casino. You can contact Cordero Meshum. He's one of the owners."

"Thanks," the trooper said, after checking the spelling of the name. "Your driving into that empty space destroyed evidence. Another rig longer and heavier than yours had parked there." He saluted and walked toward the other troopers at the barricade.

Patty put up her window. "I guess we fooled them."

"You're one hell of a liar."

"You're not so bad yourself. That fake phone number and company name was quick thinking."

"It's the correct cell number, it's just not charged, and the man and the casino exist." He sighed and rubbed his hand across his lips, before adding, "You did a great job, Patty."

She grinned at the compliment.

Chapter 14

After receiving a call from Maggie, Camden walked from the B&B through town to her diner. Despite the brisk wind that nipped at his nose and cheeks, he relished the exercise. The streets were crowded with shoppers, and kids, taking advantage of the new powder, sledded on nearby hills.

The lovely aroma of fresh baked bread teased his senses as he pushed open the diner's door. He wondered if Maggie had some kind of perfume that emitted such mouthwatering smells. Having tasted her biscuits, he knew baking must be a daily labor of love.

Maggie spotted him and nodded in the direction of a lone woman in a booth with a baby cradled in her arms. He pulled off his gloves and unzipped his parka as he made his way toward the booth. "Mrs. Darby? I'm Camden McMillan. Maggie told me you had a message for me from Josh Peterson. May I sit down?"

She smiled. "Of course, please call me Linda." She gently placed her sleeping baby next to her.

Camden took off his parka and tossed it on the bench before sliding into the booth across from her. "Sweet baby," he said.

"Thanks."

"Where did you meet Josh?"

"At a truck stop. The storm kinda threw us together. They were super to me."

"They?"

"Yeah, Patty and Josh. Patty gave me Maggie's name. She's let me stay here for the past two hours without even ordering anything but tea." Linda leaned across the table in a conspiratorial manner. "She even brought me biscuits and cheese for free." Her blue eyes twinkled and the freckled cheeks reddened.

He smiled at her animation for being treated so well. "Maggie seems to be that kind of person."

"So are Josh and Patty. She helped dig out my car. It's as though I've been blessed with meeting good people even though I can't find my...my husband."

The waitress came over. "Can I get you something, sir?"

"Your apple pie looks good and coffee, too."

"The pie's fresh," the waitress said.

"I'm sure it is," he said. "Maggie wouldn't have it any other way."

"You got that right."

Camden nodded toward Linda. "Will you join me? My treat."

"That's kind of you, thanks."

After the waitress left with the order, he said, "You told Maggie that Josh had a message for me."

"Oh, yeah, sorry. Josh said to tell you he's sorry about Mike and for you to remember the conversation that you had the last time you ran together." She frowned. "Oh, and look at the postcards."

Camden frowned. What in the hell did Josh mean? Recalling a run with Mike that happened over a year ago seemed odd if not impossible. "That's it, nothing more?"

She shook her head. "Josh was very specific. Wanted to be sure I got the words right. Funny message, huh?"

"Did Josh say where he was headed?"

"South."

"Where exactly?"

"They didn't say. You see, things were really chaotic. The electricity went out, the food ran low, and then this truck driver helped me. There was one nasty guy, but Patty told him off. She's amazing."

"I'm sure she is, but perhaps they talked about a certain route they'd be taking." The waitress brought Camden's pie and coffee with Maggie right behind her with a piece for Linda.

"Good to see you again, Maggie," Camden said.

"Always like a returning customer." Maggie nodded toward Linda. "Seems Patty and Josh helped this little gal out."

Camden nodded, although his thoughts were on Josh's message. "I was hoping to learn more."

"Yeah, me too." Maggie folded her arms. "Patty's like family." Maggie glanced toward the cash register. "I'll be back in a few."

Camden leaned back to survey Linda as she took several quick bites of pie. "When was your last square meal?"

She put down her fork and blushed. "I guess I'm real hungry. Josh is a great cook, but I haven't had a chance to eat since then." She glanced down at her baby. "I'm nursing Arlet and I get kinda tired."

He nodded, trying to be patient. "Now, tell me more about what happened during your stay with Patty and Josh. Can you give me the name of the truck stop or the names of any of the people you and they met?

Linda began to recount events. She told him about Floyd Rickter and how Patty had brushed him off. "He was really mad at her, but at least he left us alone. We think he was the one who broke into my car and stole my CD player."

"So the state troopers put out an APB on this guy Rickter?" Camden asked.

"I don't know. They were busy with accidents and clearing traffic. They didn't think I'd get my CD player back." She fiddled with her napkin. "Maggie said you might be able to help me find my husband, Peter Darby."

"She did? I don't know why she said that. I'm new in town. Have you checked the usual places, phone book, post office, employment office, police station?"

"Not yet." Linda blushed. "He got a job here; sent me a postcard saying he was trying to find a place for us to live." She stopped, then added, "That was months ago. I haven't heard from him since. I almost called the police to report him missing, but my family was against it."

"That was how long ago, exactly?"

"Nine months. When he left, I was three months pregnant. He said after he was settled in his new job, he'd send for me."

"Do you have enough money for a hotel room?"

Linda squirmed and with her head bowed over her pie, she murmured, "No." She looked up. "I thought I could get a job."

"Your husband didn't send you money after he got the job?"

"No. I had a clerical job until just before the baby came. But the hospital and doctor cost a lot. I didn't have health insurance and…"

He put his hand on top of hers. "No need to explain. It's okay." He glanced around in search of Maggie, then turned back to Linda. "Maybe you should head back home."

"I can't," she said in a sharp voice. "It's not safe for Arlet." She lowered her eyes and added, "I can't tell you why."

He sensed her fear and changed the subject. "So what will you do if you can't find your husband?"

She withered, tears filled her brown eyes, and her freckled face fell. "I… I have to be honest with you. Peter and I aren't married, but he's the baby's father. I believed him when he said he was getting a job here and would send for me, but then after the baby was born, I heard nothing." She squared her shoulders. "I got mad and decided I'd find him and make him own up to his responsibility."

"You've got courage. I hope you find him, but if not, you've got to have a backup plan. Finding work in Bromont might be difficult."

"Please don't tell anyone what I just told you. I mean, if people find out I'm an unwed mother, they'll get the wrong idea about me." She clasped her hands and looked pleadingly at Camden.

"Of course not." He took a bite of pie, trying to figure out what he could do for her. Sure she needed money, but that could be an ongoing commitment and he wasn't willing to do that. "Pie's great. Never underestimate the power of food."

Linda finished hers, pushed the plate away, and sighed.

"Can you think of anything Josh and Patty might have said or done that would give me a clue about their destination?"

"I told you south where it would be warm." She pursed her lips. "It sounded great, cuz we were freezing." She scowled. "Josh was a great listener and never asked me questions or anything. He was so easy to talk to. I think I babbled out my entire life story but he never said much about himself."

"What did Josh look like?"

"I thought you knew Josh. After all he gave you a message."

"I know his friend Mike. I'm trying to locate Josh. He has some information I need." In a manner of speaking this was true.

"Well, if he weren't blind, I'd say he was handsome, but it's kinda hard to tell behind his dark glasses. He's about your age, maybe a little older, cuz he had dark thick curly hair with strands of gray at the temple. Tall, taller than you by a couple of inches, and strong hands with nice nails. I notice hands. Do you?"

He had to smile. "Never thought about it much. I notice people's eyes."

"I guess I do too, but Josh is blind, so I studied his hands."

"Did you happen to notice if he was right or left handed?"

She frowned, hesitated, then said, "Left, I think. Is that important?"

"Could be." He nodded.

"He has real muscular arms." She giggled. "A girl notices things like that. I haven't given you much of a picture of him, have I?"

He smiled. "On the contrary, you've added a piece to a puzzle I'm been trying to solve." He was ready to move on and pay Slocum Hitower a visit, but he couldn't just leave the girl sitting in the diner. "Wait here while I talk to Maggie."

At the counter, he motioned for Maggie. He wasn't sure what he'd ask her, but knew she'd help. When Maggie finished placing a customer's order, she came over to where Camden waited.

"So, what's the story? Did you learn anything useful?"

He related some of the conversation he'd had with Linda about her status. "She needs a place to stay for a while. Can you help out?"

Maggie frowned and looked at the young woman for a time. "She says she's looking for her husband, Peter Darby. You think she's lying about that?"

He didn't answer.

Maggie sighed. "It doesn't matter. Patty sent her, so I better help her out until she can get on her feet."

He smiled. "I'll check back with you before I leave town. He placed a fifty in her hand. "This should help the girl."

"You're a sucker too, I see."

He shrugged. "I'll visit Slocum's tomorrow."

She raised an eyebrow. "You don't seem like the gambling type."

"I'm not, but apparently Mike worked there."

"Slocum's a mean son-of-a-gun, so beware."

"Thanks, but I doubt there'll be a problem." He glanced in Linda's direction. She was staring at them. "I think I'd better tell her she's got a place to stay for the time being." He started to turn away from Maggie, stopped, turned and patted the woman's hand. "You're a gem."

She winked. "The world needs more like us."

That night in his room at the B&B Camden tried to recall the last conversation he'd had with Mike, certain the message Josh had given Linda had a special meaning. The more he looked into Mike's death, the more he was convinced that the dead man was not Mike. How did that coincide with Josh's departure? It made no sense.

Linda had said that Josh was left handed. So was Mike. Coincidence? Doubtful.

He took out a pad and pencil and began writing down things he remembered about the last time he'd run with Mike. It had been early autumn. Josh was being treated on an outpatient basis at the VA hospital for alcoholism, drug addiction and severe depression. However, Mike had said that he thought their new job would help him recover.

Camden stared at the word *job*. What job? He stared out the window at the wintery weather. The job had to do with the travel trailer. Something about their being on their own, no help from the government. What had Mike meant by that? At the time Camden had thought Mike had been vague because of the uncertainty of getting the job. Now Mike's words came to him: "It's dangerous, but worth the risk. We can't let the bad guys get a foothold on native soil." Then Mike had laughed. "I sound like a Marine recruiter."

Camden put his pencil down and paced. It was Josh who gave Linda the message for him. Had Mike told Josh about their conversation? Over the past year, Mike had sent Camden postcards from various towns—no, not towns, Indian reservations with casinos. He stared at the paper where he'd scrawled ideas and words. Casinos.

Slocum's seemed a logical next step to unlock the mystery.

Chapter 15

Camden drove to the Indian reservation some twenty miles outside of Bromont. He pulled into the gravel parking area in front of a slate-roofed two-story log building, known as Hitower Casino. He'd expected a Las Vegas style neon sign, but there was nothing gaudy about the place, just a plain vanilla exterior blending into the rolling landscape.

He sat in his idling SUV thinking about the situation. What exactly did he expect to find out? He knew so little, but everything he'd learned about Mike's death made no sense. Would talking to Slocum Hitower make things clearer? He shut down the engine and got out. His boots left imprints in the snow as he made his way toward the ebony-colored double doors. He stepped aside for two men who came outside and entered a large open room that sparkled with bright lights shining on slots, and blackjack, crap, and roulette tables. Although the place was busy, a few dealers sat idly waiting for customers. The haze of smoke and the pungent smell of stale liquor hovered in the air. Wasn't alcohol illegal on Indian Reservations?

He went to the bar, located at the end of a long hall, ordered a draft beer from the broad-faced Indian bartender with a name tag that read, Lou. Camden absorbed the atmosphere and studied the clientele. Several men at the bar seemed lost in their own thoughts.

"Surprised you sell liquor," Camden said to Lou.

Lou's eyes narrowed. "You a Fed?"

Camden chuckled. "No. History professor."

"Even if you were, it's no matter." Lou grinned and pointed to a framed sign on the wall behind the bar. "Indian Council voted to allow the sale of liquor on this reservation."

"I didn't realize that was possible."

"Need a history lesson, professor?"

"Sure."

"1953, Eisenhower repealed the countrywide ban of selling liquor."

"That I do know."

"Okay. The kicker was that Indian Reservations would stay dry unless they opted to permit the possession and sale of alcohol on their individual reservation." Lou grinned. "We make money, the reservation stays out of the poor house. Everyone's happy."

Camden made no comment as to the abuses of such a policy and instead remarked, "Not too many customers."

"You looking for high stakes?" Lou motioned to a door in the far corner. "The back room's reserved for high-rollers."

Camden took a gulp of beer before adding, "I'm not a gambler."

"So what're you doing here? Can't find a decent bar in Bromont?"

Camden placed his glass on the slick counter. "Trying to find out about a friend of mine, Mike Garrick? He died in an auto accident. I understand he worked here. His death doesn't make sense."

"So whose death does?"

A guy at the end of the bar called out, "Hey, Lou, pour me another."

A pudgy man with bleary eyes and a breath that could knock over a rat, moved next to Camden and nudged his elbow. "Did you know Rhonda? Prettiest gal around and friendly. She died too, you know."

"Like Mike?"

Mr. Pudgy waved his hand in front of his face. "Not like Mike, but yeah, dead like Mike."

"You knew Mike Garrick?" Despite the man's inebriated state, Camden pressed the conversation.

"I'm talking about Rhonda, not Mike. See?"

"Rhonda? Don't think I know her."

"Then you don't come here often, do ya?"

"I'm new," Camden said. "What happened?"

The man took another swallow of his drink. "It's a big deal around here. Biggest thing that's hit this place." He glanced at the other patrons at the bar as if afraid someone might overhear. "Rhonda treated Floyd special, see. So when Floyd gets back from a truck run, he expects Rhonda to be waiting with open arms, but she took up with a new fella." The man let out a loud hiccup, wiped his mouth with the back of his hand before continuing. "One night Rhonda, her new dude and Floyd go outside. Big ruckus. Then that's the last we see of 'em. Feds came yesterday asking questions. You know what?" The man burped. "Rhonda and her new boyfriend turned up as popsicles south of here."

"Popsicles?" The guy was obviously cloudy with liquor. "That's some story." Although the story seemed farfetched, the name Floyd caught his interest.

In between gulps, Mr. Pudgy kept talking. "Floyd's in big shit, him driving a reefer and all."

"A reefer?" Camden questioned.

"God, man, you ain't no trucker, are you? A refrigerated trailer, you know, one that hauls beef and such." The man started to giggle. "Ain't that a hoot? That's why the Feds are interested in Floyd. That and the three of them going off together. They wanted to talk to Garrick, but he's dead."

Camden felt a chill. "Who was Rhonda's new boyfriend?"

"You wanna buy me a drink?"

Camden grinned. "Sure. What'll it be?" The guy might be drunk, but Camden knew when he had a live one on the line.

"Scotch straight up."

Camden waved to Lou who came over and poured a double into a glass and handed it to the man, then glanced sharply at Camden. "Last one for him. He's gotta drive home."

Camden nodded and turned back to his "new" friend. "What's your name?"

"Al."

"So Al, what about the names of these people who disappeared in an ice trailer?"

"Everyone knows Floyd Rickter. He's a hot tempered son-of-a-bitch, but Slocum uses him for stuff." He put his forefinger to his wet lips. "Shh. Don't tell anyone I told ya."

Camden nodded. "You can count on me, Al."

"Good." He slapped Camden on the shoulder. "Why did the son-of-a-bitch kill poor Rhonda? She was hot. Liked to flirt."

"Did you talk to the police?"

"Hell, no. I'm not gonna put my snoot in that mess." He nodded toward Lou, who had his back to them. "He knows all the dirt." He downed his drink and smacked his lips. "Gotta go. Wife's gonna kill me." He chortled and winked. "Not really, though." Once again he drew the back of his hand across his mouth, stood unsteadily, and backed away from the bar.

Lou turned around with a bottle of vodka in his hand. "Al, get a cup of coffee before you leave. We don't want another accident, do we?"

"Ah, sure, Lou. Whatever you say." Al teetered off toward the small restaurant at the other side of the large hall.

As Lou wiped off the counter, he said, "You ask a lot of questions about something that doesn't concern you. Why?"

"I thought what Al was talking about might have something to do with Mike Garrick."

Lou put the towel down on the bar. "Well, it doesn't, does it?"

Camden shrugged, but thought Floyd Rickter might have something to do with Mike, and what related to Mike related to Josh. He drained his glass.

"Why are you asking questions about Mike? He's dead." Lou frowned, his face transformed into a mask of hostility.

"Mike was a bouncer here."

"So? Kept his nose clean, didn't ask a lot of questions. Brought his blind friend here sometimes."

Camden ordered another beer, hoping to keep Lou talking. "Al must be a regular."

"Yep."

"Was he handing me a yarn about the murders? Were the police really here yesterday?"

"The Feds, not Police Chief Dankbar. Not his territory. Indian reservation's separate. Slocum handled them. Rickter was a customer, not an employee. Nobody here knows anything about what went on down south."

"What happened down south?"

"You must not watch TV. It's all over the news. Newspaper guys have been like hounds. Slocum sent 'em packing."

"I am totally in the dark."

Lou shrugged. "Maybe that's the best."

"Are you talking about the popsicles Al was talking about? Who was the guy?"

"This isn't a question and answer booth, buddy. If you want info, talk to Slocum."

"Good idea. How do I do that?"

Lou snorted. "You're one persistent dude." He took Camden's empty glass. "Come around after midnight and you might get a hearing. Slocum likes his privacy and nosey guys leave him tense."

Camden had a lot of questions and wondered if this was the time to notify his superiors. Too early and he didn't want to sully reputations if his assumptions were wrong. He pulled out his wallet and dropped his card on the bar with a heavy tip. "Thanks. I'll come after midnight and hope to meet your boss."

Chapter 16

Patty and Josh made good time through South Dakota, skirting the Missouri River as they cut over to the Iowa side. The roads were clear, traffic light, and the weather forecast contained no major storm warnings. When they pulled into a truck stop to get gas north of Sioux City, they filled up the tank and parked in the lot.

"Let's grab lunch while we're here," Patty said. "Otherwise we'll have to set up the trailer and that'll take time."

"Suits me." Josh put Kallie in her harness. "First, show me where the men's room is."

She walked ahead of Kallie, stopping outside the door of restrooms at the truck station. "Want me to go in with you?"

"Some things I can do myself, thanks."

"If I'm not here when you come out, wait, okay?"

"Right."

Patty left him and went inside to pick up a newspaper. When she came out, she found Josh and Kallie waiting by the side of the building. "All set?"

"Yep. Had an interesting go-round with our nemesis."

"Floyd Rickter?"

"You got it. He's been at the booze."

"You'd think with all the truck stops in America we could have avoided him."

"This is one of the main arteries south, so it's not unexpected," Josh said. "Still, I wonder if he had to stop at the police barricade or if he got through before they set it up."

"Why would it matter?"

"He drives a refrigerated truck."

"Jesus," she said. She scanned the trucking area and spotted the yellow semi hauling the reefer. "I don't see him in his cab and the engine's shut down. He must be in the café. Maybe we should drive on and eat someplace else."

"I'm not letting that bastard keep me from eating. If he wants more trouble, I'll give it to him. Come on. Show the way." Josh motioned with his hand and reluctantly Patty turned and walked toward the café with Kallie, guiding Josh, close on her heels.

Once inside Patty spotted Floyd Rickter sitting at the counter, his head bent over a coffee mug. "Let's sit in a booth at the back, far from the door," she whispered to Josh. "Rickter's at the counter."

Josh slid into the curved booth first, and Kallie settled at his feet. Patty moved in next to him. "What do you want to eat?" Patty asked, as she perused the menu. "Soup, sandwich, something more substantial?"

"A Rueben, if they have it."

"Yep. Side order of fries comes with it. What do you want to drink?"

"Lemonade."

Just then the waitress came over. "Nice dog," she said, looking down at Kallie whose nose stuck into the aisle.

Josh gave his order, and Patty asked for a steak sandwich and a diet coke. While Josh sat back, she unfolded the newspaper and began to skim headlines, hunting for any article relating to the bodies found at Oldorf's. On the third page she found it. "Frozen bodies found in deserted Minnesota RV Park." In a hushed voice, she read the headline to Josh, then continued to read the article to herself.

"All right." Josh broke into her silent reading. "What's it say? Or do you plan to leave me out in the cold?"

"Sorry. They've identified the bodies at Oldorf's. A Rhonda Crouch and, this'll blow your mind, Peter Darby. They've brought in the FBI."

Josh's hand turned into a fist, a frown creased his forehead. "I was afraid of that."

Thinking he hadn't gotten the connection, she said, "Peter Darby is or was Linda's so-called husband and father of her baby." She waited for him to respond but when he didn't she continued. "She no longer has to look for him."

"I got that part." He leaned forward. "Read the whole article to me, but softly. No point in calling attention to ourselves."

"Well, I wasn't going to shout." She glanced about the restaurant. Of course, many had turned in their direction when they'd entered, since it probably wasn't often they saw a man with a guide dog. She scooted across the vinyl seat closer to Josh and read without interruptions. "What do you think?"

"Somebody didn't like Peter Darby."

"Oh, duh. Thanks for that great input."

"Okay. I'll be serious and add some interesting info to your inquiring mind. I know Rhonda Crouch from Slocum's casino. She was a great gal, dedicated to her job. Being a flirt, having guys fighting for her attention was part of her plan."

"What plan? What are you talking about?" She stopped herself. "There's a lot you're not telling me."

He sighed. "Trust me. The less you know, the safer you'll be."

"You aren't making any sense. Safe? From what, who? Floyd?" She scowled. "Should we notify the police?"

He grunted. "And tell them that I know Rhonda? Hardly."

"I didn't mean that." With her elbows on the table and her chin in her palms, Patty's mind filtered her colliding ideas. After a moment, she sat up straighter and made her argument. "You know Rhonda. We know Linda, and she told us Peter Darby is her baby's father. And Slocum's casino is known to you and me." She stopped. "And Floyd Rickter says he knows you from there? Wasn't your friend Mike a bouncer at Slocums?"

"What're you getting at? That I had something to do with Darby's death?"

"No, silly. I'm just putting clues together. Rickter obviously frequented Slocum's. Rhonda did too. If Peter Darby went to Slocum's, he could have met Rhonda and tangled with Floyd. And as you said, Floyd drives a refrigerated truck."

"You're overreacting because I talked about your safety." Despite his words, his facial muscles grew taut and his body tensed.

Unable to read his eyes, Patty tuned into Josh's body language. "Okay, maybe I've got an overactive imagination, but you have to admit there's a lot to what I'm suggesting."

The waitress brought their food, and they stopped talking until she left.

"Lemonade's on your right." Patty pushed the glass into his waiting hand. "Sandwich at three o'clock on your plate; fries at nine." He'd taught her a few things to help him manage.

Josh took a swallow of lemonade, then put down the glass. "How do you figure Rickter fits into the picture?"

Patty glanced in Rickter's direction. "He's been to Slocum's and according to the paper, Darby was last seen at Slocum's. From what Linda said about Peter, it sounded like he was a skirt chaser. If Rhonda was a flirt, like you said, and Floyd was involved, well … need I draw a bigger picture? Plus, we know that Rickter has a violent temper and drinks a lot."

"So do a lot of people. And even your father gambled at Slocum's. So none of that proves anything. But you're right about Rickter driving a refrigerated truck and that supports your theory."

"Remember at Oldorf's I said the area where we parked must have been used by a larger rig. Well, that could have been Rickter's truck."

"All the trucks left before us, but he couldn't have been that far ahead of us, so it wouldn't have given him much time to unload his cargo. It's not enough information to give the police." Josh rested his forearms on either side of his plate.

"Wouldn't the police know by now the make of the tire from the tread marks? The troopers told us there was a set other than ours." Patty glanced at the news article. "There's nothing here that says who the police are looking for even though we did tell them about Floyd Rickter's actions at the other truck stop."

"The police don't give all their clues to the media." He sighed. "There's not much we can do even if your suspicions are right."

"We could call the police anonymously."

He picked up a French fry. "The last time we did that we got in trouble. I don't want to be hauled in by cops or the FBI to explain what we know. We got to make up lost time."

"But Josh, a phone call from a pay phone in the middle of nowhere wouldn't hurt, would it?" "I'm not sure." The fry dangled from his fingers. "They had us pegged the last time we called."

"That might have been because we over-nighted so close to the RV Park. We're in a different state now."

They ate in silence for a time until Josh said, "We could let them know Rickter is at this truck stop, he's been drinking and might be a threat if he drives. That might get the state troopers' attention without getting us involved."

"Great idea." Patty crumbled up her napkin. "I have the number the trooper gave me."

He hesitated. "Okay, go for it." Josh put his hand across the table as if searching for hers. "Don't give them your name or mine, don't over explain, don't stay on long enough for them to get a trace."

Kallie emitted a throaty growl, but Josh and Patty were too engrossed in their plan to pay attention.

"I'll be evasive." Patty started to get up when she felt a heavy hand on her shoulder.

"I keep meeting up with you two. Are you following me?" Floyd's breath washed over her. He took his hand off her shoulder and put both palms down on top of the newspaper that lay between Patty and Josh.

"Thought you were following us," Josh said. "It appears you've been drinking, sleep it off before you head back on the road."

Floyd stared with bloodshot eyes at Josh then at Patty. "I don't need you telling me what to do."

"Just trying to be helpful," Josh said.

Floyd continued to lean on the table with his elbows locked, his face close to Josh's. "You don't fool me even if you got this tart buffaloed."

Patty's chin came up, but she decided to ignore his slur. "Floyd, sleep it off or I'll report you for trucking while drunk."

He started to grab her arm, but Kallie rose, growling louder, her jaw only a foot away from his crotch. Floyd backed away, sliding his hands off the table and crumpling the newspaper in his fists. "I'm going to my truck and sleep before I hit the road again, so mind your own business or you'll be sorry." He turned away, stumbled toward the door, the newspaper still in his fists.

Patty watched him leave. "I'll make the call. He's got the newspaper with the article. What if he reads it?"

"It'll be awhile before he's sober enough to do that. By that time we'll be well out of here. Go ahead. Make the call."

As she went to phone, she decided she'd call Maggie, too. Since Patty had suggested Linda contact Maggie, then Maggie could let her know Peter Darby was dead.

Despite the dispatcher trying to keep her on the line with questions,

Patty's call was brief. She gave Rickter's name and the kind of a truck he was driving. When asked to identify herself, she hung up.

She sifted through the coins in her pocket to see if she had enough for a quick conversation with Maggie. She held her breath as the phone rang, praying Maggie would pick up instead of the waitress.

"Maggie's Diner," came the voice Patty knew so well.

"Maggie, it's me, Patty. I can't talk long. Did Linda get in touch with you?"

"Yes. Poor thing. She's a lost kitten. I'll do what I can."

"I knew you would. I found out her husband, Peter Darby, is dead, murdered."

"Jesus, girl, what're you talking about? Are you okay? Where are you?"

"I'm in a restaurant headed to Tucson with Josh Peterson—a blind guy. I'm towing his trailer. Don't worry; he's real nice."

"How do you know Darby is dead?"

"It's in the newspaper here in Iowa. He was found frozen at a truck stop."

"Dear mother of God save me," Maggie yelled over the phone. "That story's all over town. They haven't given out the murder victims' names. Are you okay?"

"Yes. It's got nothing to do with me," Patty said and crossed her fingers.

"Camden McMillan is in town asking about Josh's friend Mike," Maggie said.

"Camden? Josh gave a message to Linda for the guy. I don't have much time. Have you heard anything about a trucker named Floyd Rickter?"

"He's a suspect in the popsicle murders. That's what the newspapers are dubbing the case. Linda said he was a pain in the ass to her and you. You didn't do anything foolish did you?"

"Maggie, I did not do anything. I'm just driving to Tucson. I gotta go. I'll write soon."

"Wait. Where will you stay in Tucson?"

"Don't know. Some RV park I guess. I'll send you a postcard." The operator came on asking for money and Patty said, "Bye Maggie." She put the receiver back on the hook and sagged against the wall.

Chapter 17

As if bad luck stalked them like a curse, a weather front with wind gusts up to fifty miles an hour forced them into a truck stop seventy miles south from where they'd eaten lunch.

"So much for weather forecasts," Josh grumbled as he stepped out of the truck to grope his way back to the trailer to let down the stabilizers.

Patty zipped up her jacket and pulled on her wool hat and gloves. The howling wind tugged the door from her grasp as her boots hit the hard ground. Kallie leapt out, wagging her tail, and bounded toward Josh. Patty called out, "Kallie's headed toward you." Her voice vanished in the wind.

Kallie's nose nudged Josh's thigh and he reached down to give her a pat. As the two of them disappeared around the corner of the trailer, Patty hurried back inside. She hit the button activating the slide-outs, hung her jacket on the door peg and turned on the heat. The trailer swayed in the wind. Sagging into a swivel chair, she stretched her legs and arched her back before relaxing with a sigh.

When Josh came in with Kallie, sprinkles of ice glistened on his blue parka and his dark glasses filmed from the change of temperature.

The onrush of colder air jolted Patty out of her comfortable position. "I think someone stuck us with voodoo pins. I'm fed up with all the delays."

"Me too." Josh stomped his feet, pulled his hood back, shrugged out of his parka, and felt for the peg to hang it up. "I thought this would be a quick trip south," he said, then let out a disgusted, "ha," and made his way to the other chair. Once seated, he leaned forward and buried his head in his hands.

Patty sat across from him. "I wish you had a TV. We might learn more about the murders. I can't sit around and stare at the walls the rest of the day."

"Mike stowed some books in the bed's headboard. Not sure what they are, but you might find one to hold your interest."

"What about you?" Patty asked. "What do you do to entertain yourself? I'd go bonkers without something to read or see or ..." She hesitated. "I guess it's tough for you."

"You've kept things interesting, finding bodies, talking to the police, picking up strangers."

"Not everything was my fault and Linda needed us. There was no way you would have left her in that mess at that truck stop."

"Maybe. But I think you attract trouble."

"Oh, right, and you don't? That was a mutual decision to call the authorities about Floyd."

They sat facing each other and Patty could see her image reflected in his dark glasses. She ran her hands through her hair, trying to untangle the curls.

Josh sighed heavily. "It stinks." He stood, took a few steps, then stopped in the center of the trailer as if unable to decide what to do next. "If we were headed somewhere, it wouldn't be so bad, but these constant delays are driving me nuts. God, I wish it was over."

"The trip?"

"Yeah, that and a few other things." He rubbed his jaw, took a few steps, and leaned against the wall. "Where do you plan to go after we get to Tucson?"

"I'll see if I can get a job as a mechanic, save my money, and eventually have a home and business of my own."

"Tall order. Not sure Tucson is the right place for you."

"Too close to you?" She studied him, wondering what he was thinking and wishing she could see his eyes, despite knowing it would solve nothing. But she always had this desire. Why? Perhaps Josh was right. The eyes are the window to the soul and if a person is blind, it takes away an avenue for the sighted to understand another's character. "You never said what you plan to do in Tucson."

He turned away and over his shoulder said, "No, I never did." He walked to his bedroom, and she was left staring at his back.

Damn. "You're a clam," she yelled after him.

He slid the pocket door shut.

She rose, went to the door and slid it open again. He twirled around. "What?"

"Thought I'd look at the books you mentioned."

He slumped onto the edge of the bed, his back to her. "Help yourself."

Patty sat on the other side, leaned over and peered into the bookshelf recessed into the headboard. "He had great taste." She pulled out a copy of The Iliad, shoved it back, then took out John Steinbeck's The Grapes of Wrath. "I never read this one." She edged back on the mattress with her legs crossed and began thumbing through it. "Mike must have been reading this one. There's a book marker." She pulled it out. "Hey, it's a lottery ticket. Dated two months ago. Do you think it's worth anything?"

"I doubt it. He was always buying those and then forgetting he had them."

"Did he ever win anything?"

He chuckled. "Ten bucks once. I kept telling him not to hope for a miracle, but he wouldn't listen."

"Maybe he died before he could check this ticket out." She kneeled on the mattress. "Why don't we see if the numbers are worth something?"

"Why? It won't be any good."

"How do you know?"

"Come on. What are the odds?"

She shrugged. "I don't know. It might be fun, like solving a mystery." Josh grimaced, so she sat back. "Okay, if I keep it? Kind of a talisman." She placed it in the book to use as a book mark. "How about if I read the book out loud?"

"You sure you want to do that?"

"Of course, then we can both pass the time."

He scooted back on the bed with his back propped against the headboard, his arms folded, his dark glasses in place. "Go for it."

She began: "'To the red country and part of the gray country of Oklahoma, the last rains came gently, and they did not cut the scarred earth.'" She put the book down. "I don't think we go through Oklahoma, do we?"

"Not if we can help it."

Patty nodded then continued to read; Kallie came in and hopped up on the bed. With one hand stroking the dog's fur, Josh listened, and Patty read for an hour. The trailer shuddered as the wind banged against its metal siding, but Patty remained happily caught up in the story, until her voice grew raspy.

"Okay," she said. "I need something to drink. Want anything?"

"I'm good."

She put down the book and went to the kitchen. When she looked in the fridge, she was disappointed. "You know what I really would like?" she called out as she moved back toward the bedroom. "A chocolate shake. "I'll go to the café. Want anything?"

"In this wind and cold, you want ice cream?"

She shrugged. "Desires make no sense."

"Don't I know it." He smiled. "You twisted my arm. Make mine strawberry if they've got it. Otherwise vanilla."

Patty put on her boots and coat, sliding the hood over her head. When she stuck her hands into her pockets, she realized she didn't have any money. Walking back to Josh, she said, "Can you lend me some cash till pay day? I spent all my change on the phone call."

"The call to the police couldn't have cost much."

She swallowed. She hadn't told him she'd called Maggie but she didn't want to lie to him, so she didn't answer.

He stood and dug his wallet out of his back pocket and handed her a bill. It's a ten spot, so bring me the change."

"How do you know it's a ten?"

"I folded it in threes. A twenty gets folded in half and a five in fours."

"But how do you know what the original denomination is?"

"I have to trust people."

"Are they always honest?"

"There's the occasional crook."

She put the bill in her coat pocket and glanced at Kallie. "I'll leave Kallie with you."

When she went out, the wind almost tore the door from her grasp. She shut it with a bang and glanced about. The truck stop was full with cars sheltered among semis as the behemoths' engines idled. Patty bent into the wind and struggled toward the café some two hundred yards ahead. With her chin buried deep into her muffler and her hood pulled tight around her head, she kept her eyes on the ground. Snow swirled about her. The hum of engines was like a swarm of bees.

She heard a loud roar. Pushing her hood back, she looked to the right. A truck bore down on her, its large wheels spewing out ice and gravel. Instinctively she jumped sideways. The semi's front grill came within inches of crushing her as she slammed into the side of a car. Her head struck the side mirror, and she slid to the frozen ground. Moments passed until she willed her body to move. The salty taste of blood greeted her exploring tongue. Squinting against the peppering onslaught of blowing ice, she peered around. No one in sight. The semi was long gone. She doubted the driver had seen her.

Using the car for support, she pulled herself to her feet and edged around its front end. On wobbly legs, she staggered back to the trailer, grabbed the door handle and stumbled inside, pulling the door shut behind her. When she collapsed on the sofa, Kallie came and licked her face. She pushed the dog's head away and rested her arm over her eyes.

From the bedroom, Josh called out, "That was quick."

She moaned and sank into blissful sleep. She awoke with a cold compress on her head and a blanket over her. Squinting from the light, she realized she was in Josh's bed. She struggled to sit up, but Josh's firm hand held her down.

"Just lie still until you're feeling better." Josh sat on the edge of the bed. "You must have taken quite a fall."

"No. I mean, yes. A truck came out of nowhere. I didn't hear it with the wind blowing and all the engines idling." She gazed at Josh. "How did you get me in here? I thought I made it to the couch."

"I carried you. I might be blind, but I'm not weak."

"I know that." She thought of how easily he'd taken down Floyd, how he'd shoveled and tromped through the heavy snow. "I guess ice cream will have to wait."

He smiled, making the cleft in his chin less prominent. "I think you need a hot cup of cocoa or tea."

He moved the compress from her forehead to her right cheek.

"How did you know?" she asked.

"Know?"

"I cut the right inside of my mouth." She put her hand on his as he held the cloth.

"It felt swollen," he said.

She lifted his hand and looked at it. "You have strong, beautiful hands."

"Beautiful does not apply to a man, particularly his hands."

"They do, if a person thinks they are." She kept her hand on his and began feeling warm all over.

He lifted her hand off his and removed the compress. "Did you get a look at the truck?"

"You're good at changing the subject." She folded her hands across her chest.

"The answer might be important. Did you notice anything about the truck? Color?"

"You're thinking it could have been Floyd?" She thought for a few moments. "No way. How would he know it was me? He was still recovering from his hangover when we left." She tried to recall the details of the incident, but it had happened too fast. "I think it was just a cab without a trailer. Yes. I'm sure of it. It went by too fast for it to have been hauling a trailer."

"It could have been Floyd, if he left his trailer behind. He could have followed us then waited for his opportunity."

"But his gripe is with you, not me."

"Don't be so sure. If he takes you out, he gets at me. And after our little spat at the restaurant, he might not like you too much either."

"You're so reassuring." She pulled herself to a sitting position and wondered, not for the first time, what she'd gotten herself into.

The following morning Josh and Patty overslept. The buffeting wind had kept them awake during the night, but now the wind had subsided. While Josh was in the bathroom, Patty stepped outside and scanned the parking area before walking Kallie toward the woods at the edge of the large lot where frost clung to sprigs of weeds. The crisp air stung her lungs, but she gloried in the blue sky. The thought of Floyd lying in wait gave her chills, but there was no sign of his yellow reefer and besides only a few trucks remained. Perhaps he'd already left, if he'd been there at all.

Keeping a careful eye out for icy spots, she turned and made for the small diner with its flashing neon sign—*Joe & Josie's - Open 24/7*. The squat building's white stucco with its broad horizontal stripe of red surrounding it gave it a 1950s look. Patty hooked Kallie's leash to a nearby post and entered, feeling the blast of heat. Near the cash register the newsstand beckoned, and she stepped forward to read the papers' dates—yesterday's.

A thin, tired-eyed woman in her thirties stood behind the counter and gave her a wan smile. "What can I do for you?" she called out. "Coffee's fresh. So are the muffins. Made 'em last night."

"Sounds wonderful, but I just wanted today's paper." Patty felt the bills in her parka pocket. She never did get her chocolate shake and she'd been unable to eat dinner. Walking to the counter, she eyed the muffins under the glass lid on the counter. "How much?"

"$1.75 a piece."

Patty hesitated.

"They're big, make for a hearty breakfast." The woman pushed a strand of brown hair off her brow, her hands showing the evidence of a woman who did menial chores.

"They're good," a lanky fellow said, who sat at the counter.

"I bet." Patty decided to forego the treat. "When do you expect today's papers?"

"With this weather, nothing got through. We're lucky the storm blew over quickly. They'll probably get delivered later this afternoon."

The only customers were a woman buried in a heavy wool sweater and the trucker who had spoken earlier. He put some money on the counter, rose from his seat, and walked toward Patty. "I know you."

"You do?" Patty said, taken aback.

"Sure. We were snowbound in a truck stop up north." His smile was warm despite his pasty complexion. "Your husband had the run-in with that troublemaker, Floyd Rickter. Brutus was real impressed."

Patty smiled. "Brutus. Yes. Of course, I remember. I heard his truck overturned, and he was taken to a hospital."

"You can't keep Brutus down for long." The man angled toward the door, zipping us his heavy jacket. "Old Brutus is on the road again driving backup."

"I'm glad to hear that." She started to leave, then had second thoughts. "Have you seen that Rickter guy lately?"

"No. But I heard the police wanted to check out his reefer. Something about frozen bodies. It's enough to give you the creeps. Wonder what he got himself into?"

"Did the police pick him up?"

The trucker shook his head. "Haven't heard. I'm laying over here for a day. Need to rest or I'll fall asleep at the wheel. Can't risk my load on that. I got too much at stake. You staying?"

"No, I think we'll head out."

"Well, if you do stay, let me know. Name's Larry," he held out his leather-gloved hand. "It gets lonely on the road. I'm the red semi, hauling tractors, parked back of the lot up against the green belt."

They started to exit the diner when Larry said, "If I were Floyd and the police were hunting for my reefer, I'd dump it and go on with my cab. Head toward Mexico."

"Isn't a refrigerator trailer expensive?"

"Yep, but I think he was a company driver, doesn't own the rig. If he's on the lam, what does he care about the trailer?"

They both went outside, where Larry leaned down and held out his hand for Kallie to sniff. "Sweet dog."

They parted ways and Patty headed back to the trailer. The sun warmed the ice sheets into glistening puddles. At the trailer, she checked out the few forlorn trucks left and spotted Larry's.

Inside the trailer she removed Kallie's leash, and hung her parka by the door. "Hi," she said to Josh who sat at the table drinking coffee.

"Coffee's made, breakfast is warming in the oven." He rose, put Kallie's dish of kibbles down and sat again.

Patty opened the oven door and the heady aroma of cinnamon rolls engulfed her, making her glad she hadn't bought the diner's muffins. "You'd make a great houseboy," she said, plopping a roll on a plate. "Want one?"

"Ate already, thanks. We should get going as soon as you're ready."

"Okay." She sat across from Josh and blew on her coffee as the steam rose. "I met a trucker, Larry, who was at that stop up north where we met Brutus and Linda. Seems the news is out about the police looking for Floyd." She took a bite of the sweet cinnamon roll. "Yummy." She sighed with pleasure and licked the sticky cinnamon frosting off her fingers.

"I bet he ditched his reefer and is driving south fast," Josh said. "If he killed those people, he's headed for the border." She nodded, since her mouth was too full to speak. After swallowing, she said, "Yes. That's what Larry thought too. It's possible he was driving that truck yesterday."

"If he's around, he just might try to run us off the road." Josh stood and moved to the sink, rinsing out his cup.

"I checked the parking area," Patty said before eating the last of her roll. "His rig isn't here." She stood, taking one last gulp of coffee. "I'll do the dishes."

"Okay. I'll take care of the stabilizers. Straighten up the inside and crank in the sliders." He walked back to his bedroom and reappeared dressed in his parka and wool cap.

"Maybe I should make sandwiches for lunch, so we don't have to stop," she said.

"Good idea." He went outside in a rush, allowing just a hint of cold air to penetrate the room. Kallie sat forlornly near the door.

Patty boiled water for hot cocoa and poured it into the thermos. She made sandwiches of leftover meatloaf and cheddar cheese. Kallie's tail wagged as she stood next to Patty. "Not for you, my girl," Patty said. The trailer trembled, as the stabilizers retracted. Hurriedly, she straightened the furniture before pushing the button to pull in the sliders.

The door opened and Josh called out, "Ready?"

Kallie didn't wait to be asked, but jumped out the door and ran in circles around the trailer. Patty shrugged into her parka and with her hands full of lunch items descended the stairs. "Kallie's running free," she said.

"She'll come when we get in the truck."

"Hope so. I'm not going to chase after her again." She put the lunch in the back seat of the truck, then looked for Kallie. "She's gone into the woods," she said to Josh who stood at the passenger's door.

"Let's drive over. She'll hop in." He got in the truck.

"You hope." Patty slid into the driver's seat, hooked up her safety belt, and started the engine. Slowly, she drove toward the wooded area. "Larry's truck is close by. Wonder if he might have left food out."

Kallie came out of the woods, nose close to the ground as she snuffled from bush to bush. Patty stopped the truck near her, and Josh opened his door. "Come Kallie. Come!" He called out.

She growled, not at him, but at the truck, then stared at the woods.

"So much for obeying you," Patty said with disgust. "Damn, I sure don't get how she could be a guide dog the way she acts sometimes." She put the truck in park, letting the engine idle and got out. Leash in hand she moved toward Kallie. Fortunately, the dog was too interested in whatever she'd found by the truck's tires to escape Patty's grab for her collar. "Gotcha." As if she knew her playtime was up, Kallie followed Patty back into the truck. "Okay, Josh, that's the last time I fetch your dog. You'd better keep her in harness from now on or I quit."

"Sure."

"Sure? What do you mean? You think I'm kidding?"

"Yes."

"Damn." Patty put the truck in gear and headed out of the lot. She was fuming, but after a moment, she smiled. Of course she'd been kidding. What would she do? They were stuck with one another, for better or for worse. Abruptly, her thoughts came to rest at the next part of that phrase—till death do us part.

Chapter 18

It was after eight in the evening when Camden parked near Maggie's Diner. The neon sign reflected on the icy sidewalk, and inside a few customers lingered over coffee. When the bell above the door clanged, he was reminded of Bromont's quaintness. As he took off his coat and slid into a booth, he reveled in the aroma of fresh brewed coffee. The same homely waitress he'd seen before came over and handed him a menu. "We're out of meatloaf, stew, and beef pot pie. There's been a run on the apple pie too, so all that's left for dessert is chocolate marble cake."

He glanced at the menu, his stomach growling. "What are my choices for an entree?"

She shrugged. "The whitefish is fresh and the barbecue chicken breast is good."

"I'll go with the whitefish, a side order of spinach salad and cake for dessert."

"Something to drink?"

"Coffee, black, and water, please."

The waitress left and he settled back and searched the diner for Maggie. When the waitress brought his coffee and salad, he asked about Maggie's whereabouts.

"She had to go to Dr. Whittier's."

"She's ill?"

"No. That girl, Linda, is sick or maybe it was her baby." She shrugged. "I'm not sure."

His pulse quickened. "Hold my order." He threw a few bills on the table to cover the salad and coffee, grabbed his jacket and hurried out the door. "Damn," he swore under his breath as he flung himself into his SUV.

When he arrived at the medical clinic, Maggie told him that Arlet had stopped breathing, and it was only Linda's quick use of CPR that had staved off her death. Dr. Whittier had the baby on oxygen and now they waited for his verdict.

The clock ticked like a slow metronome as Camden sat across from Maggie and Linda in the clinic's tiny waiting room. He had no idea how to comfort Linda. His own memories of sitting in a hospital waiting to hear news of his wife and daughter ricocheted through his mind. Words were useless, but having caring people around helped.

For two hours the door to surgery remained closed. Several times Maggie had to restrain Linda from striding through that door. The young woman cried, paced, and prayed in random order. Camden brought them coffee, held Linda's hand, and whispered words of encouragement, knowing they sounded meaningless. Now and then, he glanced at Maggie, noticing how the tiny woman's presence appeared to give Linda strength.

As Camden rose to get a drink from the water fountain, the surgery door opened and Dr. Whittier came out. Linda stood, her freckled face ashen, her lips trembling. Maggie stood at her elbow. Dr. Whittier put his hand on the girl's shoulder. "I couldn't save her. Her heart was too weak."

Linda fell toward Maggie, and Camden rushed forward to catch the girl and help her to a chair. "Why? Why?" Linda yelled with tears streaming down her cheeks. "She was so sweet, so little. What did I do wrong?"

"You did everything right, Linda," the doctor said. "There was nothing you could have done. Nothing anyone could have done. She had a defective heart."

"No-o-o." Linda's wail filled the room. She stood, struggling against Maggie's grip. "It can't be. I don't believe it. I can't."

No one challenged her statement. They were all in shock. After several minutes of Linda's repeated phrases of disbelief, she straightened her shoulders. "I need to see her."

"Yes, of course." The doctor, Maggie, and Linda vanished behind the swinging doors while Camden remained transfixed in the small waiting room.

It was some time before Maggie came back out and gave Camden a wan smile. "The doctor gave her a sedative. It'll take effect soon. She's sitting by Arlet. Would you help me take her to my place?"

"Of course." Drained of emotion, Camden could say nothing more.

As if aware of the tragedy on earth, the moon hid behind a wall of clouds. On the ride through the cold dark night, the three occupants remained silent, held in a copse of black thoughts. At Maggie's small brick house, they trod over the icy ground, and entered into a house that smelled sweet and fresh. Still wearing her coat, Linda collapsed onto a couch. Maggie hurried to the kitchen. Camden knelt by the hearth and started a fire. By the time the fire flickered to life, Maggie reappeared with a cup of hot broth for Linda. She sat next to the grieving girl and pushed the mug into her hands. Linda stared straight ahead, so Maggie moved the mug to the girl's lips.

She sipped tentatively. "I don't know what to do," Linda said in a quiet voice.

"You will," Maggie said firmly. "But not tonight. Tomorrow Camden and I will help you face the day and then the next and the next."

Camden was surprised to be included. When was the last time he'd been asked to be there for someone? He stood by the hearth watching and revisiting his own agony of losing his wife and child.

After a time, Maggie helped Linda to her feet and walked her toward a bedroom. She glanced back at Camden. "Stay and we'll talk."

He nodded and Maggie closed the bedroom door behind her. Camden paced the room, looking at Maggie's collections of memorabilia from elections dating back to an *I Like Ike* button from the fifties. He smiled as he went down memory lane, scanning the different newspaper articles, logos, and paraphernalia from both political parties, as if Maggie didn't discriminate between them. There was a reason townspeople rallied to her diner and to her. She was pure midwest solid, big-hearted, sympathetic, yet tough.

When Maggie came back in the room she still wore her black slacks and yellow sweater, but she'd discarded her heavy shoes for woolly slippers. She sighed and walked over to a sideboard. "Drink?" she asked Camden. "I've got brandy, vodka, gin, bourbon, no scotch. Isn't that what men always order? Scotch?"

He shrugged. "I'll settle for brandy, thanks." He went over and took the glass she offered, then returned and stood by the fireplace to stare into the flames.

She took her brandy snifter, sat in a green high-back upholstered chair to the side of the hearth, and put her feet on a hassock. "God, what a blow. Poor mite. She's just a baby herself."

"She's had it tough."

"Tougher than you know, but she'll make it, she's got that inner drive, kind of like another girl I know." Maggie closed her eyes and leaned her head back.

"Patty Harkin?"

"Yes." She sipped her brandy. "She called me last night. They're headed for Tucson, towing Peterson's trailer. She said she dropped me a card, but I haven't picked up my mail for a couple of days. What with the snow storm, I doubt if much has gotten through." Maggie gazed at Camden as he settled onto the couch across from her. "There's more bad news for Linda. Her husband, Peter Darby is dead. Turns out he was one of the victims in that Popsicle Murder Case the media is screaming about."

"I heard about that when I was at Slocum's."

Maggie sat forward. "Poor Linda. Everything's gone sour for her."

"From what Linda implied, Darby left her to fend for herself even though he knew she was pregnant." He frowned and swirled his brandy around the glass. "What else did Patty say?"

"She asked about Floyd Rickter. He's a suspect in the murders. Hear anything about him when you were at Slocum's?"

"Yes." He rubbed his jaw, contemplating how much he should tell her. "Darby must have been involved with Rickter's girl."

"Rhonda Crouch, the other victim," Maggie said. "According to the news, they were both executed, bullet to the head. Gangland style."

"I don't like the connections between Mike, Josh, and Rickter." Camden leaned forward with his forearms resting on his knees.

Maggie's blue-gray eyes studied him. "I hope Patty's not involved."

He shook his head. "She's with Josh. She might be caught in the middle of all this, whatever this is." He drained his glass and stared into the fire. "This whole scenario about Mike is strange, and I'm not sure how it relates to Josh. But Mike is not dead."

Her eyes narrowed. "Why are you so sure?"

He rose and walked to the sideboard. "Would you like a refill?"

"No. I think I want a clear head to hear you out, but help yourself."

"Thanks." He splashed brandy into his glass and recapped the decanter. With his back to her, he said, "The description Linda gave of Josh fits Mike. The coroner's description of the body that was supposed to be Mike doesn't." He went to the sofa and placed his glass on the end table, then sat. "Dr. Whittier didn't perform an autopsy. Instead he relied on the medical records given to him by Josh. Those showed a man unable to do much of anything, let alone run. That body wasn't Mike's." He took a deep breath. "Plus the kid at the RV park who identified the body as Mike had never even met him. Conclusion—Mike's alive."

"But Patty said she was with Josh, not Mike, and Josh is blind."

"I realize that. It doesn't make sense. This fellow Rickter is somehow connected with Josh through Slocum Hitower. Mike worked for Slocum, but he may have had another agenda. Not sure what. If Mike isn't dead, then where is he? And who died in the accident?"

Her small hands encircled her glass. "I don't like it. Patty could be in danger."

"You really care about her, don't you?"

"I helped raise her after her mother died."

His concern wasn't for the girl, but for the mystery surrounding Mike. "It sounds to me as if Police Chief Dankbar hurried the investigation of Mike's death. What do you know about Dankbar?"

Maggie frowned. "He's not much good at his job, a glad-hander who rode into office on his persuasive charm." Maggie shook her head. "He's not the best chief, but he isn't the worst. Incompetent is a fitting description. Not sure he'll get elected next time around."

"Dishonest?"

She smiled. "Small stuff maybe, nothing big time."

He stared into the fire. "I need to talk with Slocum Hitower." He glanced at Maggie over the rim of his brandy glass. "What do you know about Slocum?"

She shrugged. "He stays on the reservation and employs only the local Indian population; that makes the tribal council happy and the local whites unhappy. I read where some of the reservations got caught short when the economy turned south, like a lot of companies. Trying to refi is just as hard for them as for others and many have big interest payments due." She took a sip of brandy. "Can't for the life of me figure why people gamble when they're practically broke." She grimaced and put her feet on the floor and leaned forward.

"You think Hitower's casino is hurting?"

Maggie shrugged. "If Hitower has to cut back on his distributions to the tribe, he'll be in trouble. Not sure how he'd be affected personally."

"Wonder what owners like Slocum would do if they can't refinance their debt." The thought stopped him cold. A gangland killing. The Mafia would do what it had to do. He thought of Mike and what he might have meant about keeping native soil safe from outsiders. Perhaps he did need to talk to his superiors about what was happening in Bromont. "Is Slocum Hitower connected with the mob?"

"I don't know. Haven't heard that. The reservation's small and has kept a low profile through the years." Maggie twirled her glass, letting the brandy coat the sides. "Are you going after Josh Peterson?"

"I'm not sure. Tucson's a big city. I need more information."

"True, but Patty's a mechanic and there aren't many women mechanics. That's the kind of job she'd get. A blind guy with a trailer and a woman mechanic shouldn't be too hard to find even in a city the size of Tucson."

"First, I'll talk to Slocum Hitower."

"You might be heading for trouble."

He stood and placed his glass next to the decanter. "I'm pigheaded enough to try to find out how the dots are connected, especially with two murders on the table."

Maggie stood and looked up at him. "I've never met Slocum, but I'd be careful."

Chapter 19

Clouds skittered across the sky, and in the west ominous signs of another storm loomed. Snow lay upon the land, although the road remained clear.

Patty drove through the morning hours with a throbbing headache. She wasn't about to admit to Josh how woozy she felt. Hadn't she agreed that if she couldn't get him to Tucson, she'd forfeit her pay? She couldn't afford that. But under the circumstances how could he leave her high and dry. After all, he needed her, too. At noon they pulled into a rest stop and ate lunch at a park table. The brisk air along with two aspirin helped eased her pain.

"You feeling okay?" Josh rested his forearms on the table while Kallie basked in the sun nearby.

"Sure. Why do you ask?" She pulled at her parka's collar and loosened her wool scarf.

"You've been extraordinarily quiet all morning. Maybe that hit on the noggin was worse than we thought."

"I'm sore, that's all." She was glad he couldn't see how she felt. He was perceptive enough without sight.

"We'll see. If you don't feel up to driving on, we'll stop." He hesitated. "I don't want to resort to my last option."

She'd been about to take a bite of her sandwich, but abruptly stopped. "What are you talking about? You sound mysterious."

"You don't need to know." He shifted his position on the bench so his back was to her.

"Then why say it? You get really weird sometimes, you know that."

Cars and trucks roared by on the highway, but only an occasional vehicle pulled in to use the facilities. "You know," Patty said, studying a map she'd brought with her from the truck, "we could head all the way into Arkansas and pick up Interstate 40. It looks more direct and we might not get as much snow if another storm hits." She traced the line designating 40 with her forefinger. "It goes into Albuquerque. Then we take 17 south to Tucson. What do you think?"

He turned back to face her. "Do you want to go that way because 40 goes through Oklahoma?"

"How do you know that?"

"That you want to go through Oklahoma? Isn't that what you asked about after reading *The Grapes of Wrath*?"

"I didn't mean that. I mean how do you know all the routes?"

"I told you, Mike and I had gone over this trip many times." He crinkled up his sandwich's wrapping paper. "Taking 70 west out of Kansas City seemed logical, but I'm not married to the idea."

"We can always decide when we get to Kansas City." She frowned and looked at the map again. "We'd need to take 35 southwest into Oklahoma City and then pick up 40 west." She began to map out the miles and timeline in her mind. "If nothing else goes awry, we should make Tucson easy in a week at the most."

"Perfect. Before Christmas is what I've been aiming for."

"I'd forgotten about the holidays." She stared at the traffic on the highway. "I never liked Christmas. It's fine for kids, but otherwise it's a bust as far as I'm concerned. Hate the gift giving. I always felt guilty receiving them when I knew money was scarce." She rubbed her cold cheeks with her palms. "What about you?"

"When I was a kid it was great, but then my parents died and well, like you said, Christmas is for kids." He stood and took hold of Kallie's harness. "Let's get going. Tucson won't come to us."

She packed up the food, deposited the trash in the nearby barrel, and led the way to the truck. Once settled in the cab, she drove out onto the highway, pulling in behind an old Volkswagen bus. "One minute earlier and I wouldn't have to pass that rattle trap. I guess it's the fastest he can go with that load on top."

"What kind of a car is it?"

"VW bus."

He smiled. "I had a VW bus in college. Greatest automobile I ever owned. Cheap to buy, cheap to run and plenty of room inside to have guys over for a few beers without being detected by the campus cops."

"Sounds like a misspent youth. Did you study or just have a good time?"

"You hurt my feelings. I was on a scholarship. Of course I studied, but not every minute."

She glanced out the side mirror and saw a red semi barrel up behind them, then pull back. "For a minute I thought we had a tail hugger, but he's backed off. The road's narrow right through here and there's a bridge coming up. Passing is out of the question right now."

"How fast are we going?" Josh faced forward. "Feels kind of slow."

She checked the speedometer. "Thirty-five to forty. The bus ahead is having trouble holding a constant speed. Maybe he'll pull over after the bridge."

As they drew near to the bridge, Patty noticed the semi behind her close the gap. "What the hell?" A nudge from the back sent the trailer skittering sideways. "Jesus!" She compensated.

The semi backed off. When she glanced in the rear view mirror, she saw he was coming up fast again, his front grill grinned in sardonic humor. The Volkswagen bus in front of them chugged along in an erratic 45 miles per hour. She laid her hand on the horn. The driver waved her forward—not enough time to pass with the oncoming traffic in view. Another glance in the side mirror told her she had no choice. She gunned the engine and the truck responded. As she passed the VW, its driver scowled at her. With a few seconds to spare she slid in front of the VW as cars from the opposite direction roared past, flashing their lights.

She let out her breath. "Lordy that was close."

"Why take the chance?"

"Didn't you feel that bump from behind? The idiot back there almost tossed us off the road." Her hands were sweating. "He should be reported."

She glanced in her mirror and saw that the semi had geared down. "Thank god the jerk backed off. She drove on, creating a slight gap between them and the VW. When she looked back, the semi had again sped up, swerved out, careened past the VW and barreled toward them. He drew even. "The guy's nuts," Patty yelled. "He's going to sideswipe us!"

She spotted a dirt road paralleling the highway and swung into it. The truck swerved into their lane, then slammed on its brakes; its flat bed of tractors fishtailed, clipping the VW. It plunged into a ditch behind Patty. The semi accelerated and sped down the highway.

Patty's brakes screeched as she came to a stop just short of a wood fence that led into a pasture. "The VW is in a ditch behind us. They might need help." She unfastened her seat belt, jumped out, and ran back to the bus. Its passenger side wheels were deep in sandy soil. Its engine sputtered then died. Boxes, crates, and bedding strewed across the dirt. The driver swung open his door.

She scrambled down the bank. "Are you hurt?" Her heart leaped with anxiety and her breath came in gasps.

"Not sure," the driver said. "No thanks to you." His voice held a growling anger.

"It was the semi's fault." There were moans and crying coming from inside the little bus. "Is everyone all right?"

"Gotta get our kids out." He clamored down to the ground, turned and reached back. "Julie, hand Jeffrey to me."

A pair of arms holding a child of about six lowered the sobbing boy to the man. He hugged the boy, then glanced at Patty and passed him to her. Holding the child close, she stepped back and bumped into Josh.

"Let me take him," he said.

She didn't hesitate for there was another child being handed to her by the man, then another and another. Patty continued to pass the children on to Josh. Too engrossed in what was happening in front of her, she paid no heed to what Josh did with the children after he took them. Finally, a woman crawled out of the bus and ran to the children.

Panic shifted to stunned shock as the ashen-faced woman and the slim man gathered their brood of four to them. Slowly the scene sharpened. A little girl of about seven clutched her mother's legs. The mother held Jeffrey in her arms while the man knelt down with his arms around the other boy and girl. Apparently the children weren't injured, but they were in shock, their eyes round in fright.

Josh stood nearby, dark glasses in place holding Kallie's harness. "Sounds like everyone is safe."

"Yeah, I think so." The slim man stood; his worn jeans and blue knit sweater clung to his body. His gaze shifted to Patty. "Why the hell did you pass right then? That was a crazy stunt. We could have been killed."

Patty felt his anger. "I had no choice. The semi came up behind and hit the back of our trailer. It was speed up and pass or get bounced off the road or into your bus. If he hadn't braked, I think we'd all have been okay."

The man looked down the road. The semi was nowhere in sight. "I guess. He did veer into us. Didn't even stop to see if we were okay."

"Kids seem okay." Josh said again.

"A few bruises, but they're scared." The woman still held Jeffrey. The little boy's dark brown eyes glistened with tears.

"Look at our bus. God, I don't know how I'm going to get it out of that ditch." He rubbed his forehead, his baseball cap in his hand. "And who knows if it'll run."

Josh took a step forward. "Patty, what will it take to get the Volkswagen up and running?"

"Why you asking her?" The man asked.

"She's a mechanic," Josh said.

"I might be a mechanic, but we'll still have to right the bus and get it out of the ditch. We're a long way from the next town. Have you got a cell phone?"

The couple shook their heads. The man put his arm around his wife's shoulder. "Even if we called a tow, we couldn't afford it." He glanced at the sky. "Looks like it might rain, too."

The approaching clouds meant rain or sleet and either way the ditch would get muddy and make it more difficult to haul out the VW. "Josh, I'll have to unhitch my truck from the trailer, so I can hook up a cable and haul it out." She was afraid he'd disagree, but he nodded in agreement.

"We'll have to level the bus first," she said. She turned to the man. "You and Josh will have to push the bus up enough for me to put something under the tires."

Josh spoke to the woman. "Julie, isn't it? Get the kids off to the side while we figure this out."

"Name's Steve," the man said as they walked to the side of the bus. At the top of the berm, Josh ordered Kallie into a stay, then Patty guided him to the side of the bus.

For just a second, she felt the warmth and strength of his hand and wanted to cling to it, but no sooner had he grasped her hand than he dropped it as he felt along the side of the VW. "Wait till we find something to jam under the tires," Patty said.

It took a few minutes until she found an old plank and dragged it back to the bus and Steve collected rocks and placed them near the back tire. He brushed his hands off on his jeans. "Hope this works."

Steve stood next to Josh and together they put their shoulders against the VW's side.

"On the count of three we push her up," Josh said. "Ready? One, two, three, heave." The VW rocked up and Patty stuck the plank under the front tire, then hurried to the back and stuffed in the rocks.

"Okay, ease her down." The VW sat at an odd angle, but it looked reasonably stable. "That should do it," Patty said. "I'll unhitch the truck from the trailer and tow it out."

"Not sure my engine will start," Steve ran his hands through his tawny hair.

Patty glanced at the threatening sky. "Right now let's concentrate on getting her out of the ditch and onto the side road. Then we'll worry about the engine."

"I'll help your wife get the kids into our trailer and out of the cold." Josh scrambled up the incline next to Patty and grasped Kallie's harness. As if he were a pied piper, the children followed him to the trailer. Jeffrey squirmed to be let down from his mother's arms and ran forward with the others. The woman trailed behind, a worried frown on her pale face.

After Patty unhitched her truck, she drove onto the highway and came up in front of the VW. Her wheels sank into the dirt as she backed close to the lip of the ditch. She hooked up a cable, stood and wiped her hands off on a rag she'd taken from her truck. "Okay, Steve, get in and keep your wheels straight or she might heave back on her side."

He nodded, his mouth grim. "Let's do it."

She gave him a half smile and walked to her truck just as it started to rain. Slowly, she inched forward until the cable was taut, then increased her speed. Through her rear view mirror she could see the VW's nose rise out of the ditch. It wasn't long until it was on the side road behind the trailer.

Getting out of her truck, she went back to Steve, who was trying to start the engine. "It's no use," he muttered.

"Let me take a look." She went to the rear of the VW and opened its small hatch. It was a water-cooled boxy engine. The hoses were loose, no clamps, just baling wire to secure them. The engine needed a good cleaning with gunk and she doubted if the spark plugs were firing properly. It was one sad neglected engine. Shaking her head, she went back to her truck to get a small tool kit.

"What's wrong with it?" Steve asked, as he stared at the engine.

"Just about everything. When's the last time you had it serviced?"

"I didn't. Bought it from a friend who said it was ship-shape." He frowned. "I guess I should have checked, huh?"

"Yeah. Not much of a friend, I'd say." She took off one plug and cleaned its gap with her rag, then knelt and took out a roll of duct tape. "I can wrap the hoses to make them last until you get to a service station. You need proper hose clamps and a new set of plugs, too."

Steve's shoulders slumped. "God, I don't have the money for repairs."

"Plugs won't cost much and the same for new hoses. It's labor you'll be paying for. I could do it for you." As she said this, she wondered how Josh would take the delay. Shrugging off this problem, she said, "Get in and try her now."

He did and the engine turned over. She closed the hatch and went to meet him in front of the VW.

"Thanks," he said. "I'm not much at fixing things."

"It's okay." She glanced at the luggage strewn in the ditch. "I'll help you store your gear that's all over the place, and then you can help me hitch my truck back up to the trailer." While she picked up the odds and ends, she pondered the family's situation.

By the time they'd guided her truck into the trailer's slot, sleet pelted the ground. They hurried to the trailer, opened the door, and found the children sitting around Kallie while holding mugs of hot chocolate. They were petting and scratching Kallie's belly, much to her delight. A plate holding only cookie crumbs lay on the table. Josh had set the stabilizers and the slide-outs and turned on the heat. He stood at the stove facing his guests, his ever-present dark glasses in place.

Patty took off her jacket and hung it on the peg. "Looks like a party. Any hot chocolate left?"

"Hot tea for adults. We're out of chocolate." He held out a mug which she took willingly and sat at the table.

For a time no one spoke until Steve said, "Did anyone get a look at that truck? All I remember is it was carrying tractors."

"It was red, Papa," a girl about eight said.

"Good, Shelly," the mother said. "Do you remember anything else?"

Shelly shook her head.

Patty thought: red semi, hauling tractors. Larry? Couldn't be. He was going to stay overnight, but the description fit his rig.

"You're quiet, Patty," Josh said. "You have an idea, don't you? About the truck, I mean."

"Yeah, I was thinking of Larry's truck. It was bright red with a flat bed hauling tractors."

"From your description when we were at the rest stop, I kind of figured that, too. You told me Kallie was acting kind of odd, sniffing Larry's tires. At the next town we should make inquiries about him and our other nemesis."

Patty was about to answer when the trailer was buffeted by a gust of wind. Sleet pelted its roof. The children stopped jabbering and looked at their parents, fear in their eyes. "It's just a storm," their mother said, looking at her husband. "Maybe we'd better drive on and get into town."

Taking her cue, Patty said, "Your VW's engine needs a bit of work if you're going a long way. Where you headed?

"Tulsa. Julie's parents live there and we're going to move in with them for a time."

"Papa lost his job," the oldest boy said.

"Hush, Cory," his mother said. "No need to tell folks our troubles."

"Not to worry, Cory," Josh said. "Luck sometimes follows trouble. You'll meet a lot of new kids and make good friends."

Patty could see Steve's gratitude for Josh's words, but afterward, the man hung his head. She knew the feeling. Your world was coming apart and you hadn't a thread to hold onto. It was worse for him, since he had to care for his family. She hoped he had some kind of special training, because it was tough getting a job in this economy, no matter what his skills.

"I can help Steve with the repairs," Patty said, looking at Josh. "It shouldn't take long. We have to buy spark plugs, clamps, hoses and a change of oil and the filter wouldn't be a bad idea either. That's all."

"That's all?" Josh shook his head. "You'll have to go into town for parts."

Patty saw the look that passed between Julie and Steve. If they didn't help the family, then they might not make it to their destination.

Josh said, "Okay, let's hit the road. The sooner we get this done, the sooner we'll all be on our way."

With his pronouncement everyone began collecting their things and within ten minutes, they were on the main road caravan style, heading toward the next town. While she drove and kept an eye on the VW that chugged along behind her, Patty's thoughts turned to Josh. One minute he was kind, the next curt and withdrawn. She liked the way he'd talked to Cory and felt a warm glow. Then her mind skittered to the red semi and Larry and she went cold. Had he been at the wheel? It didn't fit with her impression of him. No point in jumping to conclusions until they found out more. In the meantime they could help the family then continue on their way.

Chapter 20

It was after midnight when Camden drove into the casino's parking lot where the automobiles of choice were pickup trucks. Rubbing his hands together against the cold, he sat thinking how he would approach Slocum about Mike. So far, the more he knew, the less he understood what had happened to Mike. Enough dawdling, he scolded himself and got out of his SUV.

Unlike his earlier visit, there was a guard at the front door who had the look of a football linebacker. However, the man nodded cordially and opened the door for Camden. The smell of smoke and stale beer with the sound of blaring music combined to assault his senses.

He made his way to the bar and chose a barstool at the far end away from the ding, ding of the slots. Blackjack tables were farther away and beyond those, the roulette tables. An archway above the wide doors that Lou had pointed out to him led to the serious gambling. He wondered if that's where he'd find Slocum.

A young Indian female bartender dressed in a tux shirt with a red bow tie came over. "What'll it be, mister?" She gave a swipe at the bar's counter with a white towel.

"Beck beer, if you've got it."

"Honey, we got anything you can think of." She went down the bar and returned with a bottle and a frosted mug. "Not a hard liquor man, huh?"

"Not tonight. Is Lou around?"

"He's on day shifts. Anything I can help you with?"

"I want to talk to Slocum. I was told to come late at night." He glanced meaningfully at his watch. "Seems late to me."

She laughed. "You're a brave one. Got debts to settle?"

"No." He put a twenty on the bar. "How do I go about talking to the man?"

Instead of picking up the bill, she asked. "What do you want to talk to him about?"

"Did you know Mike Garrick?"

"Sure. He worked here."

"Do you know where he is?"

"You a joker, huh. Everyone knows he's dead." She eyed him. "You know that too, don't you?" She stood waiting for him to react and when he didn't, she asked again, "Why do you want to see Slocum?"

"Is it important for you to know that?" She didn't blink. "Okay, if it will smooth your feathers, I'm hoping he can give me information about Mike Garrick."

She looked up to the right and his eyes followed her line of sight to a video camera set at an angle, looking down the length of the bar. Big brother on the lookout for a cheating employee?

"What's your name?" she asked, ignoring his raised eyebrows.

"Camden McMillan."

She shoved the twenty back at him. "They'll come get you when Slocum's ready. In the meantime enjoy your drink." She walked away to serve another customer.

He took a gulp of beer and wondered how long it would take to be summoned by Slocum. It was disconcerting to know he was being watched and he looked for other cameras, but they were harder to spot. After he finished his beer, he paid, left a tip, and walked through the gambling halls. Old ladies sat with buckets of coins, pushing the slot buttons, a ragtag group hovered around a roulette table, and determined players appeared glued to their chairs at the blackjack tables. It all seemed so meaningless, and he couldn't picture Mike in this venue. Had the man changed that much in the year since he'd seen him? After thirty minutes, he looked at his watch with great annoyance. One more drink at the bar and that was it, he decided. There was a limit to his patience.

As he sat once again on the bar stool, a broad-shouldered Indian tapped him on the shoulder. "You want to meet Slocum?"

Camden nodded.

The man motioned with his head and Camden followed him through the wide doors that led to the high stake tables. Once inside, the man said, "Up the stairs on your left."

As Camden walked up, he perused the crowd—an assortment of attire from suits and ties to Levis and wool shirts. Everyone was welcome if they had money.

At the top another large Indian-looking fellow, gave him the once over, then pointed and said, "Over there."

After Camden moved to the side of the narrow hall, the man frisked him.

"I assure you, I'm not carrying. I don't even own a gun."

The man said nothing as he motioned him to the door on his right.

Feeling as if he were in a melodrama, Camden entered a dimly lit room. At the far end a man sat on a dais. "Mr. Hitower?" he asked.

"Yes," came a high-pitched voice. "I've looked forward to this meeting ever since you first came to my establishment. Please have a seat." The man spread his hand out toward a chair several feet away.

Camden moved toward the chair, squinting at the figure. Even in the dim light, the man's broad albino face shone from a head that seemed out of proportion to his slight frame.

"You're surprised," Slocum said. "I can see it in your face." He stood and stepped down. "Most strangers are." He sat opposite Camden, his impeccably tailored blue suit molding to his slim body. "I'm very curious about you, Professor McMillan."

"No less I about you."

"Ah, but for different reasons." Slocum took out a cigarette and inserted it into an ivory holder, then lit it with a lighter he took from his vest pocket. "You ask questions about Mike Garrick, yet he's dead."

"Is he?"

Slocum inhaled deeply. "You think not?"

"Correct."

"Do you play poker, Mr. McMillan?"

Camden shook his head. "I'm not a gambling man." He felt the nubby material of the upholstery as he rested his hands on the chair's arms.

"You should. It helps refine one's tactics in dealing with people."

"I'm not trying to be coy." Camden had no reason to kowtow to the man even if he wanted information. "I understand Garrick worked for you as a dealer and a bouncer. He got in a fight here, but as a bouncer that wouldn't be unusual. That same day his truck was sideswiped and he was killed in the crash. At least that's what the police say."

"Putting your cards on the table. All right, probably for the best. Before I tell you about Mike Garrick, tell me how you know Mike, what you think you know about his death, and why you want information."

"You want a lot."

"You want my help."

Camden shrugged and in crisp, concise language explained how he'd become friends with Mike, and why he thought Mike wasn't dead. "I hope to find Josh Peterson, learn what happened to Mike and who died in the accident. It wasn't Mike."

Slocum had listened without interrupting, puffing on his cigarette. Now he extinguished it in the nearby ashtray. "I agree with you. I don't think Mike is dead."

Slocum's candidness surprised Camden. "What do you know about Josh Peterson?"

"Josh and I had a working relationship."

"Josh, not Mike?"

"Josh and I had an understanding or I thought we did until he left town so abruptly."

Something eased in Camden's chest, a feeling of vindication for his faith in Mike. "What was this relationship you had with Josh?"

Slocum waved his hand in the air. "After I heard Mike had died, I was concerned that Josh might need help. I sent my man to see him, but he'd already left town. Later I learned about a woman who was traveling with him. Unfortunately, my source had some problems and I haven't heard anything for a few days."

"Was the girl Patty Harkin?"

Slocum nodded and leaned forward. "I'd like to get in touch with Josh, too. Usually I'd offer a man a finder's fee, but I think you'd take it as an insult." He fiddled with his cigarette holder, then pocketed it.

Camden nodded. "You're correct."

"Josh's whereabouts are important to me. We have unfinished business. I'm surprised he can survive without my help, unless Patty Harkin is now his...shall I say, benefactor. She might not understand the consequences of Josh's situation. What are your feelings toward Josh?"

"I don't know him. I have no feelings for the man other than I believe he caused Mike some grief these past few years."

Slocum pressed his hands together in front of his chin, his eyes narrowed. "Then perhaps we can come to an arrangement. Do you need funds?"

"Not particularly. I make a decent living teaching and writing."

"I see. Then you want to find Josh for altruistic reasons."

"Money isn't the issue; the truth is. Why did Police Chief Dankbar hurry the investigation of Mike's death? Why the quick cremation?"

"I have no idea." Slocum rose and walked over to a small bar at the far side of the room. He turned to Camden. "Would you like something?"

"Cognac, if you have it."

"Good choice." He took down two snifters from the glass shelf to his right and poured a small amount into each glass. After handing Camden his glass, he continued to stand as if making a decision about his next move. "You don't like my line of business, do you?"

"I'm not here to argue the merits of your enterprise." Camden took a sip of his brandy. "Smooth," he said, holding up his glass. "How do Floyd Rickter, Rhonda Crouch, and Peter Darby play into this scenario with Mike and Josh?"

Slocum moved to his chair and relaxed, setting his glass on the side table. "Why do you think they're connected?"

"I'm not sure they are, but the media seems to think that Darby took Rhonda from Floyd, so he killed them. Was Floyd one of your boys?"

Slocum laughed. "One of my boys? How quaint. Hardly. I have employees. I am not connected to the Mafia. That's what you're thinking, isn't it?"

"The newspapers said Rhonda and Darby were executed."

"I am not in that kind of business."

"Then why are the Feds interested?"

Slocum shrugged. "The Feds investigate murders relating to Indian reservations. Yes, Rhonda hung out here. Yes, Darby and Rickter gambled here, but that's as far as the relationship to me and my establishment went."

"Are the Feds still nosing around?"

"I think we are getting off track in our discussion of Mike and Josh."

Camden shook his head. "Not really. I think Floyd may be a menace to Josh and this girl, Patty."

"I'll tell you what I told the Feds. Floyd contacted me after he met them at a truck stop south of here. After that I have no idea what he or they did." He swirled his cognac in a lazy fashion. "I presume you plan to go after them."

"I will if I find out where they are."

"Tucson's a long way away, but when they get there, I'll know."

"I didn't say anything about Tucson."

Slocum smiled. "No, you didn't." He stood. "It's too bad you don't want to work for me. I think it would have been profitable for both of us. Morals are such a bother." He put down his glass. "I think we've concluded our business."

Camden put his glass down and stood. He didn't offer his hand to Slocum, but moved toward the door. "Thanks for your time. You've assured me of two things. Mike isn't dead and he never gambled."

"That may be, Professor McMillan, but his misplaced loyalty makes him a loser. Don't play the same hand. If you find Josh, you may wish you hadn't. Remember, the house always wins."

Chapter 21

Sleet continued to pummel the trailer as they drove caravan style, with Josh and Patty ahead of the VW, driving slowly enough for the VW to keep up. Cars and trucks passed them honking and glaring. Patty continually checked her rearview mirror to see that the VW kept pace. That's when she noticed the sedan tagging along behind apparently unable or reluctant to pass. "There's a car behind us that's either got a very cautious driver or has engine trouble. It was parked on the shoulder some miles back and now it's hovering in the VW's wake."

"Old or new car?" Josh asked, his voice almost a growl.

"Looks relatively new. Tinted windows."

Josh said nothing more but kept his head turned toward the scenery as if he could see it pass.

They drove on in silence until exiting at an off ramp to the business area. At a gas station they got directions to the nearest auto parts store, and pulled to the curb in front of the store before three o'clock. The VW parked in the lot.

"I'll stay here," Josh said. "Ask them where would be a good place for the kids while you attend to the repairs." He handed his credit card to her. "If he's as down and out as he appears, spending money on parts will only make the family's trip even more miserable."

She leaned over, gave him a kiss on the cheek, and before he could react, she was out of the truck. Inside the store, she and Steve quickly picked out the items they'd need. When she produced the credit card at the register, Steve looked chagrined.

"I don't know how to repay you and your husband's help, but if you give me a way to contact you, I'll pay you back when I can."

"No need," she said as she signed Josh's name. She looked up at the cashier and asked, "We need a place to repair the VW where the kids will be able to stretch their legs. Any advice?"

"Sure," the young man replied. "There's an old park on the south side of town with a parking lot across the street big enough for your trailer. It should be empty in this weather." He gave them directions and they hurried back to their vehicles.

As she got into her truck, she saw the sedan with tinted windows parked a block away. It gave her a creepy feeling. Should she tell Josh? What could he do about it even if he knew? They motored caravan style to the park that had been passed over by the town. The homes in the area were seedy with weeds in the front lawns and shutters hanging askew. Small shops with graffiti adorning their fronts looked like they were in need of customers. Still, the kids were excited to see a place where they could play on swings and throw a ball. Josh, Kallie, Julie and her kids crossed over to the park.

"Okay, Steve," Patty said. "This is going to be your lesson on fixing your van so you can take care of things yourself in the future." She set out her tools, the new plugs, hoses and clamps and got to work. An hour later with Steve fumbling his way through her instructions, the VW was ready to make its final assault on Tulsa.

"You're tires are worn, but you got a spare," Patty said.

"I know how to change a tire." Steve folded his arms across his chest.

"Didn't mean to sound patronizing. Sorry." After packing up her tools and storing them in her truck, they walked across to the park. Patty looked up and down the street — a few cars, no sedan, and only one fellow leaning against a store front, smoking. She relaxed and thought how silly she'd been to think a car was shadowing them. "I'm going to wash up in the park's restroom."

In the restroom she looked at herself in the mirror and scrubbed off the grease smudge on her cheek, then removed the plastic band that held her hair in a ponytail. When her auburn hair tumbled around her face, she put her hands on either side of the sink and stared at her reflection. "You need a haircut and a facial, kid." She grinned at her words for they sounded much like Maggie. Sighing, she adjusted her sweatshirt, put her parka back on, and went back outside. She spotted Josh with Steve and his family crossing the street to where the trailer and the VW were parked. She started after them.

From around a corner, the window-tinted sedan, tires screeching, roared toward to the group. Steve grabbed two of the kids; Julie carried the baby; Josh shoved Corey forward and let go of Kallie's harness, yelling, "Kallie, go."

Josh would have made it if the car hadn't swerved directly toward him, clipping him. He was thrown sideways. Patty ran screaming, heart pounding. When she got to his bleeding figure, she knelt. He was on his side, moaning. As she reached to him, he rolled onto his back and stared at her with the bluest eyes she'd ever seen.

"God damn you," she yelled. "You can see!"

"Sorry," he whispered, his eyes full of pain.

"Sorry?" She didn't know where to begin with her anger, her despair, her worry.

He grabbed a fistful of her hair that had fallen forward and pulled her face close to his lips. "A hit. Take Kallie. Ditch the trailer. Get away from me, from here."

His hand slid away, releasing her. His eyelids fluttered and closed. She called out, "Someone call 911."

Steve stood over her. "I don't have a cell phone. I'll get help."

Kallie came to her side and nuzzled her shoulder, while Patty remained kneeling over Josh. He was unconscious, his left arm lay at an odd angle and blood seeped from gashes on his forehead and his leg. If she moved his arm she might do more damage, so she removed her parka, stripped off her sweatshirt and pressed it against the wound in his leg. Tears ran down her face. "Damn it. Please, be okay." She wiped her nose with the back of her hand, then reapplied the pressure on his leg. "Christ, Josh, why the blind act?"

A police officer appeared next to her. "Paramedics are on their way." Other than Steve and his family there were few onlookers.

The paramedics arrived, stabilized Josh's neck, immobilized his arm, put his leg in a pressure bandage, attached an IV and placed him on a gurney. "We'll take your husband to Memorial Hospital on Euclid," an EMT said. "Check at the ER desk when you get there."

Patty didn't dissuade him of her relationship to Josh.

"Are you all right, miss? Have you got transportation?" the policeman asked.

Patty nodded, feeling as if she were stumbling around in a dream.

Steve came over and helped her into her parka. "How can we help, Patty? Want us to take Kallie?"

"No." Kallie was her lifeline to sanity.

Before the ambulance left, one of the paramedics came over. "He's awake and wants to talk to you before we leave for the hospital."

Patty hurried after the man and got inside the ambulance. An ashen-faced Josh looked at her through drooping eyelids. "One thing, Patty. There're things in the drawers under the bed, a flash drive, my weapon, other stuff. You'll know when you see them. Leave them at the hospital in my name, then scram. You're in danger, too."

Before she could answer him, he turned his head away. The paramedics motioned for her to exit. After she emerged, the man got in, closed the doors and the ambulance drove off, siren blaring. She gathered her wits, thinking about what Josh had said and why he'd pretended to be blind. She'd follow his instructions to a point. "Can I leave the trailer here overnight?" she asked the policeman.

"Give me your driver's license and I'll clear it with the traffic department."

When she handed her driver's license to the policeman, he glanced at her. "You're Patty Harkin?"

"Yes."

"The injured man's name is Josh Peterson."

Knowing relatives had more access to patients than friends, she said, "I'm his sister."

"Oh, I assumed you were his wife." He handed back her ID and went to write down the trailer's license plate number.

She turned to Steve. "I hope you get to Tulsa without any more trouble. Go ahead. Things will work out here."

"You sure? Josh really got whacked. I don't like leaving you in the lurch."

"It's okay." She gave him a brief hug, waved to his family and took Kallie by the harness. Inside the trailer, she stood, muttering to herself. "You better heal fast, Josh. You have a lot of explaining to do." She wiped her eyes. "And damn it, I care about you...you liar!"

When she searched the drawers, she found a wallet with a flash drive stuck in it. She sat on the bed and took out the driver's license—Mike Garrick. The picture was the man she knew as Josh. Everything he'd told her was topsy-turvy. "Damn you!" Shaking her head, she continued rummaging and found a cell phone uncharged, and a laptop charged. She'd check its contents later. She took the cords to charge them and went through other drawers. Under a sweater she found two fat business envelopes with wads of cash in $100 denominations. She thumbed through them and figured the total was about $10,000. "Wow. You really were holding out on me. Who the hell are you, anyway?" Her mind twisted through a maze of thoughts: a criminal on the run, AWOL, a killer, embezzler. None of those scenarios seemed to fit the man she'd been with for over a week. He'd been kind to strangers, strong in adversity, a gentleman to her. Funny how names fit people and sometimes they didn't. Mike seemed a better fit for the man she'd known as Josh.

Opening another drawer, she found his gun. What do I do with this, she wondered as she stared at it? Guns were things she didn't like to deal with. Her father had told her guns weren't something he'd have in the house. His brother had accidentally shot himself when he was twelve and that had soured the entire family against having guns around. Hunting was one thing, her father had said, handguns another.

"Okay, Dad," she said out loud. "This situation is different. We're the hunted." Still she sat, debating about taking it. She picked it up by the butt, grabbed the ammo next to it and stuck all of it into a shoe box.

She bundled up her finds into a canvas bag, then grabbed the few things she had stowed in the trailer, including the book she'd been reading to Josh—Steinbeck's The Grapes of Wrath. She gathered a few of his clothes and stuck them in a suitcase, cramming everything into the back of her truck. Before exiting the trailer for the last time, she grabbed Kallie's leash, bowl, and a bag of kibbles. When she unhitched her truck, the police were taking measurements and photographing skid marks. They might find the car, but she doubted they'd find the driver. A hit Josh had said. Floyd, Larry, someone else? Why? She gasped for air, as if she hadn't been breathing for the last few minutes.

Once she and Kallie were settled in her truck, she drove through the icy streets to the hospital. The storm had passed, but the cold lingered. She was reluctant to leave Kallie in the truck while she checked on Josh in the hospital. Glancing at Kallie, she noticed the dog still wore her harness. Patty smiled. "Okay, Kallie. If Mike can pretend to be blind, so can I."

Chapter 22

Camden had just finished breakfast at the B&B and was drinking coffee in the living room when a young swarthy-complexioned man dressed in a raglan wool sweater walked toward Camden. "Sir, you're Professor Camden McMillan?"

Camden nodded.

"I'm Agent David Parker, FBI." He flipped open a leather case to briefly show his ID. "I'd like to talk to you about Josh Peterson." He glanced at the elderly couple in the corner. "Perhaps there's a private place where we could talk."

"Not sure how I can help you, but I have questions of my own. The sitting area off my bedroom should work." He put down his newspaper, stood, and the agent followed him down the hall.

After Parker sat in a blue upholstered armchair facing Camden, he said, "You're aware of recent events that took place in a truck stop just south of here?"

"It's the talk of the town."

Parker took out a small note pad. "Can you tell me what you know about it?"

Camden frowned. "The Popsicle Murders? Nothing."

The agent winced. "Not sure I like that reference."

"Sorry. I wanted to be sure we were talking about the right murders."

"Are there others?"

Camden shrugged and waited for Parker to continue.

"You've been to Slocum's casino, talked with Hitower."

"Yes."

"Have you ever been to that casino before?"

"You mean other than the two times I've been there since I arrived in Bromont? No. Never."

"What did you talk to Slocum about?"

"My friend, Mike Garrick. If you're investigating Josh Peterson, then you must be investigating Mike's disappearance too. He and Josh lived and worked together."

"Mike died in an automobile accident."

Camden shook his head. "Maybe."

Parker's dark eyes narrowed. "What are you implying?"

"Josh Peterson gave medical records to the police that couldn't have been Mike's. The body was cremated without an autopsy at the urging of Police Chief Dankbar."

Parker leaned forward, his fingers stroked his lips as he seemed to consider Camden's words. "That's quite an accusation."

Camden shrugged. "That's how I see it."

"You think Mike Garrick is alive and the local Police Chief aided in a cover up." Parker sat back, his broad face inscrutable. "If you're right about Garrick, who did the coroner cremate? And why would the Police Chief abet a crime?"

"I have no idea. That's what the FBI needs to find out." He stretched out his legs then sat straighter.

"I'll check on Police Chief Dankbar, but who would bribe him and why?"

"Josh Peterson is the one who gave the medical records to the coroner and then he skipped town."

"That doesn't make sense, he's blind. Patty Harkin is towing his trailer south. He's with her. She's been in some trouble with the law, but nothing too serious."

"If you know where Josh is, why ask me about him? Why not ask him?"

"He's one step ahead of us, but we'll catch up to him soon."

"Have you talked to Maggie, the owner of the diner?"

"Maggie Travers, yes."

Camden smiled. In all his talks with Maggie, he'd never learned her last name.

Parker turned a page of his note pad. "What do you know about Floyd Rickter?"

"Not much. He seems to be one of Slocum's boys, although Slocum denies it. According to Linda Terrell, she and Patty had a run in with him at a truck stop."

"Miss Travers explained about Miss Terrell's misfortune. We don't plan to interview her at this time. Perhaps later." Parker rubbed his chin in thought. "We believe Rickter murdered Rhonda and Peter Darby, either in a jealous rage or because Hitower ordered it. No proof there, yet. Rickter's truck was abandoned near a truck stop with a body stashed in it, not his. A Larry Claybourne, truck driver of a flatbed of farm tractors."

The agent's openness concerning details unsettled Camden. It not only didn't seem appropriate, he knew it was not the way the FBI conducted interviews. FBI agents were usually mum about everything, giving nothing, asking everything. Oh, how well he knew.

"When's the last time you were in contact with Mike Garrick?" Parker asked.

"About a month ago. Said to look him up during my Christmas break. He mentioned a job he and Josh were doing that might help bring Josh out of his depression."

"What job was that?"

Camden shook his head. "No idea." He'd decided to keep any further information about Mike to himself. Camden had wondered why Mike had insisted he save the mail he'd sent from different Indian Reservations. They were like breadcrumbs, and he wasn't about to hand them to this agent.

"What do you know about Josh Peterson?" Parker asked.

"Not much. I think he gave Mike a hard time the last few months."

"Why do you think that?"

Camden shrugged. "A few hints now and then, nothing specific."

"Let's get back to what you know about Garrick. Did he mention Rhonda Crouch?"

"No."

"Not sure how she or Peter Darby fit in. Probably innocent bystanders or part of the love triangle with Floyd Rickter." Parker stood. "Any new information you have, contact me immediately at this number." He handed Camden a yellow piece of paper with a phone number.

Camden studied the agent. The man didn't follow the FBI's format. "No business card?"

Parker put his note pad away. "We don't advertise our presence. A few words of advice. If Josh contacts you, let me know. Except for getting word to me, stay out of the way. Forget about Mike Garrick, Professor McMillan. Go home. We'll handle things."

The back of Camden's neck ached, not a good sign. He didn't say it, but he'd be damned if he'd forget Mike or what had happened to him or what he might be involved in. Duty as well as friendship stared him in the face.

"Enjoy your holiday and return to your college. Forget Bromont, Professor. This is not your fight; you might get hurt."

His words sounded like a threat. Camden's throat went dry and he swallowed hard. "Slocum's Mafia, right?"

"Not to our knowledge. You said Mike and Josh were hired to do a job. What job?"

"I already told you I don't know."

"Okay, okay."

"Do you believe Mike's dead?" Camden asked.

"We thought so, but your story makes me think he might still be alive. Could change everything. Turn the entire case upside down. If he's connected with Slocum, he's in trouble."

Camden's hands went clammy; his heart constricted. Could his discussion with Slocum have put his friend in danger? Camden took out his wallet and handed him his business card "Look, if you find out anything about Mike, will you contact me? Cell phone number is unlisted." He tilted his head. "Of course you could get it, couldn't you?"

Parker thumbed the card and smiled. "Of course, but this makes it easier." He shook hands and left.

Afterward Camden reflected on the conversation. Some of Parker's words seemed like a threat, and the story about not giving him a business card didn't sit well.

He laced up his boots, grabbed his parka and headed out to visit Maggie at the diner. The air was cold, the sky sparkled, a gorgeous day, so why did he feel apprehensive? When he stepped into the diner, the breakfast crowd had cleared out, leaving a few old retirees chatting in a booth. Maggie was standing next to their table. He waved to her and she came over.

"A little late for breakfast," she said.

"I've eaten, thanks." He looked around the diner. "Where's Linda?"

"At my house. A friend's looking in on her." She smiled. "She's tougher than you think. She'll be okay in time. I'll give her a job as a cashier. She's good with numbers."

"You found that out already?"

"We talked."

"I bet. You're a good soul."

"I thought only the Irish were full of blarney, but I accept. So will you be staying in town much longer?"

"Not sure. I had a visitor this morning. FBI agent."

"I heard they were in town, but thought they'd left."

"Agent Parker said he talked to you."

"No FBI agent ever talked to me."

"Wait a minute." Camden put his hand on her arm. "Swarthy guy, broad face, about five ten, wore a raglan sweater."

"Nope."

The ache in Camden's neck got worse.

Chapter 23

Patty parked at the far end of the visitor's lot. After rummaging through her bags, she found an old pair of sunglasses, donned them and took Kallie's harness in her left hand, just as she'd seen Josh do. In her other hand she carried a small suitcase with Mike's clothes. Inside the bustling ER, she waited in line at an information desk. She found it interesting, but uncomfortable to see how others reacted to a blind person. For some it seemed to be a distraction from their own maladies or concerns. Others stared or looked sideways, pretending she and Kallie didn't exist. When it was her turn, she asked about Josh Peterson.

After checking, the woman said, "He's in the operating room."

"I'm his sister, Patty Harkin. Will you tell the surgeon I'm here?"

The woman nodded and started to point down the hall, caught herself, and said, "I'll get someone to show you to the waiting room."

"Thank you." Patty stood with Kallie until an elderly volunteer came and showed her to the area.

After seeing that she was settled, he asked, "Can I get you a cup of coffee or tea?"

"Coffee, black, would be great. I've just come from my brother's auto accident." She milked the situation for all it was worth and didn't feel guilty. "Would you make sure the doctor knows I'm waiting here for news of Josh Peterson?"

He said he would, left and came back with her coffee. "Would you like the chaplain to visit with you?"

Oh God, what had she gotten herself into? She smiled and said demurely, "No, thank you."

He seemed reluctant to leave her, but after hovering for a few minutes, he said he'd be back later. Patty sipped her coffee and waited. The clock on the wall ticked off minutes. It was now after six. Patty was hungry and if the wait was long, she'd go to the cafeteria. Oh, brother, that would be an interesting experience, thinking how she'd helped Josh struggle with eating. What a scam he'd pulled. Anger boiled up in her again.

She wanted to pick up a magazine, but the couple and the woman with a young boy next to her would wonder. Exhausted, she put her head back and closed her eyes. A man in green scrubs stood over her. "Ms Harkin?"

"Yes." She sat up.

"Your brother is going to be fine. He's in the recovery room and we'll move him to a room when he wakes. "He has a dislocated shoulder. For a few days he should keep it strapped to his chest. The wound on his thigh needed stitches as did the gash on his forehead. He had a mild concussion, but was aware of his surroundings when he came in. All in all from what the police told me, I'd say he was a very lucky fellow."

"How long will he be hospitalized?"

"If all goes well, I'd say he could be released tomorrow or the next day."

"When can I see him?"

"He'll be groggy for some time. Why not come back tomorrow." He hesitated. "Do you have a ride, a place to stay?"

"Ah, yes. No problem." She thought of the trailer, but discarded that idea as foolish after Josh's belief that she should ditch it. She had the money in the envelopes and a motel seemed like a good choice.

With money in her pocket and hunger on her mind, she drove to a drive-through and devoured a hamburger, fries and coffee while sitting in her truck. She fed Kallie a bowl of kibbles and gave her water, then hunted up a good motel. A shower and a bed in a warm room sent her into a state of relaxation. As she drifted off to sleep, thoughts of mayhem vanished.

In the morning she stopped by another drive-through for breakfast, filled the gas tank, and headed to the hospital. This time she parked in the main lot between two large pickups, figuring her truck would be harder to spot squirreled away among others. With Kallie's harness in her left hand and sun glasses in place, she headed to the main reception area and asked for Josh Peterson's room.

Carol W. Hazelwood

A volunteer guided her to the third floor, where she was left in front of the door to room 324. Stepping inside, she saw Josh lying on the bed nearest the window; the other bed was empty. Kallie strained forward, pulling Patty.

"Well, you're a sad looking liar, Mr. Garrick," she said. Kallie put her paws on the mattress and Mike stroked her fur.

His blue eyes focused on Patty. "You were supposed to be far away by now."

"Yeah, well, after finding the stuff you left behind, I decided I needed a lot more information before hitting the road. You treated me like a fool."

"I wanted to explain things, but there was never an opportunity."

"Oh sure, we were only cooped up together in a truck and a trailer for the better part of a week and a half. And you couldn't tell me you weren't blind. You could have driven, you could have helped out, you could have seen Floyd, you could have…damn it…you could have told me." She wasn't screaming, but her voice was raspy with anger and tears. "You could have told me the truth."

"I couldn't. You might have left and then what would I have done?" He pushed the button to raise his bed so he was sitting upright.

She dropped Kallie's harness and folded her arms. "I would have stayed. We had an agreement."

"Maybe."

"Oh? Maybe?" She whisked the dark glasses off and put her fists on the mattress, her face close to his. "You're all high and mighty. You're in the right? Hell, you're a liar and God knows what else."

"You're right. I'm a rat, a liar. Now leave my stuff. Get out of here and take Kallie with you."

"I will not."

"Didn't you hear what I said yesterday? It was a hit. I'm a dead man once they find out I'm alive and a sitting duck in the hospital."

"How—"

There was a knock on the door and a man walked in with a policeman behind him. "Glad I found the two of you together," he said. "I'm Detective Branson." He stopped and stared at Kallie. "How did you get the dog in here?"

"Ah, she's in training to be a guide dog," Patty said, stumbling over her words.

"She's what they call a Leader Dog. She'll be ready for placement soon," Mike said.

The detective sighed. "Okay, but I thought they wore an identification coat."

"The harness should be a tip off, don't you think?" Patty asked.

Detective Branson nodded. "Mr. Peterson, I understand you'll be released from the hospital tomorrow. I have some bad news. Your trailer burned last night. We believe it was arson."

Patty's jaw dropped. "Oh, my God!"

"I need to ask you, it's Patty Harkin, right?" Branson said. "Where were you about eleven last night?"

"Me?" Her voice came out in a croak. "I was asleep at a motel."

"Anyone with you?"

"Of course not." She was going to be cute and say Kallie, but under the circumstances thought it was better not to be flippant. It dawned on her that he might suspect she'd burned the trailer. "Wait a minute," she said, pawing through her purse. She handed him a receipt from the motel as well as the one from the gas station where she'd stopped for gas.

Branson took them, noting the times and the places, all far from where the trailer had been parked. "It seems rather odd, leaving the trailer and not coming back to get it later on last night." He handed the receipts back to Patty.

"I asked the officer if I could leave it there," she said. "I went to the hospital to check on," she motioned to Mike. "I didn't have the energy to hook up the trailer and drive it somewhere, not knowing where the nearest RV park was."

"Anyone have it in for either of you?"

Mike glanced at Patty as if to warn her then shook his head.

Patty looked wide-eyed and said, "No. We pulled into town for repairs."

"You meet anyone on the road who might not like how you drove?"

Patty almost choked, then forced a laugh. "About everyone who thought we weren't driving fast enough. A lot of drivers don't like trailers or RVs."

The detective nodded. "True. Where are you from?"

"Minnesota on our way to Tucson." Mike said.

Detective Branson made notes and asked for a cell number where he could reach them. Mike gave him the same number he'd given the troopers up north.

"Know anyone in town?" Detective Branson asked.

"No," Patty said.

"You have insurance on the trailer, Mr. Peterson?"

"Yes." Mike gave Branson the insurance company's name. "I'll notify them. Was the trailer totaled?" Mike asked.

"Nothing left but the frame. Tell the adjuster it'll be at the police impound lot on Jay Street. He can check in at the station. After you check out of the hospital, come by the station. We might have some answers for you."

And more questions thought Patty. She smiled as the men left, then turned to Mike. "I guess you were right about ditching the trailer."

"Yeah. I've got to get out of here now. They'll know where I am. They won't miss the next time."

"Who the hell are *they*?"

He didn't answer her question and instead said, "You're in danger, too."

"I got that part." She turned toward the chair where she'd dropped the suitcase with his clothes. "I brought your stuff, change of clothes, wallet."

"But not the money?"

"I have it. Thought I might need the funds."

"What about the flash drive and the pistol?"

"In the truck."

He let out an audible sigh. "Okay." He threw back the covers. "Let's get out of here."

"Us?"

He sat with his good leg dangling off the side of the bed, his bandaged leg straight. "I need your help."

"On one condition."

"I'm in no position to bargain."

"No, you aren't. If I help you, you tell me everything and I mean everything. If you renege, I'll dump you in the middle of nowhere." She eyed him. "And that includes why we can't tell the police about all that's happened. Agreed?"

"Agreed." He put his bad left leg down on the floor, flinching as he did so. "Can you scrounge up a wheelchair?"

"Are we going to just flee or get the doc to sign you out?"

"The fewer people who know anything, the better. My insurance will pay the bill."

"I don't like just leaving."

"If we wait, we might be leaving in a pine box."

Chapter 24

Camden called FBI Agent Sam Schiff, a man he'd known for many years. After Camden explained Agent David Parker's visit, Schiff said he'd get back to him. When Schiff called later that afternoon, he said, "You need to talk to Robert Caulfield. He's in charge of the investigation into what the newspapers are referring to as the Popsicle Murders. He'll be in Bromont tomorrow around two o'clock. Where's a private place to meet? Got a suggestion?

After a moment, Camden said, "Maggie Traver's house might be an option. She'll be at work and maybe she can take Linda with her." He gave Schiff the address.

"Camden, thanks for the call." There was hesitation in his voice. "Keep your head down. This might be bigger than you think."

Damn right, Camden thought as he hung up. He knew he should call his boss and bring him up to date, but he hesitated, afraid he might be pulled out of the investigation. For a while, Camden pondered his next move. One place he hadn't examined was the scene of Mike's accident that had occurred outside of the Indian Reservation but within Bromont's city limits. As he drove to the site, he figured there wouldn't be much evidence left, but he had to satisfy his curiosity. He pulled off onto the road's shoulder, the same side where Mike's truck had hit a massive old pine tree and caught fire. After getting out of his SUV, he went down the embankment and studied the tree's trunk. It still bore singed marks from the fire and the impact of the truck. Sap congealed around a deep gash.

Snow had since covered the truck's tracks, but the storm came in after the accident, so road conditions had probably been reasonably good. Had there been skid marks? Speeding? What was the cause of the accident? Why hadn't the Police Chief ordered blood samples to determine if drugs or alcohol had been involved?

He scrambled through the snow back to the road, looked up and down the straight road and rubbed the scar on the side of his face. Suddenly he felt woozy. The memory of his auto accident filled him with anguish—the screeching tires, his wife's scream, his daughter's small body crushed. He swayed helpless, unable to forget or forgive the drugged-out teen who had killed so quickly. Camden leaned against the side of his car; his forehead rested against the cold metal and he thought about Mike's accident. Although Camden wanted to talk with Police Chief Dankbar, he worried that instead of shaking loose the truth, secrets would be buried deeper. If Dankbar had taken a bribe, he'd never admit it and Camden had no proof, only questions and assumptions. His only recourse was to rely on the FBI findings or turn to his sources. Even though his agency and the FBI were under the Justice Department, sharing was not a top priority. For now, Camden had no intention of telling the FBI who his real employer was.

The following day with Maggie's permission Camden met Robert Caulfield at her house. Caulfield shook Camden's hand as the agent entered the house; his seamed brow and weathered face spoke of years in the outdoors. The man had an unassuming, easy manner as he sat in the comfort of Maggie's living room. Camden assessed the man before explaining what he'd learned since his arrival in Bromont. Caulfield pressed him for details, wanting to know about everything and everyone. No one was excluded. Camden was impressed with the man's thoroughness and felt as if he were wrung dry.

Caulfield pulled out several photos from his briefcase and laid them on the coffee table in front of them. "Can you identify any of these men?"

Camden pointed. "That's the fellow who claimed to be an FBI agent, David Parker."

Caulfield studied Camden before answering. "He's not. Claiming to be a federal agent is a felony."

"Who is he?"

"What did you tell him?"

"What I told you. So? Who is he?"

"Not sure you need to know."

"Look, I've given you every detail I can think of and I could be in danger. Do you want another murder on your hands?"

"You're being excessively dramatic, aren't you?"

"No." Camden rose and stood by the cold hearth. "From what I've learned, there's a cover up over Mike's death, Slocum is up to no good and there are several murders that seem related to Mike's friend Josh Peterson."

"Professor McMillan, you've done your bit here. Go back to teaching and leave this matter to us."

Camden slammed his fist against the wood paneling. "Look, you haven't told me anything. I'll find out for myself what the hell is going on."

Caulfield sighed. "That wouldn't be a good idea."

"Then tell me what the hell is going on?" He sat down again and stabbed his index finger at the photo of the fake FBI agent. "Who is he?"

"Debo Matruca. Works for Tómas Pacheco, one of the Pacheco brothers who run the Pacheco Casino."

"In Tucson?"

"How did you come up with that place?"

He shrugged. "Just putting pieces of the puzzle together. What about the other photos?" Camden edged forward in his chair.

"You don't recognize any of them?"

Camden shook his head and pointed to a photo of a man with gray-hair, flat features, protruding ears, a mole on his left cheek, and a broad smile showing stained teeth. "He looks native American."

"Juan Pacheco runs the main casino, has political ambitions, but has done nothing illegal."

"War vet?"

"Why do you ask?"

"That's the only connection I can make between Mike, Josh and Juan. If Juan needed help in something, they would have helped." Again Camden pointed to a photo of a thin-faced man with big ears and eyes set far apart. "His ears look like Juan's."

"Avoid him."

"I need to know who he is, so I'll know why to avoid him."

Caulfield leaned back. "All right, I'll explain, so you'll realize that you must leave this entire matter in the hands of the FBI." He waited for an acknowledgement from Camden, who sat with his arms crossed.

"I'll try to stay out of your way."

Caulfield studied him, then nodded. "That's Tómas Pacheco, Juan's younger brother. A petty criminal, trying to break into the big time. Uses Debo to do his dirty work for him. Stay away from Debo and Tómas." He toyed with the mole on his chin. "Surprised he's up here."

"Could Debo or the Pacheco brothers be involved with Slocum?"

"Both Slocum and Juan like their independence. Even the Mafia hasn't been able to wheedle its way into the Pacheco operations, but there's pressure from cartels in Mexico. Juan lost some authority when he was away then spent time in rehab for wounds suffered in Iraq."

Another connection to Mike and Josh, Camden thought.

"I doubt Slocum Hitower would have anything to do with the likes of Debo or Tómas," Caulfield said. "That's not my department unless it deals with the murders of Rhonda Crouch and Peter Darby."

Camden knew exactly which department ran the drug investigation, but only said, "I read where many casinos that took out large loans, can't pay them back and are looking for ways to bring in cash. Dealing drugs might become appealing."

"Maybe."

"Smuggling illegals?"

"Where'd you hear all this?"

"I read the papers."

Caulfield gave him a bland look and stared at the pictures as if hoping Camden would tell him more.

Camden leaned back and nodded to the photos. "Who are the others?"

"You've seen them?"

"Not sure. Are any of them men I've mentioned?" Camden asked.

The sides of Caulfield's mouth twitched ever so slightly as he pointed to one photo. "That's Floyd Rickter. Seen him?"

Camden shook his head. "Only heard what Linda said about him coming on to Patty and her and how Patty put him in his place." Camden felt vindicated in his assessment of the situation, but there remained many unanswered questions. "What about Rhonda Crouch?"

"Did someone at Slocum's mention her?"

"I think so. Can't remember who though. Might have been Lou, the bartender or Slocum. Was she FBI?"

"No."

"So how did she figure into this?"

"We aren't sure."

"Not sure or not going to tell me?"

Caulfield picked up the pictures and stuck them in his briefcase.

"Did Floyd murder a trucker named Larry?"

"You seem to have garnered a lot of information in a short period of time."

"You're fake FBI guy told me. Just wanted to know how much bullshit he fed me."

"Schiff said you were reliable."

"I am, but the more information I have, the safer I'll be. I don't like being a sitting duck for the bad guys or you. I want to find out about Mike. Something smells about the accident, no coroners report, no follow up by the police, everything hush-hush."

"I've given you more information than I should. I'll check on Police Chief Dankbar see if any of what you say sticks."

"Will you let me know?"

"Yes, if there's anything new."

"What about Josh Peterson?"

"He had an accident in Kansas. An agent from our Topeka office is on his way to see him at the Emporia City hospital."

"How bad is he?"

"Nothing life threatening I understand."

"Is Patty okay? Maggie, the woman who owns the diner, will want to know."

"She's fine." Caulfield stood. "I'll be in touch. Thanks for your help."

When Camden showed Caulfield to the door, the agent said, "You seem to know a lot about police procedure."

"Hey, there's tons of info on TV these days."

"You are a very interesting man. I wonder if you're more than you seem," Caulfield said.

Camden watched the man drive off and muttered to himself, "Aren't we all."

Camden hadn't mentioned Mike's postcards or why he was so concerned about Mike. Where the hell was Mike? Camden called the hospital in Emporia, Kansas, only to learn that Josh Peterson had been discharged. Did the FBI know? If not, they'd know soon enough. What else could Camden do to solve the mystery of Mike's disappearance and his business with Juan Pacheco? He doubted the FBI would tell him much more than they already had. The connection with drugs and Pacheco crossed his line of duty and friendship and he was hard pressed on how to handle the situation.

Before he left the house, he put money in an envelop with Maggie's name on it and stuck it on the fireplace mantle. Linda was going to need all the help she could get and Maggie shouldn't foot the entire bill.

He drove through slushy streets to the diner, enjoying the sun after so many days of gloom, and it couldn't come at a better time than four days before Christmas. Inside the diner the noon crowd buzzed with chatter and the clang of plates. As always the aroma of fresh baked bread greeted him. He strolled around the counter, searching for an empty spot.

Maggie looked up and saw him. "Camden, Dankbar's been looking for you."

"It's about time."

"Don't be flippant. Watch out. He seemed to want a bite of you."

The fellow on the seat in front of Maggie, swiveled around and stared at Camden. "You McMillan?"

"Yeah."

"Good luck. Dankbar can be a bear."

"I'll keep that in mind."

Maggie spoke over the crowd noise. "There's a booth in the back, grab it."

By the time Camden was half way through his lunch, the "bear" wandered into the diner. He scanned the area and walked toward Camden's booth. He was short, a pug-like face and a walk that said he owned the place. Camden knew this type, the small guy who wanted to take on every big guy in the bar.

When the Police Chief stood by Camden's booth, he stated, "You're Camden McMillan."

"That's right and you're Chief Dankbar. Won't you sit down?"

"I didn't come here to chat." His dark eyes narrowed. "I came to escort you out of town."

Camden put his fork down and sat back. "Why? I thought you and I had a lot to talk about."

"Don't get snippy and don't make this harder than it has to be. The FBI wants you to leave town and I agree. We don't need trouble makers in Bromont." The man's hands remained at his side, but he kept flexing them.

"The man wouldn't be an Agent Parker, would it?"

"That's right."

Camden hadn't figured Debo would want him out of the area so fast. "I like Bromont, nice and friendly, but I think it's got a few problems with accident investigations."

The Chief's chin came up. "I got two cops outside to see you leave town. Now. You want to leave easy or the hard way."

Camden knew the man was itching to slam him around, so he wiped his mouth with his napkin, left a tip for the waitress, grabbed his parka and headed to the front of the diner. "Maggie," he called out. "I seem to be called out of town." He motioned to the Police Chief who was right behind him. "Thanks for everything." He paused and looked at the other customers who had their utensils suspended midair. "Maggie, in the upcoming spring election why don't you run for Police Chief. The town could use a dose of common sense."

The diner went quiet. Mouths gaped, including Maggie's.

The Police Chief grabbed Camden's arm. "That wasn't smart. Everyone knows I'll be Police Chief for a long time."

Camden wasn't so sure. He glanced at Dankbar's hand and the man released his grip. "I planned to leave town anyway." Camden went to the cash register where Linda acted as cashier and paid his bill. He leaned over and gave her a kiss on the cheek. She turned bright red. "You take care of yourself," he said and went out the door with a shove in the back from Dankbar.

He drove to the B&B followed by an officer and explained to his hostess, Alice, that he had to leave suddenly. He nodded to the officer standing at the door.

She gave a furtive glance at the man, then said to Camden, "I'm sorry you have to leave. We don't get many visitors this time of year."

"You might have more if you elected a new Police Chief. How about someone really fresh like Maggie?"

Alice frowned. "Maggie?" Then she grinned and nodded. "Maggie."

The officer moved toward Camden. "I wouldn't be so mouthy about a new Chief. Dankbar's a powerful man."

"Power should come from the people." Before the man could make a retort, Camden went to his room packed and got into his SUV. He'd drive home and pick up Mike's postcards, hoping to find answers that eluded him in Bromont.

Christmas in Arizona might prove interesting.

Chapter 25

Instead of fleeing from the hospital, Mike convinced the doctor he was well enough to be released. Kallie and Patty waited in the truck until a volunteer pushed Mike's wheelchair to the side entrance. It was past noon when she pulled away from the curb.

"Hungry?" Patty asked as he settled into the passenger seat.

"Yeah, but let's get farther away from here before we find a place." Although hampered by having his right arm in a sling, he pulled maps out of the glove compartment.

"I'm glad we didn't have to sneak out of the hospital." She glanced at him. "Not sure you could have managed to remove your IV."

"Could have done it, but the damn monitor would have beeped, alerting the nurses. Better this way." He leaned back and sighed. "Kallie's been a trouper staying in the truck."

"Although you fast-talked the doc into your release, he gave strict instructions to have a doctor look at your leg in a few days. I got your pain meds at the hospital's pharmacy."

"I'm not taking them unless I'm desperate. You used cash, right?"

"Followed your instructions, yes. Are you sure your credit card, or I should say Josh's card, would be traced."

"Yes, they can and would."

"So who are *they*? You promised to tell me everything."

"I will." He kept studying the map, using his left hand, since his right arm was in a sling. "First let's find a place to eat on Highway 50."

"50 not 35?"

"It'll take us out of the main traffic flow and perhaps harder to spot. What did you do with the flash drive I gave you?"

"You said to keep it safe."

"Yeah. So?"

She smiled, thinking how great a hiding place she had for it. "It's in Kallie's box of treats."

"We'll leave it there for now." He shook his head, a grin on his face. "You continue to surprise me. You'd make a good spy."

"Not something I want on my resume."

He grimaced as he straightened his leg. "Where's my Beretta?"

"Your gun?"

"Pistol. A Beretta M9."

"Whatever. It's in a bag in the back of the truck. You haven't asked about the pile of cash I found."

"It was Josh's. I'll get the Beretta out when we stop. I want it loaded and handy."

"God, you're scaring me."

"You should be scared. I am." His head lolled on the back rest and Kallie licked his stubbly cheek. "You're a treasure. Hope you get a good home." Acting as if she understood the praise, Kallie laid her head on his left shoulder.

Patty didn't like what Mike said about the dog. What was he thinking? She'd never let him give Kallie away, never. She accelerated down the road, following the signs to 50. "It'll take us longer this way."

"I know, but it's safer. It'll take us into Oklahoma. They might not think we'd go this way. If we get clear now, they'll still try to pick us up when we get near Tucson."

"There you go again using *they*. Who the hell are you talking about?"

"*They* are Slocum's men, like Rickter, and hitting us from the south will be Tomás Pacheco's men. I'm not sure which gang made the hit on me, but either way, I'm in the middle of a drug war." He turned toward her. "And so are you."

"Shit." Patty's heart skipped a beat. "I want the whole story. Now."

"When we stop for supplies. We need food, water, and how's the gas situation?"

"You keep evading the subject. I'm not going to wait forever. If you don't come clean, I'll dump you out on the road just like I said and don't think I won't." She fumed as she turned onto Highway 50. "And to answer your question the gas tank is full."

Twenty minutes later, Patty spotted a mall with a small grocery store and pulled into the far side of the parking lot. Mike and Kallie waited in the truck while she hurried inside to buy supplies. Loaded down with her purchases, she returned to find the tailgate down and Mike rummaging through suitcases.

"Where's my weapon?" he asked, frowning. Sweat dripped down his temples.

"Calm down." She set the supplies on the ground. "That's my suitcase you've got." She took it from him and smiled as she saw the Steinbeck book nestled among her clothing. Enjoying his discomfort, she took her time refolding some items and then snapped her suitcase shut. "It's way in the back." She got up on the tailgate, retrieved his bag and shoved it at him. "Your gun's on the bottom under your laptop."

"Pistol," he corrected again, then hobbled to the passenger's door, placed the bag on the floor and got in.

Patty rearranged the gear, stowed the supplies and closed the tailgate. She wondered at Mike's attitude. He'd been so contained, so Zen-like through all their earlier encounters. Now it was as if a lid had slid away exposing his anger, his fear. Where would it end?

She let Kallie out and gave her water. Standing at the side of the truck, Patty munched on a sandwich and drank a cold soda, then walked over to a waste bin and tossed in the sandwich wrapper. Hoping Mike had composed himself, she opened the door, letting Kallie into the back seat. Patty handed Mike a soda and a sandwich, then settled inside the cab and started the engine.

"Don't you want to eat first?" Mike asked.

She shrugged. "I ate."

"I was an ass, about the weapon, I mean." He took some pills and washed them down with the soda.

"You can make amends by telling me everything." She pulled out of the lot and back onto the road.

His anger seemed to have vanished. "Okay. It's not pretty." He shifted in his seat. "You remember how I said that Josh and I joined the Marines. I changed things around a little."

"So you were the football player, and Josh was the one who was full of patriotic feelings."

"Kinda like that. He had the brains, but he was no wimp. We agreed on a try for the SEALs."

"So who rescued who in Iraq?"

His jaw tightened and his eyes grew flinty. "It was a nightmare. We were in a convoy to an assignment. The first truck hit an IED. We bailed out of our truck. Shots came from everywhere. Josh and I ran to a nearby brick wall. Then incoming mortar burst all around us. We figured we were dead meat, so we jumped the wall and landed in a ditch. We hugged the sand like fleas on a bitch. Then everything got quiet. Guys called out. Josh stood up. Before I could grab him, a grenade exploded in front of us. He got the worst of it, flash burns. My ears were ringing. I thought he was okay until I heard him screaming that he couldn't see. Scared the crap out of me." Mike turned away and gazed out the window.

Patty let things ride. No need to dig further into a hell he'd obviously revisited too often. The rolling hills of Kansas slowly passed by, and Mike dozed off. When he woke, he gulped water and opened the window, letting cold dry air freshen the cab.

"Sorry to keep after you, Mike, but if we are sitting ducks, I need the whole story."

"I know. It's difficult even for me to untangle." He sighed, then said, "It really started when I finally got my discharge papers. I'd re-upped twice. Got sent to Yemen, then the Hormuz Straits. Josh had been receiving treatment at a vet rehab center, but he refused to learn Braille. Said it was too difficult. He started drinking and taking drugs, but when I saw him a year later, he'd gotten Kallie, and she seemed to give him a new start. He got clean."

"Was he sober when you were in Bromont?"

"I'll get to that part, but you need to know about Juan Pacheco, another guy in our unit. I wasn't there when Juan got hit, but he saved his men. When I was in between tours, I visited him at his home on a reservation in southern Arizona. How two guys could handle recovery so differently amazed me.

"Juan was his usual indomitable self, refusing to give up. Despite being tied to a wheelchair, he became an important leader of his tribe. He ran the casino, no cheating by the house, took no guff from anyone, including his younger brother Tomás, who tried to hustle drugs, using the reservation as his sanctuary. Juan wanted to handle the problem internally. Didn't want any government involvement. If you know anything about our history with the Native American Indians, you can understand his feelings. The elders were on his side, but the younger crowd wanted more money, more action."

"The elders run the reservations?"

"Usually, but times are changing, and the younger guys think the old ways shouldn't apply. They want the newest things. It's tough on the elders and pressure on the entire tribe."

He glanced out the side mirror. "Car coming on fast."

"I see him."

They both tensed when a sedan came along side, slowed, then zoomed by. As it disappeared in the distance, they sighed.

As if he hadn't been interrupted, Mike continued, "When I came on-scene, other reservations were in contact with Juan, wanting help. When times were good, they'd expanded, improving their casinos, taking out loans. Everyone on the reservations had been making more money; times were good. Then the economy went bust. The tribe's income went down, loans were due."

"What does that have to do with you, Josh, Juan, and drugs?"

"I'm getting to that. The Mexican drug cartels saw an opening. Juan had the ear of many elders of reservations with casinos, but Tomás placed his men in positions circumventing Juan's ability to govern by controlling all communications. Juan can't prove it, but we both suspect Tomás is tied in with a Mexican cartel. If a war broke out between the cartel and Juan's small group, it would be no contest. Juan needed someone to travel to each of the reservations and discuss with the elders ways to avoid becoming involved with the cartel. I became that go-between and set up a time and place to meet." Mike stopped and stared out the window.

"Why not notify the DEA?"

"Not yet."

"When?"

He shrugged and looked away.

Patty let what he'd said sink in, thinking as she had from the beginning that the only hope for the Native Americans was government intervention, yet she sympathized with their dilemma. Despite her low opinion of Bromont's police, she felt Mike was wrong in not going to the authorities.

By the time they drove through Dodge City in southern Kansas and turned onto Highway 56, it was dark. The driving was hampered by small pickups and farm tractors. "How about stopping for dinner and get gas. I'll be too tired to drive through the night, and you can't drive yet."

"When we cross into Oklahoma, we can find a motel. I think we're okay until we get closer to Tucson."

After a time, Patty pulled into a hamburger place with a large empty field in the back. She left Mike standing by the truck and took Kallie for a walk. It felt good to stretch, and Kallie was eager to explore as they made their way up a long weedy path. Neon lights and dim street lamps sprinkled strange images across the landscape. The clear cold air energized her. The town's lights receded and the moonlight guided them. She continued on. Free to roam. Free from drug cartels. Free from a man she no longer trusted. A copse of trees ahead held dark shadows. Kallie was ready to hunt. She stumbled over a root. Kallie tugged on the leash. "Not now," Patty said and turned back the way they'd come.

After eating, they were back on the road and again she peppered Mike with questions. "What about Slocum? Why would he be after you?" She felt like she was batting against a cobweb.

"Juan felt that alone each reservation would be at the mercy of Tomás, but together they could handle their financial situations. If Tomás or Slocum got hold of my list of elders who wanted to cooperate with Juan, they'd prevent them from continuing in their leadership roles or get rid of them. When the cartels kill people, it gets gory. Once Slocum or the cartel take over the casinos, crime will follow."

"That list is on your flash drive."

"Smart girl. Slocum wants his own empire and is willing to go up against Tomás, but I'm not sure he knows Tomás is the front man for a Mexican cartel. They play hardball. Torture and beheadings are child's play to them. We are in the middle of a very messy situation."

With a lump in her throat that wouldn't go away, she peeled away the husk of Mike's story. "I never heard anything about drugs when I lived in Bromont. Oh sure, they existed, but not overt. Slocum's casino seemed to do well from all the gambling. God, I should know. My dad was a good customer, but he never said anything to me about drugs. Why would Slocum risk everything by getting involved with drugs?"

"Slocum kept the elders happy with large payments and plenty of jobs, but he saw a downturn, too, and he's a greedy bastard. He wants an empire. Drugs are a way to get it."

"So Slocum knew what you were doing and you needed to get out of Bromont fast. But how do those bodies in the RV park come into it?"

"Rhonda was at the wrong place at the wrong time. She was a goodhearted, lonely gal who took up with that creep Floyd. He gave her a hard time, but she wouldn't or couldn't cut loose until she met Peter Darby. Floyd doesn't do well with rejection."

"That's an understatement."

"Floyd is Slocum's enforcer, but he crossed the line when he laid out those bodies in the trailer park. I think Slocum had Rhonda killed because she knew too much about his drug plans, and Floyd didn't mind doing the deed as long as he could nail Darby, too."

"What's that got to do with you?" She lowered her beams as another car approached from the opposite direction.

"Rhonda put me onto Slocum's drug operation. My big mistake was letting Josh come to the casino. I had no idea what he was up to until it was almost too late. Rhonda set me straight and she was killed because of it."

"You think Floyd recognized you at that place we were snowed in?"

"Maybe, but he might have thought I was Josh and told Slocum."

"I don't get it. Why would he want Josh?" Since he didn't answer, she drove on thinking about all the implications. Nothing made sense to her. "Did Josh have the same information that you had? He was helping you, right?"

Mike's face paled. "Trusting him was the worst mistake I ever made."

High-beamed headlights glinted in Patty's rearview mirror. She slowed and pulled to the right, allowing the car plenty of room to pass, but it stayed behind them. Mike sat up straighter and pulled his gun out from under his seat.

Patty gripped the wheel tighter. "Not sure whether I should slow and pull off the road, or hang tough."

"Hold your speed for a while. Let's see what he's up to."

For the next ten miles the car hung on their tail. When they approached the city limits of Elkhart, just before the Oklahoma border, it pulled off onto a side street.

Patty relaxed her shoulders. "Jesus, not sure I can take much more of this. I'm bushed. How about stopping soon? The sign said forty miles to Boise City."

"Okay. That gives us a full three days to make Tucson, need to be there on Christmas Eve, preferably before. That's when the elders are going to meet with Juan."

"That's been your deadline all along?"

"Yes. Thought I had plenty of time, but...."

"Stuff happened along the way." Patty yawned. "You still haven't told me why you took over Josh's identity. You could have just left town."

"Slocum was on to me, so if I was dead, he'd forget about what I knew and how I was connected to Juan Pacheco. With the truck demolished, I needed someone to tow the trailer. I was stuck until you answered my ad."

She snorted. "Ha. My lucky day." She'd gotten out of town just like she'd wanted, never imagining she'd be stuck between two rival drug gangs. Unfortunately, she had to rely on Mike, unless she went to the authorities, and she wondered if they'd believe her. Is that why Mike hesitated now? "You have enough evidence to make the feds take notice, don't you?"

"I don't think so. Besides, I don't trust them."

"That I can understand, but it's now to the point where I'm not sure you have much of a choice."

"There's time."

She wondered how much time they really had if the meeting was going to be in three days. What would that solve? Wouldn't Tomás want to prevent them from meeting? She was afraid to ask, yet needed to know. "How did you communicate with Juan, if his brother intercepts his mail?"

It was several minutes before Mike answered. "I sent him postcards. We'd set up a simple code, thinking that Tomás wouldn't bother to read them and even if he did, they wouldn't make sense to the average reader. I sent duplicates to my friend Camden and asked him to hold them for me, but if something happened to me, he had to get them to Juan. I mailed him instructions in a letter I posted just before that storm hit."

"Camden's the guy you said you didn't know."

"Yeah, yeah. Sorry about that. I met him when I visited Josh at the vet rehab center. Camden was a professor at a nearby college. We hit it off and went fishing a couple of times together. Had time to talk."

"I meet him briefly at Maggie's," Patty said. "He was the one who told me you were dead. He was shocked. Do you think he went to visit Josh?"

Mike looked stunned. "I hadn't thought about that." Finally, he shrugged. "Doesn't matter. I was gone by that time."

Their conversation lagged until they found a small motel and checked in. The room had two queen-sized beds and felt large after the trailer. She fed Kallie, took her for a short walk and came back to the room to find

Mike in bed with the small bedside lamp lit. He had one arm over his eyes, but was obviously not asleep. Kallie hopped up on his bed.

Patty sat down on the side of the other bed. "I've thought a lot about this whole mess," she said. "we don't have a choice. We have to go to the authorities. We can't do this alone."

"I told you. I promised Juan to keep them out of it."

"That was before your life was in danger, and I might add mine, too. I don't want to die because you made a promise that no longer makes sense."

"There's another reason I can't go to the authorities." He put his arm down and looked at her. "I killed Josh."

"For heaven sakes, just because you feel guilty about the accident, is no reason to agonize that you killed him."

"You don't get it." He raised his hands and stared at them. "I killed him with my bare hands. I'd been trained to do that. I killed a friend I'd known since I was a kid. I killed him!" He grabbed the bed lamp and flung it, smashing it against the far wall. Kallie yelped and leaped to the floor.

The room went black. Headlight beams stabbed at the curtains, piercing the darkened room.

Chapter 26

When Camden pulled into his driveway, there was a car out front. He had a bad feeling about it. With his suitcase in hand, he walked to his front door and two men got out of the sedan and came toward him.

"Evening Camden," one man said.

"What are you doing here, Glen?" Camden asked, taking in Glen's tie and blue suit, a sure sign he was on duty. "I still have another week of vacation coming."

"I know." Glen introduced the stout, olive-complexioned, young man next to him as George Rocklin. "We need to ask you a few questions."

"Sounds mysterious." Camden put his key in the lock and opened his front door. He picked up his mail that was strewn across the front hall and placed it on a side table before inviting Glen and Rocklin inside. "Give me a minute to put some things away. Make yourselves at home. I'll be right with you. Can't offer you a drink, though. Nothing much in the house," he said over his shoulder, as he took the stairs two steps at a time. In his room he tossed the suitcase on the bed, washed up and looked at himself in the mirror.

Despite the many hours on the road, he had yet to decide how he was going to handle not only what he'd learned in Bromont, but what he now surmised. Mike was a friend who'd sent postcards, and until he understood what they were all about, he would serve friendship ahead of duty. If he was wrong, he hoped he'd have enough time to rectify any problems.

When he got downstairs, Rocklin was sitting on the couch as though waiting for a prom date. Glen's large hulk stood at ease in the doorway to the living room. He'd have made a good boxer and often was thought to be just that with his broken nose and fleshy lips. Not a picture of handsome, but a hell of an agent.

"So, gentlemen, what can I do for you?"

Glen took out a cigarette, but didn't light it. "We got a call from FBI Agent Caulfield. Wanted to know what we knew about you."

Camden relaxed in his big leather chair by the hearth. "Yes, I met him and we talked. My friend Mike Garrick died in an auto accident. I didn't like the way the local police chief handled the case."

"So Caulfield said." Glen didn't give much away when he wanted information, and Camden had the feeling this was going to be one of those "talks."

"May I ask what agency you're with Mr. Rocklin?" Camden asked, although he had a good idea by looking at the man.

"Bureau of Indian Affairs, Office of Justice Services. I'm investigating a suspicious fire at the Hitower Casino outside of Bromont. "

"Sounds ominous." Camden said.

The man nodded. Camden waited. It was an impasse.

Glen gazed at Camden, then his cigarette. "Sorry. I know how you hate smoking." He put the cigarette back in the pack and stuck it in his pocket. "Camden, you were there, met with Slocum. Can you tell us anything that might help?"

"I told Caulfield everything I learned. What more is there to tell?"

"The Bromont Police Chief is dirty." Rocklin acted as if that statement would set Camden into a torrent of speech.

Camden nodded and smiled. "That figures."

"Don't you want to know what this guy Dankbar did?" Rocklin was getting antsy.

Glen intervened. "Look, Camden. Help us out here."

"We'd like to know what your relationship is with Slocum," Rocklin's face was chiseled, his nose sharp.

"My relationship with the man consisted of two visits to his casino and one conversation with him. I know that Garrick worked there as a bouncer and that his friend Josh Peterson visited often."

"Slocum was moving in on the drug trade," Glen said.

"Was?"

"He died in the fire." Rocklin words were clipped. "Propane tank explosion. Took out the entire second floor. That was Slocum's domain."

"Wow. When did this happen?"

"Last night."

"I was deported from Bromont late yesterday afternoon."

Rocklin frowned. "What do you mean by deported?"

"Wrong use of words, perhaps," Camden said. "The Police Chief thought I was trouble and gave me an escort out of town." Camden fingered the scar on his cheek. "You can see I couldn't know anything about a fire."

"I'm not saying you do, I'm asking what you might know that could help my investigation." Rocklin seemed unaware Camden was upset at his line of questioning.

"Look, Rocklin," Camden said. "If you talked to Caulfield, you know that Tomás Pacheco's boy, Debo, was in town. Tried to pass himself off as an FBI agent. He's the one you should be questioning."

"Caulfield told me about Debo," Rocklin said. "We think either Garrick and or Peterson were in on the drug plans, but we aren't sure how. Caulfield said you didn't think Garrick was dead. Is that true?"

"That's what I think, but I can't prove it. If he's alive, then where is he and who did the coroner cremate?" Camden looked at Rocklin. "Have you been able to talk to Peterson?"

"FBI lost him." Rocklin's face flushed. "There's a girl named Patty Harkin with him. Do you know her?"

"Met her briefly. I doubt she's involved."

"Hard to know. She took off with Peterson. Local police say she had some petty crimes against her and an assault and battery charge that was dropped."

Camden knew where Peterson was headed but he wasn't about to tell Rocklin or Glen. Not yet, anyway. "I thought Caulfield was investigating the so-called Popsicle Murders. How do drugs fit into the mix?"

"We were hoping you'd be able to tell us," Glen said.

"Glen, if I knew I'd have been on the phone to you."

"Do you know a man named Floyd Rickter?" Rocklin had taken out a little notebook.

Detectives rookie's primer question, Camden thought with derision. "Heard about him when I was in Bromont. I understand he's the main suspect in the murders."

"You never met him?"

Camden leaned forward. "Rocklin, how could I have met the man when he was long gone before I ever got to Bromont?"

"I understand. I'm just trying to cover all my questions." He placed his card on the coffee table in front of the couch and stood. "If you think of anything that might help, please call me."

"What are you doing about Debo Matruca?"

"We're looking for him and so is the FBI." Rocklin glanced at Glen. "I gather your department is in on this, too?"

Glen nodded. "Everyone is cooperating. Rocklin, would you please wait outside for me?"

"Sure. Nice to have met you, Mr. McMillan." The young man swiveled on his heels, gave one backward glance at Camden, went out and eased the door closed behind him.

"Where do they get such young guys?"

Glen shook his head. "Are you telling me everything?"

"What do you want me to say? I come home from vacation, lose a good friend, and the Justice Office of BIA questions me as if I know something about a possible arson case."

"Okay. Look. Take the rest of your vacation." He sighed. "But I'm warning you, if I find out you know something about a drug war, the fire or anything else we need to know about the Bromont area, and don't give us the information, I'll have you fired and charges brought."

Camden stood and walked Glen to the door. "I know the score, believe me."

After the car drove away, Camden leaned against the wall. Shit, what had he gotten himself into? He shook himself as if to regain his thoughts, went into the den and sat at his desk. He removed a file from a drawer and took out the postcards. Nursing a scotch on the rocks, he thumbed through the packet of mail. He'd discarded the junk mail. And glanced at the catalogues and magazines, the bills and a few personal notes. He picked up one envelope on hotel stationary, his name and address printed in block letters with a post mark of Bromont. He tore it open.

I might be in some trouble when you get this letter. The postcards were meant for you to read and use the information as best you can. Your profession in no secret to me. Whatever you hear about me, believe half of it. I had my reasons. Josh is dead. Cartels are moving in. I'm trying to get to Juan Pacheco, Tucson, AZ, but I might not make it. If I don't, I hope you will intercede on the Native Indians' behalf. You've been a good friend. SEAL SWC Mike.

Camden leaned back, thinking he shouldn't be surprised that Mike knew about him. When you become friends, words slip out unintentionally and Mike caught onto things quickly. He rose and went to the kitchen, removed a frozen dinner, and zapped it in the micro oven. Not the most appealing of meals, but it would hold him till he could get to the store. After eating his skimpy meal, he spent the night studying the postcards he had laid out in front of him on his desk. Seven. He'd looked at the map and each came from a different Indian reservation with a picture of the local casino. But the first and last had the picture of Mission San Xavier outside of Tucson. It made no sense. It was like he was starting all over from the beginning. "God damn it, Mike," he said out loud. "Couldn't you at least give me a clue?"

He buried his head in his hands and reread Mike's last letter. Why sign it SEAL SWC? Sea Air Land Special Warfare Command. The individual letters might mean something. Could they be the decipher? Finally when he applied them to the postcards, the information on the cards made sense. Mike had encoded the names of the men from different tribes who were coming to a meeting at midnight on Christmas Eve at or near Mission San Xavier. For some reason he hadn't let Juan or anyone else to know who they were.

He picked up the phone and made a reservation for the first available flight to Phoenix.

Chapter 27

The glare of headlights stabbed at Patty and Mike's bedroom window. Mike pulled his pistol out from under his pillow. He nodded toward the window and whispered, "Take a peek and see who's out there, but keep to the side, don't make yourself a target."

Patty rose, stepped over Kallie, who had perked up her ears but remained quiet. There was a sedan parked in front of their door, back doors open. A man passed by their door and entered the adjacent room. Muffled words came through the thin walls. The man came back outside, leaned into the backseat and emerged with a sleeping child in his arms.

Patty leaned back, sighed and shook her head. "It's a family. They had a child in the back seat. I think that's why they left the headlights on."

"Stupid jerks." Mike lowered his Beretta.

They heard the car doors close, the beep of the lock mechanism, and eventually the headlights died. Thumping and a child's cry, then a hushed quiet. Still fully clothed, Patty sat on the edge of her bed, feeling her heart rate slow. The room slipped back into darkness, and Kallie jumped up on the bed. Patty laid back listening, thinking, stroking Kallie for reassurance. Hours later she heard Mike's soft snoring.

She rose, went into the bathroom and turned on the light. Once long ago she'd stared at her image in a bathroom mirror at Maggie's Diner and thought she'd hit the depths of despair. God, how little she knew what real trouble was. Okay, get a grip, she told herself. There's always an answer, isn't there? She opened the door a crack, the shaft of light fell across her suitcase with the book. She scanned the room and spotted Mike's laptop. *What the hell, I'm not going to sleep anyway.*

She'd noticed the sign when they'd checked in that the motel had WiFi. Even now at one in the morning, the office light glared showing it was open. She picked up the book and the laptop and eased out the door. The night air was crisp. She knocked on the office door, then entered. An old man, behind the desk reading a magazine, looked up and smiled a toothless grin.

"I couldn't sleep and didn't want to wake my...," she didn't bother to finish her sentence. *No need for him to know her relationship to Mike.* "Do you mind if I sit here read and check my email?"

He shrugged and nodded.

She settled into an old vinyl couch, plugged in the computer and took the lottery ticket out of the book. It took a while, but she eventually pulled up the Minnesota lottery website and began scanning recent winning ticket numbers for the various awards. No match on Powerball, or Mega Millions, or Hot Lotto. "Damn, not a single hit,"she muttered.

The old man looked up.

"Sorry," she said. "Just some disappointing news." Undeterred she checked old, unclaimed tickets. And there it was. "Oh, my God." She put her hand over her mouth to suppress a scream. It was for Gopher 5, the amount, if not divided among other winners, was $530,000. So far no other claimers. She searched the site to find out how to claim her prize. *How was she going to get back to Roseville, Minnesota, to claim the money?* Shaking, she took out a pen and signed the back of the ticket, then wrote down the information she'd need. Closing the computer, she unplugged it and sat staring into space.

"Everything all right Miss?" the old man asked.

She nodded. "Absolutely. Some good news." She stood and walked toward the counter. "May I use your phone to call Minnesota? I'll pay for it, cash."

He studied her for a moment. "Okay, but I want to hear the cost from the operator myself."

"Sure." She took the phone and dialed Maggie's home phone. *At one-thirty in the morning Maggie would be home, but would she answer the phone?*

She let it ring five times and almost gave up, but on the sixth ring, Maggie answered the phone in a groggy voice. "Yes?"

"It's me, Patty. I need your help." She didn't wait for Maggie to answer. "I'm going to send you a package Federal Express. If anything happens to me, open it. Otherwise just keep it safe for me."

"Are you in trouble?"

"No…well, yes. What I'm sending you is good. I can't explain the rest."

Maggie continued to badger her for more information. Patty resisted the urge to tell Maggie everything, and besides the old man had his ears tuned to her conversation.

"A couple of things you should know. Report Slocum to the authorities, not the police, maybe the DEA." Patty glanced at the old man, whose eyes narrowed.

"Slocum's place burned down," Maggie said.

"What?"

"Yesterday. They think it was arson. Feds all over the place."

"Slocum's dead?"

"They aren't saying. Scuttlebutt is that no bodies were recovered."

"Wow." Patty thought for a minute. "I'm on my way to Tucson. Going to meet a guy named Juan Pacheco. I have a dog, a golden retriever with me. I think I'll have to put her in a kennel during my visit. I'll give the kennel your name and number for a contact just in case. I'll send you some money to cover her costs to fly her to you. Take care of Kallie, that's her name. You'll love her."

"Wait a minute. What's going to happen to you? Look Patty, I don't know what's going on, but you get yourself to the authorities, Feds or local police, don't care which."

"Sorry, Maggie, not yet, but soon. Bye." She hung up afraid that she would tell Maggie more than she should.

The old man took the phone, dialed the operator and asked for the charges. Satisfied, he hung up. Patty paid him and included a generous tip. When she walked out of the office, her heart was lighter, if not buoyant. She stood looking up at the stars, thinking.

The lottery ticket belonged to her, not Mike. Hadn't he said it was Josh who bought them? Mike had lied to her, he was a killer, and had hooked her into the middle of a drug war. What allegiance did she owe him? She could bug out now and head north. Leave Mike stranded. Would she? The answer no longer seemed black and white. She still had time to decide. She walked back to their room, unlocked the door and entered.

The overhead light was on. Mike sat on the end of the bed, his Beretta pointed at her.

Chapter 28

Two days before Christmas Eve at three in the afternoon Camden's plane landed in Phoenix. He rented a compact black sedan, drove to Tucson and checked in to a Comfort Inn. That night he visited the crowded Pacheco Casino. Contacting Juan was his top priority, but making that happen might prove difficult. Mike had sent postcards in code to the man, which probably meant Juan was under surveillance either by his brother Tomás or the Mexican drug cartel.

He'd researched Juan and found he was chairman of the reservation's southern district that bordered Mexico. Camden hoped he'd be able to arrange a meeting, but was unsure how to make contact. After perusing the different areas of the casino and playing a few slots to blend in, he went to the bar and ordered a beer. His biggest fear was meeting Debo Matruca, the fake FBI agent who worked for Tomás. If that should happen, Camden might get a one-way ride to the cemetery.

He tried chatting up the bartender, a woman of immense proportions, but got the cold shoulder. Other patrons seemed intent on their own problems or not interested in talking to a stranger. He went to the restaurant, but again struck out. Dealers were notoriously closed mouthed, and he had no intention of making himself conspicuous. Dawdling at several different betting venues, he scanned the rooms for a likely candidate to pump for information about Juan. He made one more pass through the casino. As he was ready to leave, he spotted a face from the photos Agent Caulfield had shown him. What was Floyd Rickter doing here? Was Slocum in town? Was this about revenge for destroying the Hitower Casino or something else? Caulfield doubted Slocum would join with the Mexican cartel. Was he wrong?

Camden had two options, call the FBI now or follow Rickter and see where he went. His duty told him one thing, his instincts another. He waited and watched. When Rickter left the casino, Camden tailed him through suburbs of Tucson to a house in an upscale neighborhood. He drove past as Rickter pulled into a driveway. Making a U turn farther up the street, he cut his headlights and parked across the street a few houses away. As Rickter approached the front door, it opened and the entry light shone on a white face. Camden smiled. Slocum wasn't dead. But why was he here? The meeting on Christmas Eve or something else?

Slocum and Rickter were the FBI's concern, but Camden's contact was with the DEA. He called the local office, gave the information of Rickter's whereabouts and the make and license number of his car. They'd send it on to the FBI and the Tucson police.

The dead of night seemed like the opportune time to take a look at Juan's house on the outskirts of the town of Sells. The road south had potholes and the flat desert terrain made the two hours pass slowly, giving him a chance to think about why he was here and wondering what he could do about the information he had. How reliable was it? What had Mike gotten himself into? He had only a few answers but a lot of questions.

By the time he arrived in Sells, he was stiff and sleep nagged him. Perhaps he was taking too many chances, but he needed to know if Juan was a free man or under Tomás's surveillance.

Once in Juan's neighborhood, he slowed to a crawl. There were no curbs, only dimly lit street signs as he cruised past modest homes with cacti and rocky front yards. Dogs slept on bare ground or roamed the gravel roads. Eventually he found Juan's house, encircled by an adobe wall. A man, half asleep, sat by the gate. Whether he was guarding the house to prevent people from entering or from leaving was difficult to know. Camden drove by, turned the corner, and parked, cutting his engine. He rolled down his window and sucked in the cold air. Thick high clouds foreshadowed an oncoming winter storm, fulfilling the prediction for snow tomorrow.

A scruffy dog walked over and sniffed at his tires. Reconnoitering on foot would be a major problem. Instead, he drove off to circle the block, trying to find another entrance to the compound. In the dark, he couldn't find a place to scale the wall unseen. Frustrated, he drove back to his motel and fell into bed at three in the morning.

His alarm went off at eight. Looking out the window, he saw snowflakes drifting down to the lot below. He ordered breakfast through room service, took a shower and dressed, all the while thinking of how he would handle his call to Juan at the number listed in the Indian reservation's directory.

Feeling that nine o'clock was a decent hour to call, he punched in Juan's number. A man answered in a curt voice. "Pacheco's."

"Hello, this is Bob Simon, I'd like to speak to Juan, please." Without waiting for the man to speak, he continued, "I'm a Marine buddy of his. He'll remember me."

"He's busy right now."

"Aw, come on, bro, ask him, he'll want to talk to me. He and I had some tough times together in Iraq. I was there when he got hit. I've come a long way. Can't go home without touching bases with Juan. Gotta tell our buddies Juan's doing okay."

There was silence on the phone, some talk in the background and then the man said, "I'll see if he's available."

I bet you will. This was a long shot, but Camden had to try it. Actually, when Juan came on the line, he was surprised.

"Hello, Bob," Juan said, as if he knew exactly who Camden was.

Was this really Juan? He had no way of knowing, but it didn't matter. If it was Juan, he'd understand the message, if not, then Camden wouldn't be out much.

"Hey, you ole Indian," Camden said. "Glad you're home. How are you doing?"

"As well as can be expected."

The man was hesitant and Camden didn't blame him. "Did you get my postcards?"

"You sent postcards?"

"Yeah. From all the casinos we visited in our travels this past year. Didn't you get them?"

"Oh yes, of course."

"My wife, Leah, and I are in town for the holidays." He forced a laugh. "Do you remember how you kidded her about her name and started calling her Dea."

"Of course, I remember. She was a good sport."

"Right. Anyway, we'd like to get together with you."

There was a click on the line. Someone had picked up another phone and was listening.

"It's a surprise to hear from you," Juan said. "Is your daughter, Michelle, with you?"

Okay, Juan had to be asking about Mike. "She ran off with some guy, and I haven't seen her in awhile. Can't figure what she's up to. Hope she'll catch up with us here in Tucson, and Josie isn't here either. The two of them pulled a disappearing act on her mother and me. How do you like that?"

"Sorry to hear that. It must be difficult for you."

"You can say that again. Don't know what we'll do without them. How about you joining us for dinner tonight? We can come pick you up." Camden heard murmuring in the background.

Finally, Juan said, "I'm afraid that won't be possible. I'm tied up with family right now."

"Oh, yeah, I remember you had a brother. How's Tomás?"

"He's very successful. Lives close by and visits often."

"Glad to hear you have support. Maybe you and I could meet during the day."

"It's a busy time. But there are many events you should see while you're in the area. There's a docent tour at the San Xavier Mission at 12:30 on Christmas Eve day. You shouldn't miss that."

"Oh, sounds interesting. I guess there'll be a lot of tourists. Isn't there a mass on Christmas Eve?"

"No. Only in the morning. The mission closes at five o'clock. Didn't know you'd be interested in mass."

"Just an idea."

"Are you still smoking that awful pipe?" Juan asked.

"Ah, yeah. Can't seem to quit." Camden realized this was Juan's way of IDing him at the docent tour. What other messages could he relay. "You know, if you can get away, call me, and we'll drop everything just to have a visit." He gave his cell number to Juan.

"Well, it's been good talking to you, Bob," Juan said. "Give my regards to Leah. If you see Michelle or Josie, tell them I'd love to see them. You're one lucky dude, but don't let your wife drag you into more than you can handle."

"I'll tell her. You take care of yourself. Bye." Beads of sweat ran down Camden temples. He wiped them away and fingered the scar on his cheek. He'd have to wait until the tour to find out what was going on. He'd pick up a pipe and hope Juan would contact him before the Christmas Eve meeting of tribal leaders at or near the San Xavier. Trouble was in the offing for those in attendance.

He picked up the phone and called Glen in Minneapolis. After explaining to Glen what he'd seen and what he'd learned, he got a severe reprimand. Glen's voice got so loud that Camden had to hold the phone away from his ear.

"FBI Agent Caulfield is in Tucson. Get your ass over to the meeting at the local DEA's office in two hours. Clyde Wycoff is the lead man."

Chapter 29

Patty froze in the doorway, then smiled. "God, you sure can scare the crap out of people with that peashooter of yours."

"I intend to." Mike didn't lower the pistol. "Come in, close the door, then sit on the bed."

She did what he asked, but was mystified by his tone and his actions. "What's the matter?"

"Who did you phone?"

"What?"

"You heard me. I saw you in the office talking on the phone. Who did you blab to? The feds?"

"Are you crazy? I called Maggie."

He frowned. "Why?"

"Because you got me in a lot of shit, that's why. And Kallie isn't going into some animal pound like you suggested. I'm going to find a good kennel and have her taken care of until I can get her again. If something happens to me, I want Maggie to take her." She was so mad, she spluttered. "I'm taking Kallie since you want to dump her."

He put the Beretta on his knee. "I never said I'd dump Kallie."

"Yes, you did. You said you hoped she gets a good home. Well, I'm going to give her a good home, and if not me, then Maggie will."

"God damn it, woman. You jump to conclusions. I was going to give Kallie back to the Guide Dog Foundation."

"No." She clenched her hands and glared at him. "She's been away from that for too long."

"Okay, okay. We can talk about that later." He seemed to relax. "You snuck out of here, so what was I to think? Did you tell Maggie about me?"

"No." Patty fingered the laptop and nudged the book aside. "You are so paranoid. I've put up with all your shit and I've had it."

"You took my laptop. Who did you email? Did you broadcast that I'm alive?"

"No. That would be stupid." She took a deep breath. "As you've mentioned many times, I'm in trouble, too. I checked for news. There's a storm coming in, a big one."

"You didn't need my laptop for that. You plan to turn me in?"

"I am not turning you in, damn it, but I've made a decision. I'll drive you to wherever you need to be and then I'm leaving. No way am I staying around to get gunned down by some gang."

"The cartel doesn't gun people down; they slice them up in tiny pieces."

"That's a cheerful bit of news."

"I'm glad you're going to get out. This isn't a game."

"I never thought it was." She took off her parka and tossed it on the bed. "One thing is bugging me. I've been with you for almost two weeks. You might be a liar and done some awful things in the war, but I don't see you killing someone just for the hell of it. Why did you kill Josh?"

"Does it matter?"

"It does to me."

He shifted on the bed, scooting back to lean against the headboard, but he didn't put his pistol away. It lay next to him. "Josh was in on what I was trying to do for Juan, talking to elders, finding out who could be trusted, who was in charge of the finances, particularly the loans. I documented everything." He nodded toward the laptop. "It's in there and backed up on the flash drive I keep with me at all times."

"What does that have to do with killing Josh?"

"Hang on and I'll tell you. Slocum learned about what I was doing, I'm not sure how. Maybe from Josh. But somehow that doesn't make sense, since Josh didn't start working for Slocum till after we'd been there awhile."

"If not Josh, then there must be a leak somewhere in Juan's organization."

Mike nodded. "Or I misjudged one of the people I talked to during my tour through the seven reservations." He shook his head. "I've thought about it, but it doesn't make sense."

"Why would Josh work for Slocum? I thought he was your friend."

"So did I, but Slocum found out that Rhonda told me about his getting Josh back on drugs. I knew what Slocum wanted: the names of the seven honest men who want to keep their casinos from falling under the cartel's influence. If Slocum got hold of that list, he'd be able to get control of the casinos. I was too busy snooping to check on Josh. Half the time when I got back to the trailer in the morning, I was beat and went to bed. I should have noticed Josh's taking drugs, but I didn't."

"So Rhonda was killed because of what she told you about Slocum and Josh?"

"Probably. The night I killed him, he'd asked to go with me to the casino. I'd taken him there before, but after what Rhonda said, I was suspicious. I checked and found he'd stashed my computer inside my truck. I confronted him and he laughed. We were on the road to the casino. I pulled over, switched on the cab's interior light, grabbed his arm and pushed up his sleeve. Needle marks. Something inside me turned to ice." Mike stopped talking and stared at his hands. The clock ticked on past two a.m.

"You don't need to know the details," he finally said. "He confessed he was trading information for drugs and money." Mike glanced at Patty. "That's the money you found in bundles and have been using like it was yours."

"What a bunch of crock. You know damn well I've used it to buy food and lodging for us, not for extra stuff." They glared at each other; the overhead light stark and bright against the worn brown carpet and brown bedspreads. "You're on a vendetta, aren't you? Whose side are you on?"

"Juan's. I owe him my life. And you bet I want revenge. I want to nail creeps like Slocum and Tomás."

"So why not give what you have to the feds? I guess that would be the DEA from what you've said."

"Not till I talk to Juan."

"God, you are so stubborn."

"Turn out the light. If snow's on the way, we need to get an early start in the morning. If it keeps up, it might help us slip into Tucson unnoticed."

She rose, clicked off the light and fumbled her way back to bed. Fully clothed she threw a cover over herself. "I've been thinking."

"Now what?"

"If you already set up a meeting with the elders and Juan, why do you have to be there?"

"I could miss it. But I vouched for the men's safety. If Juan can't make the meeting for some reaon, then I'll have to take up the slack. Get them to join together and fight the bank that has them over a barrel. One thing I haven't told anyone is that I know who owns the bank that made the loans to the casinos."

Chapter 30

When Camden walked into the meeting room at the DEA's office, Caulfield was standing by the floor to ceiling windows that overlooked a plaza. He smiled and said, "I had you pegged right."

Camden nodded to Caulfield. "Thought I handled it rather well."

Caulfield shook his head. "You had too much information for a visitor trying to find out what happened to his friend."

DEA's lead agent, Clyde Wycoff, in his forties, tall, gangly, and balding stood behind his wood desk. In a soft voice he introduced himself, three other DEA agents, and Police Chief Mark Powers. Then motioned for everyone to take seats at a long table.

Wycoff nodded to Caulfield. "Let's start with your involvement."

"The house Camden reported seeing Floyd Rickter enter is leased to a Robert Perth. The real estate agent said the man paid in cash and never met him. Transaction was done over the phone and money delivered by a messenger. Slocum Hitower might be here to avenge the arson fire at his place. After we got Camden's message, Chief Powers put the house under surveillance. There's been no activity since the police arrived. When we get Rickter, he might give up Slocum, but right now we have no evidence linking Slocum Hitower to what the media is calling The Popsicle Murders."

"What about Josh Peterson and his driver Patty Harkin," Camden asked.

"We're looking for them. They haven't committed a crime as far as we know, but we've determined that Josh was the victim of a hit and run in

Kansas. The doctor who treated Josh said the man was not blind, but the police confirmed that they had a guide dog with them."

Camden rubbed his scar. "Did you find out anything more about the truck accident that killed Mike Garrick?"

"Oh, yes. The Police Chief had the truck towed to a chop shop out of town. We found evidence that the fire had been intentionally started."

Camden nodded. "So the accident was staged."

"When we confronted Police Chief Dankbar, he admitted he was too quick on his actions regarding the accident and suggesting there was no need for an autopsy. He claims this was due to a heavy workload, but there was no law enforcement problems during that time. The man's lying. We're checking his bank records. Eventually, we'll nail him. He has overstepped his authority in too many cases." Caulfield looked at Camden. "I understand someone suggested the city council should recall the Chief and install a Maggie Travers."

"No kidding." Camden grinned.

"So how does this tie in with what's happening here in Tucson?" Wycoff asked.

Caulfield nodded. "I'm not sure how Slocum ties in other than the revenge motive."

"We've warned the casino operators to beef up their security," Police Chief Powers said and turned to Caulfield. "The FBI has the responsibility to investigate major crimes on the reservations."

"True, but right now it's all assumptions and no hard evidence," Caulfield said. "If we run roughshod over the local Indian's authority and come up empty-handed, we'll be in trouble. However, I am contacting the other district chairmen on the reservation and see what they know about the Pachecos. We'll also send a team into the casino to do a spot check on what's going on."

Camden interrupted. "Juan requested Mike Garrick set up this meeting on Christmas Eve. It's strange. Why have seven responsible elders from the reservations with financially troubled casinos meet together?" Camden hesitated, then added, "If Mike is alive, I believe he's on his way here for that meeting."

Wycoff leaned forward. "What's Juan's purpose for this meeting?"

"That's what I keep wondering," Camden said. "The only thing I can think of is that Juan's brother Tomás has such a strangle hold on him that he can't communicate without his brother's knowledge. If Juan has an answer to the casinos' financial problems, he probably wants to talk to them face to face. But my gut tells me the meeting could go very wrong."

Wycoff said, "We know Tomás has ties to the Los Coyotes Mexican drug cartel, but we can't prove it in court. That cartel has been pushing across the border through the reservation's southern district. We've got five ugly cartel killings in the last few months. In fact we were called out to the reservation three days ago. Some kids found body parts strewn over the desert. No head found yet. Haven't ID the remains yet. We will." His voice trailed off. Those seated at the table knew the cartels were growing in number and power, while law enforcement staff had been cut.

Camden asked, "What about this meeting on Christmas Eve? Can you cover it? And what about Juan's house? It looks like he's under guard."

"Our personnel is stretched thin," Wycoff said. "We have no legal grounds to raid his home and we only have your friend's encoded postcards and your telephone call to Juan. To put men onto something so iffy could risk other operations."

Camden placed the postcards on the table, each with a picture of a casino. He looked at Wycoff, then Caulfield. "Why don't we pull the tax records on each of these casinos?" He pointed to the postcards. "We might be able to come up with clues about their financial situation."

Wycoff nodded to two of his agents at the far end of the table. "Get the names of who the leaders are on each of these reservations, backgrounds, anything you can dig up. Let Camden know what you get."

Camden fingered his scar. "I have a bad feeling about the meeting. If the cartel kills these men, then nothing will stop Los Coyotes from running those casinos."

"Killing all of them would be a brazen act," Wycoff said, his voice rising for the first time, then he sighed. "But I wouldn't put it past them. The bastards get bolder everyday."

Angered by the law's impotence against the cartel, Camden said, "We can't let these seven men gather until we know it's safe."

Wycoff surveyed the group. "I'd like to coordinate our actions with the tribes police, but I'm not sure how secure their communications are and all it would take is one person to squeal to the cartel and we'd be sitting ducks. On the other hand, if the meeting goes forward and they get massacred, we'll all be held responsible." He paused, twiddling with his pen. "Any suggestions?"

"I'm to meet Juan's representative tomorrow at San Xavier," Camden said. "I might get more information then. It's cutting it close, but I don't see any other alternative right now."

"Let's see what you learn. Report back to me immediately." Wycoff glanced at the other DEA agents. "Talk to your informants, see if we can learn who these seven men are and where they're staying. Cross reference the tribal elders with the tax and financial records. And let's put a man out at the San Xavier Mission. Rotate them through shifts."

Police Chief Powers' cell phone rang. He excused himself and walked to the far corner of the room. "Secure the crime scene," he said into his phone. "No media within five blocks. I'll be there in twenty minutes. FBI Agent Caulfield will be with me." He glanced at Camden. "And a DEA agent, too." He hung up and said, "My men entered Slocum's house and found a body."

Chapter 31

Patty drove through a light snowfall, taking Highway 25 to Santa Fe and on to Albuquerque. As they approached the capital, police seemed to be out in force. It made her nervous, but she soon realized they were slowing traffic due to highway construction. Mike seemed oblivious to what went on around them and drew what looked like diagrams on a sheet of paper, arrows going here and there.

Patty asked, "What are you doing?"

"Thinking on paper."

"About what?"

"Some of the questions you asked started me thinking about the box I've gotten myself into."

"Like what?"

"This meeting, for one." He tapped his pad of paper, stared out the window. "I need to do some checking. When we get in the center of Albuquerque, we need to find a big drugstore where I can get a cane and a cell phone."

"You've got a cell phone. It's just not charged."

"I need a throw away, one that can't be traced."

"So you aren't too sure about what you're up against or what's really going on?"

"Both."

Patty had the urge to head back to Minnesota where everything had started. She'd had no money and been desperate for a job, but the only dangers she'd faced were hunger and homelessness. Now that she had money to look forward to, her old home town seemed like a refuge. The miles passed, and she ached to stretch her legs, run, anything to alleviate her anxiety.

Despite the snowfall, she enjoyed the peace of the desert scenery. Clouds obscured the Sandia Mountains on their left as they drove into Albuquerque. They hunted for signs to a shopping center and eventually she took an off ramp to a large mall and parked.

"That one should have what you need," she said, pointing to a chain drugstore. "What kind of a cane do you want?"

"One that's adjustable or I'll be leaning over like an old man. And buy a 100 minute card for the phone."

"Got it. Anything else?"

"Since I lost all my clothes, I could use another shirt. This one's getting grungy."

She wrinkled her nose. "I agree."

He jotted some numbers on a sheet of paper and handed it to her. "My pants' waist and inseam measurements. Make sure the shirt has buttons, no t-shirt. I still can't lift my right arm."

She took the paper and smiled at the other items he'd written down. "You do need a shave. Going to get all duded up for the big meeting?"

"Just do the shopping, all right?"

"I'll do my best." She started to get out of the truck, then hesitated. "I need to find a Fed Ex office, too."

"Why?"

"I need to send Maggie money to bail Kallie out of the kennel. And yes, I will use some of Josh's wad of cash."

"You don't know what kennel you're going to put Kallie in yet."

"I know, but I might not have time to do this later." She extracted more of Josh's money that she'd kept in her backpack. "Okay?"

He nodded. "Good to have a backup plan."

"Right." She closed the door and went shopping, feeling uncomfortable about not telling him about sending Maggie the lottery ticket. Then she shrugged, thinking about what he'd got her into.

After buying the cane and the phone, she went to a department store in the same mall to buy Mike's list of things. She enjoyed shopping, picking up a pair of khaki pants, a sport shirt and a sweater for him. It had been a long time since she'd had money to shop. She even went to women's wear and bought herself a denim jacket with coyotes embroidered on the front.

Loaded with packages, she returned to the truck to find Mike leaning against the fender with Kallie at his heels. "Looks like you bought out the store."

She grinned. "Absolutely." She placed the bags in the truck and handed him the cane. He took it with his left hand, extended it as far as it would go, and limped around the car. "It'll do." His right arm was still in the sling and when he moved it, he winced.

Back on the two-way street, Patty said, "There's a Fed Ex office about four blocks from here."

Mike nodded, and turned on the phone to register it under a false name. "The reception should be good here in town."

"Who're you calling?"

"Nosey."

"Hell, yes. Right now, my life seems to hinge on everything you do."

"Okay, Juan Pacheco. I'm not sure I can reach him if his brother has him under surveillance, but I've got to try."

"Do you really think they could trace your call if you used your other cell phone?"

"They'd know the number, that's for sure."

When they arrived at the parking lot in front of the Federal Express office, Mike said, "Send your letter and the money to Maggie while I call Juan."

He'd told her what he was involved in and what he'd done, so secrecy on his part seemed pointless. Although now she seemed to have more secrets than he did. Would she take the lottery money without telling him?

Their trip together had spun through some interesting transformations and she wondered how her relationship with him would end. But they really no longer had what she could call a relationship. She wouldn't call Mike a friend, but what would she call him? Travel companion? Hardly a companion. Companion meant you had some kind of a relationship and they didn't, unless you called being in danger of being killed by some cartel a relationship. Not a partner. She was only a what? An aide is as close as she could come to a description.

She pointed to his notepad. "Can I have a few sheets of paper from your pad?"

"Sure." He turned the page he'd been writing on and tore off three sheets.

"Thanks. This shouldn't take long." She left him to make his call and walked into the Fed Ex office. At the table, she wrote Maggie two letters: one explained the lottery ticket and how she was sending her money to bail Kallie out of the kennel if necessary; the other gave her consent for Maggie to claim the lottery ticket in the event Patty was unable to do so. She'd thought long about this last letter, realizing that under the circumstances she might not make it out alive. She placed money and the papers in the envelope and addressed it. Before she took it up to the clerk, she studied the third piece of paper Mike had torn off. Taking out a pencil she softly shadowed the paper with the graphite. What appeared were some of Mike's notes. Arrows led back and forth from Slocum to Josh, Tomas and Juan. In the corner was the name Camden with a question mark. She had no idea what it all meant, but thought it was interesting and put it in her pocket. After paying, she went back to the truck and found Mike sitting transfixed. She got in and asked, "All set?"

He shook his head. "I'm not sure."

"What do you mean?" She waited, but he didn't elaborate. "We drive on?"

"Yeah."

She maneuvered through the Albuquerque traffic and headed south toward Las Cruces. After that, Tucson would be a morning's drive. "I don't know about you, but I'm about done in. By the time we stop tonight, it'll be late." She made small talk, while Mike remained in a mute funk. "The first thing I'm going to do in Tucson is find a decent kennel. Maybe we can check them out on line before then." She glanced over at him. "Okay?"

"Yeah."

"Can you fill me in on what's going on? I'm not exactly unaware that we're heading for more trouble."

He sighed. "I'm afraid we are and I don't know what I can do about it."

"You got hold of Juan?"

"He's got everything lined up, but he asked me questions that have me second guessing myself. He wants the names of the seven men who will be at the meeting. Why? He also wants to know where they're staying. He doesn't need to know that. He has a banker ready to take over the loans. That wasn't the original plan. When I agreed to find the reliable people at each of these casinos, he thought they could pool their resources, get a lower rate and pay off their balloon payments. Now he's talking about another bank assuming the loans. Why? Which bank? He ignored my questions."

"Are you sure you were talking to Juan?"

"Absolutely."

They lapsed into an uncomfortable silence, until Mike said, "Another thing. How did Slocum know I was helping Juan before I even arrived?"

"Are you sure he knew?"

He shrugged. "That's what Rhonda said and she had no reason to lie to me."

"So one of the seven coming to the meeting told Slocum."

"Why?" He stared at her.

"How the hell should I know. The whole thing's creepy, and frankly, I think ill-conceived." She drank the last drop from the plastic water bottle, then threw it in the back seat where Kallie promptly chewed on it. "She's as bored as I am."

Mike wrestled the bottle from Kallie and stashed it under his seat. "I don't think it was one of the seven."

"Then who? Juan? That doesn't make much sense, does it?"

"Tomás could have found out. But why would he want Slocum to know what I was doing unless they'd joined forces?"

"If Tomás knew about the meeting, wouldn't he want to get rid of you and Josh?"

"Except that it was Slocum who sent Rickter after me." Mike stared out the side window, then turned toward Patty. "If Slocum thought Josh had all the information I'd gathered, he had the opportunity to take over the loans. Whoever controls the loans, controls the casinos."

"So, Slocum thinks Josh has run out on him and sends Rickter after Josh."

"Except Rickter was already at the truck stop when we got snowed in," Mike said.

"Rickter learns that it's you and not Josh and contacts Slocum for instructions, right? Game on." She passed a slow truck and then asked, "Could Juan have joined up with his brother?"

"I don't see that happening. Juan was a Marine, tough as nails, dealt with being a paraplegic. Giving up is not in his DNA. What would make him turn?"

"Does he have family they could get to?"

Mike frowned. "He never talked about family or even a girl friend. When I visited him, it was just him, no one else except his brother who hovered around."

"You were the one who said the cartels are ruthless." She felt Kallie breathing on her neck and reached back to scratch her behind the ears. "Okay, let me ask you this. What happens if the seven men aren't around to stop the loans from being taken over by the wrong people?"

He nodded. "Now you see what I'm worried about." He mumbled to himself. "Get off the highway at Socorro so I can find a place that has WiFi."

"Are you notifying the Feds?"

"Not sure. First, I need to check something, then I'll decide."

Chapter 32

Police Chief Powers, FBI Agent Caulfield and Camden arrived at the crime scene in separate cars, then walked up the driveway to the rental house together. They stooped under the yellow crime tape strung across the entrance and checked in with the lead officer. Since he had no protective gloves, Camden kept his hands in his jacket pockets. The foyer had tiled floors and a high ceiling with a glittering chandelier. He thought it ostentatious, but then the entire size of the house reeked of wealth. Why would the homeowners rent? Did they need the money or just wanted it occupied while they were off on some exotic trip? It should be checked out.

He followed Powers and Caulfield into a large room with stucco faux-painted walls in a dull yellow. The body lay sprawled on its back. Powers introduced Camden and Caulfield to the coroner and Officer Quinn, a police techie.

"Shot in the back of the head." The coroner snapped another photo, while others dusted for fingerprints.

Officer Quinn looked up from his notes. "No ID, pockets rifled. We might get some fiber off the victim's clothing that may belong to the perp. He fell or was pushed forward, then turned over."

"How do you know that?" Camden walked to the other side of the body.

The coroner pointed to the purplish-red color on the abdomen, "Once lividity occurs it doesn't change. Therefore the body was prone on the floor long enough for lividity to set in, then turned over."

Caulfield studied the body. "How long before he was turned?"

The coroner shrugged. "Anywhere from twenty minutes to four hours. I'll know more when I get him on the table."

"Not the act of the cartels. Looks more like an assassination," Powers said, bending over the body. "You finished with him?"

The coroner nodded. "We're about ready to transport."

Powers glanced at Caulfield and Camden. "Do you know who he is?"

Camden nodded. "Slocum Hitower."

"The FBI believes the shooter may be Floyd Rickter," Caulfield said to Quinn. "He's killing his way up to our top ten most wanted list. When you dig out the slug, see if it matches the ones that killed Rhonda Crouch, Peter Darcy, and the truck driver, Larry Claybourne. I'll send that information over to your lab." He looked closer at the body. "Rickter used a Kel-Pec P-11."

Quinn flipped his notepad closed. "The entry wound might fit a nine-millimeter. Looks like it's from a hollow point cartridge. What did this Rickter use in the other crimes?"

"Hollow point." Caulfield stared at the body.

"Guess he doesn't care about our matching the ballistics," Quinn said. "The bullets still lodged inside."

"Richter probably only cares about who's paying him and how much." Caulfield paused and added, "Unless his temper kicks in and he reacts violently." He turned to Camden. "You saw Rickter enter here and left a message with the DEA. Wouldn't it have been better if you'd called me, the FBI or the local police?"

Camden knew his excuse would sound lame but gave it a try. "I didn't know you were in town. I thought Rickter wasn't going anywhere. After all he was Slocum's boy and Slocum was here." He sighed. "In hindsight, yeah, I should have made a different decision."

Caulfield's eyes narrowed. "Are you protecting Garrick?"

"Hell no. I wasn't sure he was alive until our meeting today." Camden, realizing they might think Garrick killed Slocum, added, "We don't know where Garrick is, but we know Rickter was here."

Powers turned to an officer standing nearby. "Officer Manuel. What time did your patrol get here?"

The man stepped forward. "Call came in to our patrol unit at three fifteen in the morning, sir, and arrived on site twenty minutes later. We didn't see a car that matched the bolo. No one entered or left while we were here. We checked the perimeter; windows and doors were locked. Nothing out of place, lights out. At that time we felt we had no cause to enter without a warrant."

"I called the DEA office about one a.m.." Camden felt rotten about his poor judgement on notifying the authorities. "You can check the logs."

Caulfield shook his head. "Too damn much time."

Powers attention went to Officer Manuel. "You were outside for several hours. What made you decide to enter the house this morning?"

"We had probable cause when a neighbor stopped and said she'd heard what sounded like gun shots during the night. With that and the possibility of a wanted fugitive inside, we rang the bell." He smirked. "When no one answered the bell or our pounding on the door, we jiggled the front door handle and it opened."

Powers turned to Caulfield. "This happened on my turf, so we'll take the lead."

"We will be involved, but my men are stretched thin." Caulfield studied Powers. "Keep me informed. Autopsy, forensics, weapon used, everything." He didn't wait for Powers to agree and instead turned to Camden. "Let's start looking at those tax reports, financial records and names that Wycoff's men have been working on."

They left the crime scene, drove back to the DEA office, and settled into desks behind computers. From his university days, Camden enjoyed research, even found it soothing, but Caulfield was the kind of guy who wanted to be where the action was.

Caulfield bent over the computer keys, fuming. "Each of these casinos has a loan outstanding, but we have no idea what the terms are. If they can't meet their obligations, what happens? Foreclosure? Is there a balloon payment? What?"

"Take a look at this," Camden said, as he pointed to a report one of the DEA agents had uncovered. "It's the loan applications. A Consuelo Regina signed for the Midland Independent Bank."

Caulfield leaned over Camden's shoulder. " Never heard of it. Check it out."

Camden read further, checking the list of names the agents had assembled of the Indian reservations' elders, especially those involved with the finances.

"If we contact the tribal officers and any one of them are in with the cartel, it'll tip them off that we're onto them," Caulfield said.

"Is that a bad thing?" Camden asked. "If it stops seven murders, it would be worth it, wouldn't it?" He watched Caulfield's face. "You're thinking that the cartel would pull in its horns and wait for another opportunity."

"Something like that."

"The cartel people are cocky sons of bitches, so they just might go ahead." Camden thought how far removed he now was from his former life. Six years ago he'd taken a leave of absence from his university postion and trained to be a DEA agent. The death of his wife and daughter at the hands of a meth-head teen had been his impetus. Afterward he'd returned to the University and worked undercover in the DEA's northern area, watching student activists, returning vets and the gangs. Recently the drug cartels had invaded the north, making killings more violent, as if each gang had to prove they were worthy of a cartel's interest.

Camden had met Mike while running and a friendship had evolved, separate from his DEA job. Mike's relationship with Josh went unnoticed by him until Josh's name came across his desk with a list of other vets who had drug problems and were connected to the drug world. Josh joined Camden's watch list. Because of his friendship with Mike, Camden had requested to have someone else assigned to Josh. His boss, Glen, refused, saying Camden was in the perfect position to get information. In time, Mike must have learned about Camden's true career. Why else would he have sent the postcards?

Caulfield's voice interrupted his thoughts. "I'm wondering who this Consuelo gal is?" He continued to check the FBI data bank. "Slow process," he muttered and walked away to get a cup of coffee from the machine in the hall while the computer ran through the data. He returned to his desk and squinted at the screen. "Bingo."

Camden leaned over and saw the image of a woman in her thirties, long black hair, dark eyes with a brooding look. "Attractive."

"She's Chaco Seltano's daughter. He's head of the Los Coyotes cartel." Caulfield read through the file. "No criminal record, but the relationship sends up a red flag." He put his fingertips together and leaned back. "From what we've got so far it looks like they set up a bank, loaned money and collected interest. When the balloon payment comes due, they'll not only get their money back, or if the payment can't be met, they'll own the casinos. Not only will they be able to launder money, but they get control of the casinos. Cute."

"But if Consuelo is with Los Coyotes, it means that the cartel will have the casinos in its pocket anyway." Camden remained puzzled. "So why the meeting?"

"Juan called the meeting, right? Tried setting it up without his brother's knowledge." Caulfield made notes on a sheet of paper. "He knows the cartel's involved with the original loans and wants to get them out of the deal. If he has another legitimate source to pay off those loans, he'd need these men on board."

"It sounds screwy to me. Why meet with them in person? Why use Garrick as the errand boy? What's wrong with the phone or email?"

"Interference from Tomás."

"Maybe." Camden was not satisfied with that conclusion, but went back to his bank search. "Got a Midland Independent Bank." He pointed to the screen. "It looks legit—proper forms, directors, taxes filed for the last five years. Consuelo Regina is the CFO."

The men gathered their notes. "Okay," Caulfield said. "Continue crosschecking the tribal elder officials with the banks, pull up their individual bank records. Dig for a connection. It's no coincidence that Consuelo is Seltano's daughter. Odd that her name hasn't cropped up before this. When I deal with a woman's involvement in a crime, I think of Kipling's poem, *The Female of the Species*— 'the female of the species is more deadly than the male.'" He stood and grabbed his jacket from behind his chair. "I've got to make a few calls to Washington. If Consuelo Regina is tied to Los Coyotes, we'll be able to freeze the bank's assets under the Foreign Narcotics Kingpin Act. I'll let you know if I get orders for an operation. You got my cell number. Call if you get anything." As he walked out the door, he said over his shoulder, "I've got to touch bases with Powers. Rickter's got to be found before he kills again."

Amen thought Camden.

He continued sorting names and culling those less likely to be involved. It was nearing 6:30 and he was famished. He turned off the computer, put his notes into a file and grabbed his suit coat off the peg. He'd heard of a good Southwestern Mexican restaurant nearby that he could walk to. But before he could leave the building, Wycoff came through the door and motioned Camden to follow him into his office. Camden groaned, realizing something had happened for Wycoff to have a sour look on his face. Before Camden had a chance to close the door, Wycoff said, "They still haven't found the head, but we've identified the body parts found in the southern area of the reservation. We don't have to worry about Tomás Pacheco anymore."

Chapter 33

While Mike used a coffeehouse's internet connection in Socorro, Patty strolled through the old town with Kallie, learning its history from mural tiles in a small park. If it weren't for their predicament, she'd enjoy seeing the Bosque Wildlife Sanctuary nearby, but this was no vacation. Her gut told her Mike would refuse to call the authorities. At times she wondered if she should alert them. Would it put them in more jeopardy or solve their problem with the cartel? How would that help with the likes of Rickter? She'd decided to leave Mike to his fate, hadn't she? Take the money and run. Isn't that what she'd decided? He didn't care about the lottery ticket. He was obsessed with this crazy meeting to get casinos out of debt. Casinos took people's money, usually from the poor, so why should he care? Loyalty to Juan, to the SEALs? She'd had her fill of gambling with her father losing money and putting them in the poor house. Wasn't it about time gambling paid her back by way of the lottery ticket?

She sat on a bench and Kallie nuzzled her hand. "Yeah, I know, Kallie. The problem with all this is that I like the guy. Don't ask me why after everything he's done, but how the hell do I stop caring?" She stayed in the park for several minutes, thinking about all that happened and what might happen in the future. "Come on, girl, at least I'll get you in a safe place."

When she returned to the coffee shop, Mike was still on his laptop. He didn't look up until she stood next to his table. "Can you do a search for kennels in Tucson?"

He frowned, his jaw set, his dark eyes black as ink. "I did that. Found two that looked good. One was booked solid, so I got her into the other one. We can check it out when we get there." He closed his laptop and stood. "You ready to go?"

She nodded and walked out ahead of him, feeling his eyes boring into her back. What was eating him now? Once they were in the truck, she asked, "More indecision about what to do?"

Instead of answering, he stuck his laptop in the back next to Kallie and stowed his cane next to his door. "I checked the search history you did last night."

"So?"

"There were a lot of games with different rewards. How much was our lottery ticket worth?"

She bit her lower lip, knowing she was a lousy liar. "The ticket was good for a small amount."

"How small?"

She started the engine and backed out of the parking lot into the street. "A couple thousand."

"You weren't going to tell me?"

"No, I wasn't." She let out a deep sigh. "Look at what you've done to me. I'm in danger. You never cared about the ticket anyway. I deserve some reward."

He laughed. "I guess you do. Keep your reward. I don't care, but I don't like being lied to."

She stared at him for a moment. "Now you know how it feels. Only I didn't lie, I just didn't mention it. That's not the same thing." She pulled onto the main highway and silence hung between them. Finally she asked, "Is the meeting still on?"

He nodded. "A slight change."

"You talked to Juan?"

"No."

"Are you going to leave me in the dark? I thought I was going to drop you off at the San Xavier Mission. Where now?"

"I'll let you know when you need to know."

"God damn it. You trust me or you don't."

"Trust goes both ways."

"You're a hypocrite."

He shrugged. "I've been called worse."

She shook her head, wondering what had happened to the former easy manner they'd established earlier. Okay, their relationship had been uneasy, but at least it had been sociable. Now they were slicing and dicing each other. "Can we call a truce?"

He adjusted his seat belt and turned toward her. "You're right. We've both lied. I have gotten you into something you shouldn't even know about and I need you because of my injuries." He sighed. "I wish I didn't, but that's the way it is." He took a drink out of his water bottle.

A glance out the rearview mirror made her swallow hard. "Don't turn around. We've got a tail. It's a New Mexico cop."

"Are you speeding?"

"Nope." She wanted to gun the engine, but knew that would be stupid.

"Is he closing?"

"He's just hanging back about two car lengths. Any brilliant ideas of what we should do?"

"Act normal, keep to the speed limit and let's see what happens."

Patty smiled as cars began to build up behind the cop. "He's going to have to either pass us or pull us over. Traffic is getting heavy, and I bet the other drivers are getting antsy." Suddenly a silver Porsche convertible sped past, going at least ninety. The cop kicked on his siren, flashed his lights and roared past them. "Thank God for sports car drivers."

"When we get to Las Cruces, we'll pull off onto a side street and find an abandoned truck."

"I'm not trading in my truck for some heap."

"That's not what I mean. We need a New Mexico license plate. Your Minnesota ones stick out like a neon sign. As soon as we rent a car in Tucson, and you drop me off, you can put back your own plate."

"It's illegal."

"Yeah, but it's better than getting picked up by the highway patrol or the cartel. We were just lucky the cop hadn't gotten a BOLO on this truck."

"BOLO?"

"Yeah. A be-on-the-lookout bulletin."

"Am I going to be glad to dump you!"

"Thanks."

"I didn't mean it in a bad way."

"Don't try to be nice."

She chewed on his words, but decided to avoid another verbal battle.

When they got to Las Cruces, they exited, drove to a seedy part of town and began the hunt for a likely candidate for license plates. The sun was low in the sky, but it had stopped snowing.

Mike pointed to a side street with ramshackle houses and she turned into it. Halfway down there was an empty lot with a rusted pickup, tires deep in weeds. She parked. "It looks deserted."

"I'll take Kallie out," Mike said. "It can act as a reason for our being parked here."

Patty went to the back of her truck to get a screwdriver from her toolbox and grabbed a can of WD-40 as well. Using his cane, Mike hobbled along the dusty street with Kallie. Feeling as if the world was watching her commit a crime, Patty checked the front and back of the rusted out truck. Luck. The back license plates had the year's current sticker. She knelt and began to loosen the screws after giving it a good spray of the WD-40. When she had both plates in hand, she went to her truck and exchanged her Minnesota plates for the battered New Mexico ones.

Mike opened his door to let Kallie jump in the back. "Nice job. You just might have a career in crime."

"Oh, shut up."

He got in the truck and slammed his door, while she packed all the items away and wiped her hands on a rag. She closed the hatch and got into the cab. "Now that I've done the evil master's bidding, let's stop for dinner."

"If we get arrested, you can use that line." He ruffled Kallie's fur as the dog placed her head on his shoulder. "Due to our four legged passenger, it'll have to be a drive-thru."

"I don't care. A juicy hamburger would do me just fine."

"Would you be up to driving on into Arizona? That way we can have enough time to get Kallie into a kennel and find a motel south of Tucson. I want to be as near San Xavier as possible and I need to check in with my friends."

"You've got friends?"

He sighed and shook his head. "Don't blame you for being skeptical. Of course it all depends how the meeting tomorrow night goes if they continue to be my friends."

"You're not going to call the authorities, are you?"

"I thought about it, but I think it's safer to keep them out of the loop. If things go sour, then I'll call in the troops."

"You might not have time."

"Possibly. But if they come too soon, the entire operation could blow up."

"Aren't you putting an awful lot of faith in Juan? What if he's been compromised? You know, gone over to the dark side."

"I don't want to think that, but in case you're right, I've set up plan B."

"And that is?"

"I'm going to bring Juan to them. They won't be at the mission." He held up his hand. "You'll still drive me there and drop me off. Juan has a van with a trusted driver he's depended on for years. I'll have them drive me to where the seven elders are staying. You drop me off as agreed and hightail it home to Minnesota."

She'd be glad to be rid of him, wouldn't she? A part of her wanted to be there at the end, despite the danger. Not knowing the final outcome was not sitting well with her. The journey had been crazy from when that nutcase Rickter had shown up. "Have you wondered what happened to our friend Rickter? It's creepy that he's vanished. Maybe he gave up."

"I've been wondering about him, too. He's not the kind of guy who stops something because he loused up a few times. In fact that probably wet his appetite. Maybe the police picked him up, but I think he's around, biding his time. That's one of the reasons we changed the plates and that's why we're going to rent a car. You'll drive me to San Xavier in a rented sedan. No one should expect that." He looked out the window, before he added, "I hope."

Chapter 34

It was late in the evening, leftover pizza boxes were in the trash, water bottles stood like soldiers on the rectangular table in Wycoff's office. DEA agents Sam Lovelace, Eugene Welch, Camden and Wycoff sat with files and papers strewn in front of them; laptops had been accessed and now lay idle. Through the large windows, city lights sparkled off the glitter of falling snowflakes.

"The question remains," Wycoff said, "should we send two agents to Juan's house and inform him of his brother's murder or do we wait until after Camden meets his representative at the mission at noon tomorrow?"

"We can't let Camden go alone." Eugene crunched up his paper napkin and tossed it into a wastebasket.

Wycoff nodded. "Eugene, you will drive separately, dress and act like a tourist."

"What if things go wrong?" Eugene's intent gray eyes narrowed. "Shouldn't we have others around as backup?"

Camden fiddled with his pen. "What do you expect to happen? It will be daylight with tourists around. I don't think we need an army there."

Eugene persisted. "I'm not talking about a lot of manpower, just enough to quell a disturbance. God knows, if the cartel is there, anything can happen."

There was a knock on the door and Caulfield entered. "Sorry I'm late." He sat at the far end of the table.

Wycoff leaned back and rubbed his forehead. "Glad you could make it. We're deciding if we should tell Juan about his brother's death."

Caulfield nodded. "I heard about that. It does put a different slant on things." His attention went to Camden. "Do you think Juan may already be in the cartel's pocket?"

Camden shrugged. "I have no idea, but it goes against everything we've learned about the man."

"Cartels can be persuasive," Wycoff said. "If he knew what happened to his brother, he might have thrown in the towel."

Camden shook his head. "He didn't get along with his brother, but when I talked to Juan, it sounded as if someone was monitoring the call. Since we now know it couldn't have been Tomás, who was it? Someone from the cartel?"

"Once Tomás disappeared, Juan had to know something was amiss." Sam Lovelace had been quiet during most of the meeting, reading files, listening. "But he might not know how he died."

Eugene put his elbows on the table. "Tortured and then cut up would give anyone pause."

"Juan might have canceled the meeting," Sam Lovelace said. "Why have it, if the cartel already has the casinos in its hip pocket with foreclosures looming? January fifth. Isn't that the due date?"

"Right." Camden nodded and made notes on the pad in front of him. "I agree with your assessment, Sam." Camden picked up a sheet of paper. "We've narrowed the list of elders who might be attending, but haven't been able to locate any of them."

Wycoff looked at his men one at a time. "Here's where it's at then. Juan may or may not be in charge of his own destiny. If he holds the meeting as scheduled, the tribal elders may be in danger. The cartel may want to either intimidate them to go along with the bank's foreclosures on their casinos or—kill them. Camden goes to the meeting tomorrow afternoon. Eugene will arrive ahead of time and blend in with the tourists. We'll have men available if needed. Afterward Camden will report back, then we'll decide the next step. In the meantime, Sam will try to locate the tribal elders."

"What about Garrick?" Sam asked, "We don't even know if he's coming."

"Oh, he's coming." Caulfield smiled, as all heads turned toward him. "We got a report from the New Mexico police. Patty Harkin's truck was spotted outside of Las Cruces, a man, a woman and a dog inside. We told the police not to intervene, allow the truck to continue and alerted the

Arizona police and gave them the same instructions. This evening their truck was seen at a motel near Benson. It now has New Mexico license plates. We've asked the police not to approach or hinder their travel in any way. We've sent an FBI surveillance team to follow the truck and report to me."

Camden felt both relief and despair and stared down at the table. He said nothing, but prayed Mike would contact him before he committed any other illegal acts. Was Mike afraid of the authorities or the cartel? Had he been in touch with Juan? If so, did he know about Tomás? "I might learn about Garrick when I meet Juan's representative tomorrow."

"Before we adjourn, we need to talk about Floyd Rickter." Caulfield leaned forward, placing his forearms on the table. "We've interviewed employees at the reservation's casino. Just as Camden reported, Rickter was seen talking with Debo Matruca. As you know Matruca is, or I should say, was, Tomás's righthand man. According to witnesses, the men were not only cordial with one another, but spoke at length. This says to me that they've joined forces. The question is have they joined forces with Juan or with Los Coyotes. We're sure Rickter killed Slocum, right? Why would Juan have Slocum killed? I think the answer is Los Coyotes wanted to get rid of the competition. Same reason they killed Tomás." He glanced around the table at the set faces. "That's my take. Any questions or disagreements?"

"It makes sense," Wycoff said, then asked, "Anyone else want to chime in?"

"It sounds like Garrick is walking into a trap." Camden knew he sounded as if he were defending his friend, but it needed to be said.

"Maybe," Caulfield said, but didn't elaborate.

"Nothing more we can do tonight." Wycoff stood. "That'll be it for now. We'll meet tomorrow after Camden and Eugene return from San Xavier."

Chapter 35

After six hours of sleep and a quick breakfast of coffee and donuts, Patty and Mike were back on the road and entered Tucson's city limits about noon. Mike navigated them to the kennel and after Patty was satisfied that Kallie would be well taken care of, she made arrangements with the kennel owner about contacting Maggie. Having done all she could, Patty watched Kallie join the other frolicking dogs, then hurried out the door.

Once in the truck, she gripped the steering wheel and held back tears. "I can't believe I'm weepy over a dog. Me? I never even liked dogs."

Mike smiled. "Hey, think of it this way. Kallie helped you get over your fear of dogs."

"I never said I was afraid of them."

"You could've fooled me. First time you came into the trailer, you were all trembly when Kallie smelled you up and down."

"The trailer was dark and I didn't know what I might come up against."

"Okay. I get it." He reached over and rested his hand on hers. "Anyway, Kallie needs to be around other dogs for awhile."

"Yeah, well, let's get the show on the road." She wiped her eyes with a wad of tissues and started the engine. "Where to?"

"There are motels near the airport. We'll find one that's busy and has several floors."

Patty pulled out of the parking lot and drove down the street. "Maybe I'm paranoid, but a sedan's been following us ever since we left the motel in Benson. At first I thought nothing of it since Interstate 10 is the main road into town, but he's behind us again. Want to lose him?"

"I've noticed him, too. Let's drive to the motel. If he's with the cartel, he would have moved on us before this. I think it's the police or DEA."

"Jesus. How did they know where we were? "

"Remember that New Mexico cop who trailed us for a long time. I guess changing license plates didn't do much good."

"Great. How much trouble am I in because I changed the plates? I do not want to go to jail. Don't you get it?"

"Jail would be a better choice than other things I can think of."

"Like landing in the hands of the cartel."

"Yeah or Rickter."

"Jesus, you make me want to turn myself in to the cops." She followed his driving directions while she stewed. "If the cops know who we are, why haven't they stopped us?"

"They obviously want to know where we're going. So we'll let them know."

"I don't get it. You've been hiding from them for weeks, now you don't care if they know where you are. Explain."

"We check into the motel, leave the truck in the parking lot and take a few bags in with us. Near dinner time we call a cab and hope they're watching the truck and not the front entrance. We take the cab to a restaurant. We'll eat. The elders will drop off a car in the back of the restaurant. We'll use that car to go to San Xavier."

"You're not going to rent a car?"

"If the authorities are onto us already, they'd have a trace on the card number and my name and know immediately what kind of a car we were driving. It's not much, but using a different vehicle might let me get to the meeting without the feds interfering. After you drop me off at San Xavier, you drive back to the restaurant, leave the car with the keys under the seat and get a cab back to the motel. We'll pay cash for two nights so you can get Kallie the day after Christmas and leave the area. Any questions?"

"I sure hope everything works out."

"If it doesn't, you'll be in the safe hands of the authorities."

"Oh great. Just what I've always wanted. Christmas with a bunch of cops."

He grinned.

At the motel, Patty registered, dropped Mike at the entrance with his bag and laptop in hand and parked the truck. As she grabbed her suitcase, she noticed the car that had followed them pull into a parking space eight cars down. Ignoring the man who remained seated behind the wheel, she walked into the lobby, and she and Mike rode the elevator to the third floor. After drawing the curtains, she peeked out the window and saw they had a corner room that overlooked the front street and the area where she'd parked.

She put her small suitcase on the bed and opened it. "I plan to take a long soak in the tub, so if you want to get into the bathroom first, be my guest."

"I'm fine, but I need help getting the bandage off my shoulder." He took out his Beretta and put it on the table between the queen-size beds. When she'd removed his bandage, he moved his arm back and forth, wincing with the effort. "It's much better, but I'll wrap it again with my weapon secured to my chest. I need to be prepared. The weapon will be difficult to get at, but at least it will offer some protection if I get a chance to use it."

"A chance to use it?"

"I mean, if it's necessary."

After Patty was through with her tub soak, she dressed in black slacks, a black turtleneck sweater and put on a thin silver necklace that had been her mother's. It was the only thing she had from her.

Mike took his turn in the bathroom. When he came out he was clean shaven and wore the new slacks and sweater she'd bought him.

"You look better." She slipped on her new denim jacket with the coyotes embroidered on it.

"My wardrobe is limited, but you look…uh…real nice."

She guessed "real nice" was as good as he could do. How long had it been since someone had complimented her? Then he ruined it.

"It's a little ironic that you bought a jacket with coyotes on it. The cartel is called Los Coyotes."

"God, Mike, you sure know how to flatter a woman." She stopped, reflecting on what he'd said. "How do you know the cartel's name? You never mentioned it before."

"I should know it. I've been researching this loan business. It's not a name I'd throw around. Sorry it slipped out. Just mentioning it can lead to trouble. Remember that." He hobbled over to the window and peeked out through the curtain. "That guy is still waiting for us. Thank God the motel's busy. Should keep our tail from realizing we've left." He continued to look out the window. "That must be our taxi now. He turned and picked up his laptop.

"Don't you want to leave it here?"

"It doesn't get out of my sight. Let's go."

They took the elevator and walked into the lobby where Mike stopped at the desk, paid the clerk for postage and dropped a letter into the mail slot.

Patty stepped to his side. "What did you mail?"

"Insurance for the elders."

They went out and got into the cab. As they drove off, Mike looked back and smiled. "So far so good."

The cab pulled up to a small restaurant called Maya Quetzal on 4th Street. Mike paid the driver and ushered Patty inside. "It's Guatemalan food."

"Kind of far from where we're heading tonight," Patty said.

"That's the idea."

They were shown to a table and deliberated over the menu. Patty worried that the FBI would barge in and arrest them.

Mike seemed at ease. "I think I'll have the churrasco. What about you?"

"Is this the equivalent to the man ate a hearty last meal?"

"I hope not, but we have time, so let's enjoy these last few hours."

She sighed and stared at the menu. When the waitress came, she asked, "What's the seafood tapado?"

"Very good choice." The waitress started to write it down.

"I mean, what's in it?"

"Oh, si. Coconut soup, with red snapper, shrimp, bananas, bell pepper."

"Sounds great. Thanks. I'll have it."

Mike ordered the charbroiled steak, then added, "I'll have a glass of your house red wine, and she'll have a glass of your house white. We'll both have the flan for desert."

The waitress flashed him a smile.

Irked, Patty said, "No flan for me, thanks."

The waitress gave a curt nod and walked away.

"Do you think we should drink with what's ahead of us?"

"Patty, the meeting isn't until midnight. If one glass makes you drunk, then you aren't the gal I think you are. Relax, enjoy."

"What makes you think I drink?"

"Intuition."

She had no retort and for the rest of the meal they enjoyed the food, the conversation and the wine. Mike tempted her with a bite of his dessert, but she refused and sipped her coffee. "When are you going to call the elders?"

"They know where to go and when. How do you think I found this restaurant?"

"They're nearby?"

"You don't need to know. Just in case you're asked."

"Who would ask me?" It was a stupid question and one she wished she hadn't asked. Of course, the FBI, the DEA, the cartel, they'd all want to know. It brought her thoughts back to her errand for the night and the last time she would see Mike. The food felt like lead in her stomach. "I'm freaking out, thinking about all the things that could go wrong."

He leaned forward. "It's going to be okay. You'll be out of this soon."

"You won't."

"Maybe I will be."

"Mike I want you to know that in spite of everything, I...I care about you."

His dark eyes sparkled. "If things had been different, well...."

She swallowed hard. Damn, she was going to get teary-eyed.

But his next words brought her back to reality. "I'll pay the bill, go to the restroom, then out the backdoor. I'll meet you there." He paused. "Okay? "Ready?"

She wasn't, but she stood and went to the restroom. A few minutes later, she stepped out the back door and into the cold night. It was snowing. A dark shape hobbled toward a Honda and she joined Mike by the side of the car. They stood side by side with snowflakes melting on their hair and shoulders. His arms went around her; her body melded to his. His lips teased hers like a feather, then pressed down with ardor. It wasn't what she'd expected, but it's what she wanted.

Chapter 36

The following day Camden drove to the mission, his Glock in his shoulder holster. Although he'd been trained to use it, he'd never shot at anyone during his six years in the DEA. In the present situation he was glad to have it. The pipe he'd bought as a prop nestled in his leather jacket pocket. Snow had fallen in the mountains above Tucson, leaving an appealing white cover on the surrounding barren hills. Two inches more were predicted for tonight, Christmas Eve. He only wished he could enjoy the holidays, but had a gnawing feeling that tonight might be one he wouldn't want to remember.

From the highway he could see San Xavier del Baca Mission gleaming white against the hovering dark clouds. He turned off the highway and followed the signs. A few cars were in the large dirt parking lot directly in front of the Spanish colonial building and tourists milled around the grounds. To his left was a ticket office where he stood in a short line to buy a ticket for the noon tour. As he walked to the entrance, he took out the pipe and studied the massive mesquite-wood entry door. It was a few minutes before noon, so he wandered around, looking at the ornate Moorish-inspired building and studying the tourists, thinking he might spot Juan's messenger.

A boy of about eight tugged at his sleeve. "Are you Mr. Simon?"

Startled, Camden pulled back. "What do you want?"

The boy frowned. "Aren't you Mr. Simon?"

"Yes, but—"

"Your friend's up there." He pointed to a hill on one side of the mission.

"What do you mean?" He grabbed the boy's arm.

"Let me go." His dark eyes flickered in fear. "He said he waits for you, that's all."

Camden released the boy and looked toward the hill, but didn't see anyone. The boy ran off, and Camden was left wondering if this meeting was a ruse. Perhaps the man was behind the crumbling ruin walls on the hill. He moved aside as tourists came out of the cathedral entrance, including Eugene, who passed him with a nod.

Camden turned away and walked to the bottom of the hill. He stopped, felt for the gun in its holster, and then began to hike up the dirt path leading to the top. The melting snow had turned the red soil into a slick mess. He slipped. "Damn." He hadn't worn shoes for these conditions. As he went down on one knee, his felt the wet mud seep through his khaki pants. By the time he reached the top, his heart thudded from frustration and exertion. Looking north, he saw agricultural fields and the city beyond. He put his hands on his hips, disgusted with being set up, then bent over to get the mud off his pants. He heard steps and looked up.

A man had stepped out from behind the crumbling stone walls. Camden froze as he faced a man with dark glasses covering most of his face. The guise didn't matter. Rickter's face was etched in his mind. Camden swallowed hard and tried not to show fear.

"What's your name," Rickter asked.

"Bob Simon. And you are…?"

"You only need to know is Juan sent me."

"I'd sure like to meet my old friend."

Rickter sneered and stepped closer. "I bet you would. You're DEA, right?" He worked the zipper on his windbreaker up and down, revealing the gun in his waistband. "Let's not play games. Garrick sent you postcards. Too bad he had an accident. Juan wants to reschedule the meeting. Where are the elders?"

Camden sidestepped the question. "Why reschedule?"

Rickter shrugged, tugged at the zipper of his jacket as if undecided as to whether he should pull out his gun or not. "Time of year. The holidays. Juan wants the meeting in January."

"After the fifth?"

Rickter glared at Camden, his mouth agape.

Someone must have told Rickter when the balloon payments were due. Was Rickter now working for the cartel or Juan? In his years with the DEA Camden hadn't faltered in the face of violence, but never had his courage been so severely tested. "The DEA would like to speak with Juan directly. We could come to his house if it would be more convenient."

Rickter brushed the back of his hand across his mouth. "Why the DEA? Juan doesn't deal in drugs and besides he's sick."

"As sick as his brother?"

"His brother?"

"Yeah, Tomás."

"I haven't met the guy. Didn't know he was sick. "

Whoa, now that's interesting, thought Camden. The cartel hadn't clued Rickter in on how they'd killed Tomás. Why? Maybe they didn't want to scare him. Had they used him to get rid of Slocum and promised him a piece of the pie? Or could he be working for Juan? Maybe Juan doesn't know about his brother. "Has Juan talked with Mike Garrick recently?"

Rickter shrugged. "So what if he has?"

Either Juan told him or the cartel had listened in on Camden's telephone conversation with Juan. "We can settle matters easily once Juan meets with me."

Rickter gave a smarmy smile. "That's not going to happen. We need to let the elders know about the new plans for the meeting. Where are they?"

"We don't know."

A worried look crept into Rickter's eyes. "You don't trust Juan?"

"I've never met Juan. We can't contact the elders, because we don't know where they are."

Rickter's eyes narrowed and turned flinty. "The DEA doesn't know where they are?"

Camden shrugged. "We aren't perfect."

"So the elders will be at the meeting?"

"Juan sent you here merely to ask me where the elders are?"

Rickter hesitated, then said, "Tell us where they are, and they can be home for Christmas."

"I told you, we can't locate them."

"That's crap. I'm not stupid enough to believe you."

Camden sighed. "This isn't getting us anywhere. I need to talk to Juan."

"I told you he's unavailable." Rickter unzipped his windbreaker. His hand moved toward his waistband.

Camden's gut tightened. "We seem to have reached an impasse."

Rickter zipped up his windbreaker. "You're playing games. We don't like games. The elders have to cooperate. It's in their tribe's interest. Tell them that."

"Sounds like an ultimatum."

"Take it how you want. If you don't tell us where the elders are, they might not be happy about the outcome." Rickter moved a step closer and continued to play with the zipper of his windbreaker. Camden caught a whiff of alcohol and stepped back.

He hadn't learned much, except that no one seemed to know where the elders were. A good thing. On the other hand, if the meeting went on as planned, they'd have to have men at the mission to protect the elders. He obviously wasn't going to learn anything more from Rickter. He turned to leave, but worried about being shot in the back as he headed back down the hill. He prayed that with tourists wandering around the man wouldn't be that brazen. Shit. Camden began his descent, struggling with the treacherous footing and his desire to run for cover. He continued on, slipping and sliding on the wet dirt.

When he reached the front of the mission, he turned a corner, heaved a sigh of relief and leaned against the building's white plaster. Despite the cold weather, sweat dripped down his back and he gasped to catch his breath.

Eugene, who'd been waiting in the garden, hurried over. "You look done in. Are you okay?"

Camden looked at his trembling hands. "Rickter. Up there." Camden nodded toward the hill from behind a pillar, then scanned the hilltop. "He's gone." He hoped Eugene didn't notice how scared he'd been. "We might be able to pick up his trail on the other side of that hill." They took off running, hands on their weapons. Their shoes slithered through the muddy slope. By now both of Camden's knees were caked with red muck. Eugene had thick treads on his boots and faired better. At the top they checked the area behind the walls with guns drawn. Nothing.

"Damn." Camden holstered his gun and punched in Wycoff's number on his cell and explained the situation.

"I'll alert Caulfield, the BIA Justice Services and the tribal police," Wycoff said. "Agent Valdez lost contact with Garrick and Harkin after they checked into a hotel. They took a taxi. We've contacted the cab company, but the driver went off duty. We've got a search warrant for Garrick's hotel room and Harkin's truck. You and Eugene get over there and talk to Valdez."

"We could drive around, see if we can pick up Rickter's trail." Camden said.

"FBI is on that and right now we have to concentrate on this damn meeting and Juan's involvement with the cartel."

"We could raid Juan's house," Camden said.

"Caulfield's already on his way there."

"So the FBI's taking the lead?"

"Can't be helped." Wycoff's tone was full of frustration. "He's supposed to let me know what he finds. When you finish your search of the hotel and the truck, join the FBI at Juan's. Have Eugene go with you. I don't want anyone driving around solo with Rickter on the loose. Time is running out and we still have no idea where the hell the elders are." Wycoff rang off.

While Camden drove, Eugene fiddled with his seatbelt. "I can't believe Wycoff let the FBI take the lead. Drugs are our domain, aren't they?"

"Take it easy. We aren't the only players in town." Camden slowed to avoid a pothole. "Wycoff and Police Chief Powers decided against a road block to the mission. Instead the police will monitor both routes into San Xavier. There shouldn't be much traffic tonight. The tribal police will patrol the back roads and the BIA is loaning us a few men."

"It still sounds sounds iffy to me." Eugene grabbed the bar above his door as they hit another pothole. "We should have people on-scene."

"I agree, but we're not in charge."

When they met Agent Valdez in the motel's lobby, Camden refrained from telling Valdez his opinion of his sloppy surveillance. The desk clerk had been shown the search warrant and gave them the key to Garrick's room. Once inside, they spread out, each taking a different area to search, but only found dirty clothes and an old ace bandage in the bathroom. Frustrated, they went out to the parking lot where Valdez and Eugene walked ahead to unlock the truck while Camden answered his cell phone.

It was Wycoff. "Juan's house is deserted, but the tribal police found Juan's van abandoned on a residential road. No sign of a struggle and no body. They've left the vehicle for us to search. Anything at the hotel?"

"Not so far. We're about to go through the truck."

"Be quick about it. I want you and Eugene down at that van." He gave Camden the directions. "I'm sending a tow to impound the van and bring it in for analysis."

It was dark by the time they pulled up behind a tan-colored van. Its handicapped license plate visible in their headlights. They showed their credentials to Officer Nez who was waiting for them at the side of the road. "Our men are canvassing the houses nearby. So far nobody heard or saw anything. We checked the vacant lots, only old footprints, animal tracks." His attention came back to the van. "We looked inside and didn't see anything unusual, but we left the thorough inspection to you."

"Anyone touch anything inside or out?" Camden asked.

"Not without gloves. We know Los Coyotes and this man Rickter are on our reservation and don't like it one bit. Juan Pacheco is one of our heroes and finding his van abandoned is a bad thing. We'd been told his brother was killed. Everyone's on alert."

"We appreciate your cooperation," Camden said, as he and Eugene pulled on latex gloves.

When Eugene opened the van's back doors, the inside light went on. "It's got a lift, but no wheelchair."

"I'll leave you to it," Officer Nez said and walked away toward nearby houses.

Camden peered inside. "That's a good sign. If the cartel has him, they would have left the chair." He shrugged. "But maybe not. See what you can find. The forensic's team will dust for prints. I'll check the front seats." Camden opened the passenger door, studied the interior, then opened the glove compartment, but found nothing but the registration papers. With a flashlight in one hand, he pulled out scraps of paper from under the seats, checked each one then placed them in a baggie.

An agitated Officer Nez ran toward them. "There's a body behind a house." He pointed to shadows of a gathering throng down the street.

"Officer," Camden said. "Stay with the van while we take a look." After stripping off their gloves, Camden and Eugene hurried to the site, pushed through the gathering crowd and flashed their IDs. An officer shone a light on a body. Before Camden could tell him not to touch anything, the officer leaned down and flipped the body onto its back. His beam of light played across the face. Women screamed; men groaned. A bullet hole between the eyes explained it all.

"Who is it?" Camden asked the officer, whose face had paled.

"Gordito Ohono, Juan Pacheco's driver."

"Officer, please have the people move back." Camden knew there was little hope of finding any evidence at the scene the way the crowd had milled about. "Eugene take their statements." As Camden viewed the body, he wondered if this could be Rickter's doing. But why? If the cartel didn't have Juan before and now they do, why had Juan stayed in seclusion? Why hadn't he met Camden instead of sending Rickter? Had he been the one to send Rickter?

He called Wycoff and reported their findings. After listening to Camden, Wycoff said, "Caulfield is still at Juan's house. I'll let him know. Sounds like the murder scene is already contaminated. Do the best you can to secure the scene and wait for the forensic team, either ours or the FBI's. At this point everyone is cooperating and pulling double duty."

Camden and Eugene did the best they could in the dark, getting the homeowners to turn on all their backporch lights and asked for more flashlights or lanterns. The DEA's tow for the van arrived and hauled it away. It was almost nine by the time Caulfield and two other FBI agents arrived. Camden filled them in on what they'd done so far.

Caulfield took Camden aside. "We found blood on Saltillo tiles inside Juan's house and a cigarette butt with lipstick. Consuelo Regina is a smoker. Other than that there was nothing to explain what happened to Juan." He rubbed the back of his neck. "God, I'm tired and hungry, and the hell of it is, it's Christmas Eve. Let's sit for a minute." They walked over and got in the back seat of Caulfield's car. "Tell me about your meeting with Rickter."

"Wycoff told you?"

"Summary, that's all." Caulfield leaned his head back, while Camden detailed his talk with Rickter.

"The guy's a loose cannon, that's for sure. I couldn't figure out if he's working for the cartel or Juan." He glanced at Caulfield. "Now that we've found Juan's van with his driver murdered, it seems Rickter must be working for the cartel."

"We won't know if it's Rickter's handiwork until we get a ballistics report."

Camden checked his watch again. "The only lead we've got is the San Xavier meeting. I need to be there, not sitting here."

Caulfield nodded. "I agree. Can I get a ride with you? My men can finish up here and stay until the coroner transports the body. They can join us later."

Camden signaled to Eugene and he, Caulfield and Camden drove off in Camden's car. They were all hungry and stopped at a drive-thru for a quick bite and eventually pulled into a side street near the mission a little after eleven. The falling snow made it feel like a peaceful Christmas Eve.

Camden's phone rang. Wycoff was on the line. "Where are you?"

"We're waiting near the mission, but a bit far away from the parking lot. Caulfield is with us."

"Things are literally exploding in your area. There's a large warehouse fire off the back road to the mission, a house robbery on the reservation, and an accident on Highway 19 near the exit to the mission. It's tying up traffic in both directions. Powers had to pull his men off the stakeout to handle the situations. These events could be diversions, so keep your eyes open. If Caulfield has anyone available, get them to help out. Do the best you can. I'm on 19 now and hope to get there soon, but it's blocked solid and nothing's moving. I'd get a helicopter, but they can't fly in this weather." Wycoff hung up.

Camden relayed the information to Caulfield and Eugene.

Caulfield shook his head. "My men are on the way, but it'll be awhile."

Camden held his phone in his palm. "I don't believe in coincidences."

"Me neither." Caulfield stared out through the front windshield.

Eugene leaned over from the backseat. "Let's get closer to the mission."

"I don't know how without being seen," Caulfield said.

Eugene tapped Camden on the shoulder. "What about the hill? I could get up there and have a good view of the area. If I see something, I'll call."

"Too far away. In the dark you couldn't see, what was happening."

"Then let me go to the mission. There are plenty of places to hide. I'll call if anything happens."

"It might be our best chance." Camden nodded. "Keep your weapon ready. Good luck."

Eugene got out of the car, eased the door closed and walked off into the darkness, while Caulfield and Camden sat and waited, hoping that peace would reign this midnight of Christmas Eve.

Chapter 37

Patty followed Mike's instructions to the mission's back road. It was early, but he wanted to scout the area before midnight. She pulled the old Honda to the side of the road when she heard police sirens. The police streamed past and through the falling snow, they could see an orange glow from a large fire off to the west.

Mike leaned forward, turned on the radio and punched buttons until he got the local news. The newscaster made it sound like a crime spree had erupted in Tucson. "A five car pileup on Highway 19 has blocked traffic in both directions near the Vail Street off ramp. The police have cordoned off the area, looking for the hit and run driver who caused the accident. On the east side, a huge warehouse fire off the back road to San Xavier Mission was started by an explosion from an incendiary device. And this just in—a home burglary and a kidnapping on the reservation south of the casino. Christmas Eve is not quiet tonight, folks."

Mike turned off the radio. "Odd, don't you think?" He stared out the window.

"Not what you want to hear on Christmas." Patty pulled back onto the road.

"That's not what I meant. All those incidents are near or around the mission."

"So, stuff happens. Those crimes can't all be related to your meeting Juan." She slowed to look for the sign to turn into the mission.

"Diversions draw firepower away from that target."

"That's war. This is…. Okay, I see what you mean." She peered through the windowshield as the wipers cleared away the snowflakes.

"Don't turn at the sign," Mike said. "Keep going straight ahead. We'll double back after a few blocks."

They passed the turnoff to the left and continued down the road. "Turn right at the next street, then right again and stop."

As she turned right, the street lights went out. Darkness. Not a Christmas light gleamed from a window. "It's pitch black outside." Patty strained to look ahead as her headlights caught the drifting flakes.

"Shit. Not a good sign." Mike braced his left arm against the dashboard.

She continued down the street, turned right again and pulled to the curb. "What now?"

Mike looked at the car's clock, twenty minutes before twelve. "Turn off your headlights and kill the engine." They sat in silence. The soft snow gathered on the windshield. "We stay here until a minute before mildnight, then drive to the mission parking lot. The gate should be open. If not, we drive past and leave the area."

She shifted in her seat to look directly at him. "There's something I have to tell you. I should have before this. It's about the lottery ticket." She couldn't see his face in the dark, but sensed him stiffening. "I didn't tell you the entire truth about how much it's worth."

"You thought you put one over on me?"

"Well, yes. You see…."

"It's worth over a half million."

She sat mute, unable to catch her breath and stared out at the snow falling. Finally, she gathered herself. "How did you know?"

"Something I didn't tell you. I have a memory for numbers. Came in handy when dealing cards at the casinos. I was hoping you'd tell me."

"And if I didn't?"

"I'd chalk it up to another lesson learned about my fellow human beings."

"And you'd just walk away from half a mil?"

"Money won't help me where I'm going."

"God, Mike, don't say things like that. You make it sound like this meeting will be the end of you."

"One way or another. Yeah. I killed a man in cold blood. Don't forget that, Patty."

"Who's to know? I won't tell anyone."

"I gave Camden enough evidence for him to figure it out. He's a good investigator."

She grabbed his hand. "You can use the money for attorney fees."

He shook his head. "Patty, come on, you're a realist. Life doesn't go as we plan. If it did, you and I would ride off into the sunset."

"Damn it. Then let's do it, now. Forget all this meeting jazz."

He clasped her hand tightly. "It's almost midnight. I turn into a pumpkin, and you start a new life with money in your pocket. Buy an auto shop." He laughed. "Hey, Kallie will make a great partner."

She gritted her teeth to hold back tears. "Stop it. This is a nightmare."

He sighed. "I'm sorry…back at the restaurant's parking lot. I shouldn't have let you know how I feel about you."

"I'm glad you did. We'd been sparring for too long."

He leaned over and kissed her cheek. "It's time to go. Remember, you drop me off and drive away. No turning back." His hand lingered in hers, then he withdrew it. "You promised."

She wiped her tears away, nodded and started the car.

The road seemed deserted as they drove down the entrance into the mission. Their headlights flashed on the open iron gate to the parking area. At the far end of the lot near the mission, they could make out a parked car and a van.

"They must have been here awhile—no tire tracks in the snow," Mike said. "Pull up near them, but not too close." He pushed at the Beretta stuck under his bandaged arm. She stopped the car. He opened his door, used his cane to help him stand and looked over the top of the Honda as a man came around the back of the van.

"Juan's in the back." The man nodded to the rear of the van.

The Nissan sedan that had been parked next to the van backed up, spun around and stopped broadside behind Patty, blocking her exit. Mike slammed his cane onto the hood of the Honda and yelled, "Go. Ram that car. Now."

Patty slammed the gear into reverse, wishing she had her truck. Unable to gather speed, the Honda barely made a dent in the sedan's side. Her headlights spotlighted a man running toward them from the mission. A shot rang out. The man fell. Snow caked her windshield, making it difficult to see. She felt for the door handle and was about to exit when a man ran at her car. Rickter's face was seared in her memory. She locked the door, but he swung at her side window with a tire iron, smashing it. As he reached in and opened the door, she hacked at his hand. He yelled, but managed to fling the door open, grab her arm and drag her out of the car. With her free hand, she chopped down on his arm that held the tire iron. He dropped it. She broke free. With an open hand she struck at his throat. She missed and hit his chest.

His fist cracked against her face. Stunned, she dropped her arms and tasted blood. He punched her in the stomach. Doubling over, she sank to the ground, retching. He yanked her hair, snapping her head back.

"Fuckin' bitch. I finally got you." His laughter crackled through the icy night. He released his hold on her and shoved her into the ground. When his boot came at her, she rolled into it, held his foot and yanked him down, then mashed his face into the slush. He slithered away and threw himself on top of her, straddling her. His fist hammered her face. She parried some of his blows, but with each whack she grew weaker.

A voice cut through the fog that engulfed her. "We gotta leave."

"She's mine, Debo. I'm gonna teach her who's boss."

"Not now. We gotta get outta here. I had to shoot a guy hiding by the mission."

"Cop?"

"How the hell do I know. Let's go. Car's coming."

Patty struggled against arms that lifted her then dropped her like a sack onto a hard surface. She curled into a fetal position, hurting. A thud. Silence. Darkness.

The engine roared. Tires screeched. Inside the trunk, she was tossed against the hard metal interior as the car swerved back and forth, then ran straight. She put a hand to her throbbing face and licked her puffy lips. She tasted the wet salty stickiness of her blood.

Her body and head ached and her thinking process had slowed. *Gotta get out. How?* She felt around the dark space. Nothing. Cold seeped into her. At each turn and stop, she braced herself. Her watch glowed in the dark. A few minutes to twelve thirty. The car rolled to a stop; the engine turned off. A door slammed. She had to be ready for him. *Kick or go out head first?* When the trunk opened, she leaped at him, aiming for his eyes. He was ready and twisted her arm behind her back.

"Keep fighin' bitch. It'll be more fun." Rickter laughed.

"Take her inside. You can have her later. First we get information." It was the other voice, the man called Debo.

She squinted at the flashing neon casino lights. Rickter pushed her through an open door, shoved her inside and slammed it behind her. She sagged to the floor, hearing distant sounds of laughter and music. The dim overhead light revealed boxes, crates, a small window on one side and two doors—the one she'd entered and another on the opposite side. The walls of the store room were concrete blocks. She heard a moan.

"Mike." She stood and staggered toward him. "You're okay," she managed to say before sinking down next to him. He sat against a large crate, his face bloody.

He looked at her through puffy eyes. "Patty? I thought you got away. Who beat you?"

"Rickter."

"Damn it. He's here?" He put his arm around her shoulder and pulled her to him. "I'm so sorry I got you into this."

She rested her head against his chest. "He took me by surprise. Usually I can take care of myself. Not this time." It was difficult to talk with her bruised mouth. "So much for walking into the sunset."

"We'll get out of this." He nodded to the far window. "Can you fit through that?"

She studied its narrow opening. "Maybe."

"Help me get my Berretta. Thank God, they didn't find it."

With the hint of hope, Patty loosened his bandage and removed the Berreta. He took it with his left hand. "Okay. Now, get out that window."

The far door opened and a shaft of bright light pierced the dim room. Mike slipped his weapon into his sling.

Chapter 38

A man rolled into the room in a wheelchair. The door closed behind him. Mike leaned over to Patty. "It's Juan. Move away from me."

She edged away from Mike, who remained sitting with his back against the crate, his right arm in the sling and his left hand holding his right. Juan was supposed to be on their side, wasn't he?

Juan rolled closer. "Mike, good to see you. They messed with you. Sorry."

"Juan, you're looking good." Mike spoke in a monotone. "They haven't done a job on you?"

"No. They took it out on Tomás. They killed him."

"Too bad. I thought he was their fair-haired boy."

"For a time." Juan pulled his body to a more erect position in his chair. "If you'd told me where the elders are staying, we wouldn't be in this fix." He nodded toward Patty. "She'd be safe."

"So what do you suggest?"

"Give 'em what they want." Juan raised his chin. "We'll be out of it then."

Mike emitted a low guttural laugh. "I'm not that gullible, and you aren't either. What are you up to?"

"I'm trying to make this easy. There's no need for your girlfriend to be harmed more than she has been. They'll let her go."

Juan had a look in his narrow eyes, a look that frightened her. Unable to hide her anger, she blurted out, "Rickter works for you now, doesn't he?"

Juan swung his attention to her. "I heard you were a mouthy troublemaker." He grinned, but had a wicked look in his eyes. "Rickter's been very useful. He took care of the competition."

"Slocum?" Mike frowned.

"Didn't you know he was dead?"

"No. How could I? Rickter killed him?" Mike's face showed nothing, but his voice was harsh.

"After Rickter bungled taking you out, he had nowhere to turn. Slocum couldn't protect him, we could. Loyalty can be bought. I thought loyalty was your mantra, Mike. But you haven't been loyal to me."

"Loyalty?" Mike spit out the word. "It was your plan from the beginning, wasn't it? You used me. I got the names of the elders who'd fight to keep the cartel out of their reservations. You never did have a banker who'd refi their loans, did you? You wanted the elders tucked out of the way. Were you going to kill all of them?"

Juan's smile didn't reach his eyes. "They'd be taken care of if they didn't listen to reason."

"Why? What made you turn? What happened to you?"

"Christ, you ask that? You of all people! Look at me. In a wheelchair, forgotten, on disability, a pittance. My duty to country and what did it get me? And for what?" Juan's breathing was rapid, his voice trembled with rage. "For fighting for a bunch of rugheads who'd kill if you turned your back. And Josh, blind, nothing to live for except drugs and booze." He caught his breath. "What happened to him?"

Patty waited as the silence seemed to suck the air out of the room.

Mike finally said, "I killed him."

"What?" Juan wheeled back a few feet. "I don't believe it."

"He had the information I'd gathered. Wanted to give it to Slocum in return for drugs."

Juan nodded. "I wondered how Slocum found out about my business."

"Funny, isn't it." Mike spoke in almost a whisper. "You saved my life."

"In the heat of battle we do stupid things."

Mike's voice got stronger. "Buddies in war, killers in peace."

"Tell me where the elders are and join us."

"That's not going to happen."

"You realize what will happen to her." He nodded toward Patty.

"She doesn't know where they are."

"But you do. You want to watch what Rickter will do to her?"

"That'll solve nothing. I sent the information, detailing the loans, the cartel, your involvement to a friend of mine in the DEA."

Juan pulled a pistol from under the robe covering his withered legs. "It won't matter. We'll have control of the casinos before the feds can act, and juries can be bought." He rolled his chair toward the door and over his shoulder said, "I'll let Rickter and Debo take over. You won't like it."

"Wait," Mike said.

Juan spun his chair around to face Mike. "You've come to your senses, remembering that I saved your life."

"Never." Mike slid his Berretta out from the sling.

Juan stared, then raised his pistol. Shots rang out and Patty wasn't sure who'd fired first or who'd been hit until Mike gasped. Blood seeped from his chest. She glanced at Juan and saw him slumped forward; his weapon on the floor.

She crawled over to Mike, took off her jacket and pressed it against his chest.

"Patty, forget me." His voice was thready. "Get out."

"What about you?"

"Get help. Now!"

The door crashed open. Mike shoved her away and fired several times. Debo's large body fell, wedging the door open.

"Hurry," Mike said.

Patty pushed a crate under the window, climbed onto it and pulled herself up. Grasping the frame, she wriggled through. Her torso lay in the snow. She scrambled forward, scratching at the cold clay soil, inching out her hips, then her legs. She kicked with her feet at the cement wall around the window and sprawled on the icy ground. While on her knees, she looked back into the room, but couldn't see a thing. The sound of firing, echoed through the silence of the dark night.

"Mike!" she yelled.

She stood transfixed, hearing the shrill sounds of sirens. *Thank God.* Running back toward the storeroom door, she stumbled and fell. *Mike, please be okay.* Scrambling back to her feet, she hurried to the back of the building, As she turned the corner, the store room door burst open and Rickter ran out. She waited, thinking Mike would follow him, but no one appeared in the doorway. Rickter headed toward the Nissan and got in.

Bastard. I won't let you get away. The police gathered at the front of the casino, but began to spread out. *Mike'll get help. I have to get Rickter.* Truckers stood by their semis gaping at the scene. Dodging between parked cars, she tried to find one she could use. Rickter backed around and headed out of the lot. An unhitched semi cab had its engine running with the driver standing a few yards away. Just as she climbed into the cab, the driver turned and yelled. She put the truck in gear and sped off with him running behind screaming and waving his arms.

Rickter was about two hundred yards down the road; his taillights were her target. Ignoring the slippery road, Patty floored the semi's engine and closed the gap. The powerful engine roared. She whacked into Rickter's back fender. The Nissan fishtailed, then straightened. She grinned, feeling like an avenging angel. She slammed into his car harder. The Nissan skidded, then swerved across the road. Flashing lights glared in Patty's rearwindow, but she avoided thinking about who was behind her and zeroed in on Rickter's car. When she slapped into his fender again, she kept her foot on the accelerator, sending his Nissan sideways. She kept the pedal to the floor. Grinding metal threw off sparks that flickered against the white snow. Rickter accelerated and burst free of the semi's bumper, but the big semi clipped the right rear of the car, spinning it off the road. An adobe building loomed out of the desert brush. Patty smiled. The Nissan smashed against the adobe wall, then tumbled sideways over the old bricks and landed upside down. Inside it somewhere was Rickter.

She threw the semi into reverse, backed up a few feet, then turned off its engine and leaped to the ground. Arms flailed from under the wreckage. Flames shot upward. She heard screaming—police cars, sirens blaring, closed in around her.

Chapter 39

Late morning Christmas day Patty was escorted from her jail cell by a female police officer to a car waiting at a side entrance. "She's all yours, Agent Caulfield."

"Miss Harkin, I'm FBI Agent Robert Caulfield. You're now in my custody. I presume you don't plan to try to escape."

"Why should I? Where would I go?"

He nodded and removed the handcuffs, then took her to the passenger side of a black sedan. He shut her door and walked around to the driver's side and got in. "I'm taking you to the hospital."

"I'm okay. I just look bad." She stopped. "Mike? Is he there? Is he all right? They wouldn't tell me anything. I've been going crazy not knowing."

"He's there." He started the engine and drove out the gate. "We need you to tell us everything that happened during your time with him."

"Hasn't he explained things to you?"

Caulfield shook his head. "He's been unconscious much of the time."

"How bad is he?"

"It's not good."

Patty's breath seemed to leave her and she put her head back on the seat. "It was all so pointless. He realized Juan had set him up from the beginning, but he still hoped to the very end that he was wrong." She glanced out the side window.

"You haven't asked about Rickter?"

"Why should I? I hope he's dead."

"If he dies, you could face a murder charge."

She shrugged. "I don't care. The bastard deserves to die. Do you know how many people he killed?"

"Oh, yes. I'm well aware of his killing spree. He's on the FBI's most wanted list."

"Not surprised."

"If Rickter pulls through, he'll be brain damaged, a cripple, and will probably get life in a federal prison."

"Even that's too good for him."

He glanced at her and shook his head. "You did try to kill him. Stole a truck. Changed the plates on your truck. You could go to prison."

She had no idea how many years she'd get. After finally having money, sitting in prison for years would be a cruel irony.

He turned a corner and stopped at a red light. "Of course, you nailed Rickter for us. He might have gotten across the border."

She turned toward him with a small smile on her lips. "You acting as my lawyer?"

He grinned and shook his head. "Sounds like it, doesn't it. I'll see what I can do." He grew serious again. "You're one feisty woman. Even if you get off from the Rickter case, you'll have to account for stealing the truck."

"I bet he's ticked."

"Maybe we can persuade him to drop the charges against you. If, well…." He hesitated, then said, "We need you to tell us your side of everything that happened with Mike, Slocum, Rickter, even Juan. And what you know about Josh. His death in that accident is suspect."

"So that's the trade off?" She studied him. "I don't know a lot of details. Mike held things close, didn't confide in me much." No way would she tell about Mike's confession about killing Josh.

"You probably know more than you think after all those weeks."

"We went through a lot together. My questions about Juan helped trigger Mike's realization that the guy was no angel." She pulled at the seat belt and glanced out the window. "Other than that, I'm not sure how I can help."

"Tell us everything. It'll help fill in the gaps." He didn't say more until they drove into the underground parking lot of the hospital. "The press has staked out the front, so we'll go in the back."

He ushered her into an elevator, then they went to the Critical Care Unit. A uniformed policeman stood in the corridor with a tall slim man who looked vaguely familiar. He came forward and put out his hand. "Patty Harkin. We meet again."

After shaking his hand, she said, "I'm sorry, I don't remember you."

"Maggie's Diner. You asked for my newspaper's want ads. I read about Mike Garrick's death and talked to you about it."

"Oh, my God. That was so long ago. Sure, I remember, you babbled about Mike and I wasn't very sympathetic."

He smiled. "I'm Camden McMillan, an old friend of Mike's."

"How's he doing?" she stammered, fearing the answer.

"I gather the two of you grew close. I won't kid you. The doctors don't hold out much hope."

She sagged against the wall. He reached out, but she shoved his hand away. "I'll be okay." After a few moments, she asked, "Can I see him?"

Camden nodded, took her elbow and escorted her past the policeman and into CCU. He pulled back a curtain and nodded to a nurse, who left them alone. Catching her breath, she stood and stared at Mike. IV bags with dangling tubes stuck into his arm and wires hooked up to a monitor made him look like a lab experiment. His face was ashen. She walked forward, leaned down and kissed him gently on the lips.

"Hi, Mike. It's me, Patty."

His eyelids fluttered, but didn't open. She took his hand and stroked it. His fingers moved. She tightened her grip, hoping to get a response. Camden pushed a chair near the bed and motioned for her to sit. She remained standing.

"Talk to him, Patty. He might respond. I've been here for hours and several times he's become conscious and seemed to understand what I was saying, but couldn't answer. We found his laptop under the seat of the Honda you drove to the mission. It gave us the information of how to contact the elders, but all the other files were erased. Everyone's cooperating except of course, Consuelo Regina. She's involved with Los Coyotes, the drug cartel."

Patty gave him a blank look. Why was he telling her this now?

"I'm going to leave you alone with him. If he regains consciousness, ask him what he knows about the connection between Los Coyotes and the reservations."

"Some friend you are." Her anger surged. "You want me to pump him for information. That's why you bailed me out of jail."

"One of the reasons, yes." He didn't evade her glare. "Mike thought he was doing something good. Help him accomplish what he set out to do." He turned and walked away, pulling the curtain closed behind him.

She sighed and gazed at Mike's face, a nice face, despite its purple bruises. She pushed back a lock of his dark hair from his forehead, studying his features, etching them in her memory. To find someone she really cared for and have him taken away felt like a knife driven into her. She sat in the chair, kept hold of his hand and began to talk as if he could hear her.

"You know, Mike, right from the start you were a pain, ordering me around, being secretive. Well, not just secretive, but lying to me. I sure was mad at you. And then you told me the truth and I began to understand why you were doing what you were. Even, you know, Josh. That got to me. It really did."

"Yeah." It was a low mumble.

She stared at him. "Mike? You're awake?"

"Yeah."

She stood and leaned over him, cradling his cheek in her hand. "You'll pull through. You're strong. You can make it. We can walk off into the sunset together, just like we talked about."

"Dreamer." His voice was a whisper. "Tell Cam. It's in the mail."

"Don't leave me."

He smiled and slowly shook his head. His hand relaxed. The monitor no longer beeped; it hummed in a deadly drone; the heartline went flat. Doctors and nurses rushed in, pushing her aside. She stood in the far corner, watching, feeling numb.

NOV 1 1 2021

CPSIA information can be obtained
at www.ICGtesting.com
Printed in the USA
FSHW020256270919
62361FS

9 781593 308728